AMERICAN Day DREAM

Margot Eve Pepper

FREEDOM VOICES
www.freedomvoices.org
San Francisco, California

This is a work of fiction. While historical facts and public figures are portrayed accurately, any resemblance to persons living or dead is unintentional and coincidental.

Edited for Freedom Voices by Jess Clarke, Kitty Costello and Eric Robertson.
Cover design by Christine Joy Ferrer. Production by Jess Clarke.
Cover photograph: "The City at Dusk" ©2010 by Curtis Fry.

©2015 by Margot Pepper
All rights reserved.
ISBN: 978-0-915117-22-2

Published by
Freedom Voices
P.O. Box 423115
San Francisco, CA 94142
www.freedomvoices.org
books@freedomvoices.org
www.margotpepper.com

Library of Congress Cataloging-in-Publication Data

Pepper, Margot, 1962-
American day dream / Margot Eve Pepper.
    pages cm
ISBN 978-0-915117-22-2 (alk. paper)
I. Title.
PS3616.E59A83 2015
813'.6--dc23
                            2014041163

For the 99%
especially Jess, Jeanette
and Rafael

"In a time of universal deceit, telling the truth is a revolutionary act."
—George Orwell

Photo ©2015 by Margot Pepper

I

THOUGH HE COULD hear alarms sounding, Ian W. found it too painful to open his eyes, particularly the one with the blocked tear duct. Light occupied more space than his cranium allowed, as though his brain had swelled beyond the capacity of its container. The pounding seemed inextricably tied to the excruciating shriek of sirens. Had he been the victim of some dreadful accident? Eyes still sealed in agony, Ian sat up slowly on the flimsy cot, the throbbing more acute with each motion of the broken springs. Ian's panicked grip informed him that indeed what he lay on was akin to a camping mat on a coiled metal frame, not the foot or so of luxury wonder-foam top on his Divine® king bed at home. His eyes snapped open, scrutinized with horror the chipped walls dabbed with remnants of gouged out graffiti. Yet what did he expect from an emergency hospital ward with his level of coverage—the Hyatt Regency?

"Lockdown complete on 80. Lockdown complete on 80, copy?" The noise from the loudspeaker thundered over the alarms. Ian clasped his ears, cradling his head.

The alarms on the floor stopped. As he had grown accustomed to upon waking over the last few months, Ian wiped the crust that had accumulated on his left eye. He blinked rapidly, suddenly realizing the alarms had not belonged to an ambulance, but to the building in which he was currently housed.

"Lockdown complete on 90," blared a voice from somewhere above. More alarms desisted.

"Do you copy? We're outta here," the first voice bellowed. Somewhere more alarms stopped. Still the pounding persisted. Now the throbbing seemed to echo the reverberation of some disparate din resounding around him like a hundred warring walkie-talkies. Were people being evacuated?

In spite of his body urging him otherwise, Ian summoned the strength to rise. He swung his long legs around on the cot with a start, injuring the funny bone at his knee on the drawer of a small writing desk, nearly knocking it over. In the process an empty tin cup rolled off the desk, some books between two bookends slid to the right, and his wallet fell to the floor.

It was then that he caught sight of the steel bars where a wall would have otherwise been, at the head of his bed. The sight of the bars distracted him from the electric twinge of pain in his knee. Instinctively, he looked for the door. To his horror, it looked very much like a jail cell door, save for the top three feet where there seemed to be only wood. So he was in the jail wing of a hospital. Obviously, some gross mistake.

He wiped his constantly tearing left eye with the back of his hand. Besides his head, everything else in his body seemed to be intact. Carefully, he swung his legs in the opposite direction and attempted to hobble over to the front of the cage to see whether he might secure some help from the source of the dull roar of amplified voices beyond, but the floor underneath him began moving in the opposite direction. The surprise of the motion caused him to lose his balance and twist his back in order to avoid falling backward. Instinctively, he managed to fall toward the bed and sit down again.

"Hey! I'm in here!" he called out. The alarms throughout had stopped and now Ian could hear radios, walkie-talkies and voices on the floor around him. No, it didn't seem to be an evacuation.

Again, he assessed the flooring that was parallel to his bed and led to the bars. Judging by the rollers he spied through a hairline gap in the cement floor, it was a mechanical walkway. Gingerly, he tapped his toe on the rubber surface. It remained still. He put more weight on it. Nothing. With a few more motions he discovered the walkway seemed to pose a threat only if one started to mount it sideways, in the direction to approach the bars, not if it was approached in perpendicular fashion.

The bars were odd, he mused; only four feet high. They were buried within the remaining three feet of cement at the top of the wall. Then again, it wasn't intended to be a jail, but rather a hospital, he reasoned. Perhaps the wing had been converted from one originally housing injured juvenile offenders—the age of incarceration had been reduced so over the years.

Ian stared at the wood portion of the door above the bars. The wood was sturdy, clearly four inches thick, but didn't wood go against basic principles of security? Then again, hospital patients were lower security because of their ailments.

Ian noticed some cracks in the cement by the ceiling where rust had bled through. So the bars spanned from floor to ceiling inside the cement. Ian puzzled over this. They must have been buried within the wood of the door then, as well.

He continued to inventory his surroundings. He swung his legs around on the bed to face the desk. To the left, high on the wall opposite where he sat, was a flat interactive screen. To his right and behind him, the chipped porcelain of the rusty wash basin was practically on top of the foot of the bed with a stained lavatory to the right.

Ian popped up to the screen and pushed on the power. Nothing happened. The power cord and source were buried within the wall, so it was no use searching for those. He noticed a small door to the right of the set and discovered a small closet with a bar from which hung, to his astonishment, his business jacket, leather jacket and many of his favorite suits. The shelves also contained familiar changes of underwear, socks, T-shirts and workout gear. He glanced at the books on the desk—some of his favorite photograph and art books. Rather than reassure him, the sight of his belongings sparked a fight-or-flight reaction in him, causing his heart to race, his neck to burn and his breath to grow shallow. He bounded to his feet and stood on the walkway. Not a motion.

He turned and faced the cell bars. Stillness. He took a step, and with a groan, the walkway met his stride. After some effort, he made his way to the bars. It took him some time to fight his way back on this bi-directional treadmill to the john. Changing directions seemed to make the walkway rise out of the ground and assume a grade as steep as the walk up Columbus Avenue, in North Beach. He jumped off and the platform sank again. A thought came to him as he zipped up his trousers. These costly treadmills were obviously intended to keep inmates in shape over a lengthy term. What was wrong with him that he should be hospitalized at length? And why not just a regular prison? What crime was he accused of having committed?

A heaviness began to settle in his gut, burning it like molten asphalt. If this was a hospital of sorts, where was the blood pressure gauge? Where were the disposable rubber gloves and wipes and trays used by nurses—the myriad outlets and wires for heart and oxygen monitors? Nothing about the room was hospital-like in any way. In fact, the contrary, judging from the unhygienic condition of the sink and latrine.

A wave of panic overcame Ian and he seized the bars. Their immutability greatly disturbed him, seeming to him an outrageous violation. He had to stoop somewhat to grasp and peer through them. "Hey!" he yelled, craning his neck. From Ian's cell, he could see the cells opposite, across a chasm about 100 feet wide, whose depth he couldn't discern. Some thirty or forty floors above, rays of sunlight poured down from a tremendous skylight into the wide atrium in the building's center. Almost echoing the color scheme of the filtered light, balconies of white opaque glass obstructed his view directly into the cells across the atrium, except for that foot of bars above the balconies, below the cement. Through this one-foot gap, he could peer into cells directly across from him and on the floor below as well, but not below that. Up above, the floors jutted out in pyramid fashion, so he could only see the underside of the floor of the prisoners' cells. Not a great place to be in an earthquake, he thought to himself.

Ian couldn't tell whether the cells were empty or if the captives were lying or sitting on their cots. He could hear muted droning, which at first he had assumed was for communications between the guards and from their superiors. There seemed to be dozens of different programs running simultaneously. He strained his neck to see farther. He heard arguing and the sounds of a walkie-talkie. A door opened and closed and the arguing stopped.

"All clear," a voice said.

"Copy."

There were no guards to be seen in the few feet of visible corridor across the chasm or to his immediate left or right.

"What's going on?" he called out. Contrary to his expectations, his words did not echo but were utterly absorbed, as though by carpeting far below.

The disparate sounds from the various programs were disconcerting. They sounded like the showroom where he had purchased his own multi-screen. He had always felt sorry for the salespeople in stores like that. Particularly after the advent of the interactive sets. He simply could not stay here.

Ian moved to the farthest corner of his cell, wiped his eye and peered through the bars. In the cells next to him, there were no signs of life, save for the drone of two competing screen programs. In time, he thought, this would all resolve itself. He didn't seem injured and he had done nothing wrong, he reminded himself.

Ian scrutinized the wood portion of the cells to see whether any looked as though they were newer than the rest, which might hint at previous escape attempts. Strangely, from the outside, the top three feet of the cells appeared new and tastefully done. The top portions of the doors looked as though they could have belonged to an elegant apartment building or hotel. They reminded him of something familiar which, perhaps because of the interference from his headache, he couldn't place.

Fighting the treadmill, Ian sat back on his cot. From this vantage point, as well as from the john, he could see only the opaque milky-white plexiglass of a balcony outside his cell. The privacy was somewhat of a relief.

Ian swung his legs over to the other side of the bed. He caught sight of his wallet lying on the floor under the desk and stooped to pick it up. He placed the wallet in his trouser pocket and sat back down on the cot. Under the desk he noticed a few jacks and a grounded power outlet, as well as a docking station with speakers for a MEphone®. Strange, he thought. By force of habit, he felt for his own mobile in his shirt pocket. Of course it would have been taken from him since he'd been jailed for some erroneous reason, which he would presently clear up.

His camera! And MEpad®! He had a sinking feeling as he thought of his briefcase in the hands of the authorities. At least all his photos were backed up on the net.

He opened one of the three desk drawers. The first was filled with papers and his photographs. The other two contained albums of his favorite pictures as well as some photograph and art books. Again he was overwhelmed by a feeling of being invaded. How could the officials have known his preferences? Perhaps they were apparent after a close examination of the contents of his MEpad and MEphone.

Only— his favorite underwear? The black ones, the tiger ones? They had been inventoried in his travel lists. He had also purchased

them online. Ian could feel his face flushing. Wasn't it standard practice
to shame inmates? But why was he being held?

Judging from all the accessories, his stay was intended to be a
lengthy one. Still, such luxuries? Perhaps his notion of jail was just
outdated—from movies like the *Birdman of Alcatraz* and *Papillon*.

He had a thought. His MEphone. He had tried to call Barb and...
had been in a rush to leave to get to the ferry and somehow left his
briefcase at work with his phone and yes! His camera and pad as well!
The thought of his devices being at work instead of in the hands of
authorities was a small relief. Only that made the sudden appearance of
his preferred possessions all the more unsettling.

Ian leaned back against the wall on his cot and let escape an audible
sigh. He wiped his eye and cradled his head, as though trying to put
things together inside: Yes, today had to be Thursday, his day off. He
remembered very clearly standing on the ferry's lowest deck, where
bicycles were parked. He had been hanging over the railing, looking at
the sun play on the water, the flecks of gold multiplying to become an
infinity of sparkles, gold dust. He remembered having become
mesmerized, high. As he watched San Francisco and the Bay Bridge
shrink behind the wake of foam, he felt as though he had been flying
with the gulls over the wake. How alive he had felt, how gloriously at
peace after such a pleasant afternoon. He remembered it distinctly,
because, regardless of his surroundings—be they the soothing Samovar
Tea Lounge framed in the perfumed wisteria and magnolia of the Yerba
Buena Gardens, the Penthouse jacuzzi of the Monterey Plaza Resort
observing the biologists name-tagging otters in the bay, or drinking in
the reflection of the Pier's firework-like Ferris wheel lights on the dark
ocean from the fire pits at the Loews Santa Monica Beach Hotel—he
had learned that it was nearly impossible for him to fully enjoy the
moment. Part of this was due to his habit of photographing the
moment instead of beholding it directly with his own eyes. There
always seemed to be a lens between him and the world, except when he
was reviewing his work. Thus, he had come to the realization that he
was the happiest when he was reliving his life in his photographs,
relishing events in retrospect, minus the blemishes, touching them up
when necessary.

He had once mentioned this to his old photography teacher. She
only smiled her usual cryptic Cheshire-cat smile. "So that's your secret,
why you can't be without your camera. Maybe that explains why your

work is so alive. We benefit from your loss!"

His ecstasy in situ that sunny afternoon was interrupted by the presence of a bicyclist. He had been fumbling with his beat-up-looking bike and his exit ticket flew overboard. Ian laughed along with the young man and, after quickly assessing the desperate condition of his clothes and pack, offered him his own ticket.

"That's okay," said the boy, looking down, then smiling again.

"Why don't you take it," Ian said, pulling out another from a book of tickets. "When we exit, I'll explain what happened, and if they allow you off the ferry without it, you can return my ticket to me."

Only Ian could not remember exiting, nor speaking to anyone about the overboard ticket. Instead, there had been some kind of jolt. Yes, on the way out of the port, they had passed a Chinese cargo boat the length of several city blocks that one of the deckhands said had taken a week to get to San Francisco. Two tug boats were guiding it under the Golden Gate, toward Oakland, to be unloaded. Ian remembered the majority of containers had been labeled Bear-TT, probably containing MEphones and MEpads.

There had been a jolt, yes. Had the ferry hit the cargo boat? He tried to remember what had happened next.

His headache had subsided a little; it seemed not to bother him as long as he sat still. In this stillness, his mind went blank. A sensation like pins and needles overcame him. For the life of him, he could not remember any of the details that normally followed: stepping off the ferry, the pleasant shaded jaunt along Ark Row, past the steep shop roofs, under the ficus trees, their potted bases adorned with impatiens and fuchsias, winding his way to the bay, where he could see his house.

He searched his aching head for clues and found none. Had he hit his head? Why was he in jail then, and not in the hospital? What could he have possibly done to end up here? Or had some struggle ensued after his false arrest which injured his head and erased his memory? Worse still, had some blow to his head made him do something foolish?

"What is this place?" he demanded. He fought his way over the conveyor again to the bars and tried in vain to shake them. He craned his neck up and down the corridors.

His head began pounding again as though the pressure of his pulse had no outlet. Then he saw someone's chin, then blue-black hair through the foot-high gap of bars between the balcony's white glass and the cement and wood portion of the cell diagonally across the way.

"Hey!" He screamed at the prisoner who kept stooping down or bending, perhaps changing attire. There was no response. He strained to catch a better look. He could almost swear the inmate was a woman, because of the curve of the neck and cascade of hair.

"Hey," he screamed again. "Can anybody hear me! Help!"

No response.

"Hey! I have the right to a lawyer and to know why I am here!"

He endured another twenty minutes of broadcast noise.

"Somebody! This is wrong!" He began whimpering. "Help! Help!" he suddenly called out desperately. Then, "Fire! FIRE! There's a fire here in my cell! Do you hear? We'll all burn up!"

The screens didn't seem louder than his yelling, but they must have been. "This is wrong!" he screamed again. "You're headed for a lawsuit!" He battled his way back to his cot.

Eventually, after several more attempts to make himself heard over the white noise hum of screens, he resumed searching his own mind for an answer.

What incriminating act could he possibly have committed? In his younger days, he delighted in living on the margins like most teens, but now, as much as he hated to admit it, the system had him on a tight leash, comfortably numb. He was never even late for a credit card payment and never showed up late to work. He simply could not recall a single criminal act or questionable confrontation. Nothing unusual at all. OK, he had joined in on the private mobile conversation a business man on the ferry was having at loud volume about where to eat lunch.

"Me? I'm not a steak man myself. I prefer the crepes at Ticouz. Oh sorry, I thought you were inviting me along," Ian had said sarcastically, hoping the man would quiet down so Ian could enjoy the view in tranquility.

Ian was startled by the sound of outside footsteps, then the electronic whir of a card opening his cell door. A tall, bald, African American guard handed him a tray of food. His features were good-looking, and he had a regal air about him.

"Nice! Room service!" Ian joked.

There was a tense moment.

"No jokes, right, in jail? It's so nice here, I… I forgot I was in jail."

The man looked at Ian hard. "What's that?" He raised an eyebrow at Ian.

"Nothing," Ian muttered.

The guard gave Ian a sideways smile. The other half of his face was scrutinizing Ian intently. He reminded Ian of a panther.

"Except—" Ian cleared his throat. "Sir, would you mind telling me—" Ian stumbled, but the guard only turned, talking to someone at the other end of the device attached to his ear as he walked away. "Sir!" Ian called after him. He pounded the top of the door with his fist to get the guard's attention, but only injured his wrist in the process.

Ian's head felt as though it would explode. He sank back down on the cot, wiped his leaky eye, then cradled his head. From where he lay, he was sickened by the faint smell of what looked like a scoop of dog food in the tin by the door. After what seemed like an hour of debate, he summoned the strength to rise and fetch the small tin of water. It tasted incredibly good and cool, and he lapped the last drop up desperately.

The rest of the day dragged on; he kept reaching in his shirt pocket to check his messages or rearrange his calendar engagements in vain. He managed to fall asleep several times, waking each time in a fit of sweat, with insatiable thirst and increasing faintness, his head pounding harder and his left eye struggling to see as though from underwater. He realized he had left all his pseudoephedrine in his briefcase. Was he suffering a malady after all from some accident? He seemed to be floating in and out of delirium.

II

THE FOLLOWING MORNING three policemen with tinted glasses came to his cell. He wondered about the glasses; was the light from the tremendous skylight at the top of the building that bright? Or were they supposed to look like stereotypical cops? It was difficult to take them seriously. They reminded him of a self-conscious Hollywood action film.

"Sirs, if you don't mind my asking, why exactly was I admitted to the hospital?" Ian inquired, searching the guards' glasses for the eyes behind the reflection. He could not be certain if the guards could hear him because of the devices on their ears. Now and then they would talk at each other or the air. He recognized the one with the head like fine polished wood.

"I have a right," Ian continued, "to know why I'm being held. It's in the constitution, you know. Or have they stopped teaching it…?" he trailed off.

The older, heavier cop with sagging grey jowls sniggered. "Please put on your coat and tie," he mumbled.

Ian followed the orders almost eagerly; perhaps he was being released or at least being granted his day in court. He was relieved that his headache and fever—if that's what it had been—had diminished to a dull, almost imperceptible throb, though he still felt weak. He wiped his eye and glanced around. "Am I being released? Or will I be meeting my attorney?"

The older cop waved him on with a motion of his heat ray. Ian remembered seeing a special that showcased modern "non-lethal" anti-terrorist weaponry and he knew the Active Denial System or ADS had the ability to make its victims feel as though their skin was burning. Prolonged fatal applications made blood feel like it was boiling, searing nerves. Ian puzzled: either a weapon once used to torture Afghanis was now being used routinely on jailed U.S. citizens like himself, or, worse, they considered him a terrorist without any rights.

"Where are we going? I have a constitutional right to know why I'm being held."

Again, no answer. Perhaps because they thought him a terrorist? He'd clear that up in court soon enough.

The policemen led him down a hallway, through some locked double doors to a bank of five elevators. Inside, Ian was impressed by the lift's bay windows. The elevator stopped several times to pick up various well-dressed people, some in suits as though off to work.

"Late shift today, finally?" a balding man holding a briefcase inquired of a woman in a green surgeon's suit. The woman nodded, grinning, then glanced at her feet. Two men who were more casually dressed, but in a hurry, stepped in, one talking on a mobile. Then entered two women in expensive dresses and heels, one listening to a Clear Tunes device, another talking on her MEphone. The surgeon was forced to move closer to Ian and the policemen. She smiled awkwardly at him as though she didn't know he was being escorted by the uniformed men.

Suddenly, the elevator was flooded with light as it emerged from the cement shaft into the building's atrium. Ian turned around and saw, through the glass walls of the elevator, the familiar lobby of his office drifting toward him. He could see his coworkers in their cubicles and his manager busy at work in his larger work station. Everyone was slaving away, except in Ian's cubicle, which was empty. Was he dreaming? Since when did the Embarcadero Multiplex house a jail?

A sinking sensation overtook him. He was late! And the explanation would likely get him fired. He reached into his empty shirt pocket for his MEphone, then withdrew his hand quickly, as though he had received a shock.

As he waited nervously for the elevator doors to open, Ian could see the pink table cloths and potted ficus trees in the restaurant next door to his office. The waiters were busied with closing one of the sections, as they did when the breakfast rush was over, in preparation for the new lunch configuration. The view was the self-same one Ian occasionally enjoyed upon descending in the glass elevator after having had lunch or dinner in the building's rotating restaurant on the top floor.

Baffled, Ian searched the faces of the other elevator riders. One of the women in the nice dresses looked nervously at her Clear Tunes device for the time.

"Excuse me. Do you have the time?" Ian asked timidly, glancing sideways at the policemen, but they now seemed to be ignoring him.

"Ten thirty-two and twenty-seven seconds."

Ian gasped. He had never been late before, much less two hours!

The doors opened and everyone rushed out. Ian paused and looked behind him at his armed escorts. "You're late!" one of the policemen said sternly into Ian's ear. Reflexively, Ian bolted out toward his work station.

When he entered the office, Alice, the blonde office manager, peered over her glasses and smiled mischievously. She was big-boned, with a big nose and big smile. "Well, look who finally decided to show up for work. Is everything okay?" She asked in her New York accent. "Late date with your MEphone again?" She swung her bouncy tresses over her shoulder.

Ian looked nervously over his own shoulder. There was no sign of any guards. Had he been released? A mistake that the legal system wanted flushed down the memory hole?

"Great!" Ian responded, almost giddily.

"Work's piling up," Alice cautioned. "It's been crazy since Pat's been gone."

On the way to his work station, a few of his coworkers greeted him casually. Others seemed too absorbed in their work to notice he was late. Everything seemed as it always was—with the exception that Ian's supervisor was out, which actually made things more pleasant.

Hurriedly, Ian found his way to his cubicle, sat down and started up his work MEpad. Yes, judging from the large number of messages in his inbox, yesterday had been Thursday, his day off. The screen stated that it was Friday.

Ian sank into his leather chair nervously and rolled backward as far as he could in the cubicle, tilting his head back to get a good look at the upper floors from which he'd just emerged. His office was designed in open-air style, like the restaurant next door, sharing the ceiling of the tremendous lobby.

To his relief, everything looked as it always had. Nothing but a combination of the elegant time-share, condo and hotel rooms overhead that made up the Embarcadero Multiplex. Working in the cubicle, though somewhat confined, was actually very pleasant, because of the loftiness of the encompassing atrium lobby, over 100 stories high. From his particular cubicle, which had one of the best views, often Ian would gaze up at what looked like an inverted right angle pyramid of floors, with each subsequent floor jutting out several feet farther than the one below. The effect, from the lobby gazing upward, was like staring at an M.C. Escher print. No door was visible. In fact, from his vantage point, it looked as though he had the entire complex to himself. Seldom had he seen anyone walk the balconies above. Even the glass elevators floating up and down the hundred-something floors always appeared empty because of the special tinted glass. The sanctuary-like setting was hardly a jail. What had come over him, he wondered. Was it a stroke? His heart began palpitating, his left eye tearing again, blurring his vision.

Ian closed his eyes and breathed in deeply. A tear released itself from the right corner of his left eye. He wiped it with his knuckle and glanced with relish at his desktop and inbox. Besides mail, there were the photos to edit. He'd leave the best for last, in order to revive his energy at the end of the day. Automatically, he began answering the messages, working on the tasks required, before eventually pausing to consider the hallucination he had just experienced. So if this wasn't a jail, where had he been?

He had to talk to someone about what had transpired. Barb. He'd call on his break. He returned to the messages in his inbox, and presently losing interest, he found himself reaching into his empty shirt pocket to check his own personal messages.

Suddenly he remembered his MEphone and looked in the bottom drawer where he usually hid it, under the papers. To his delight, his entire briefcase was there, with his MEphone, MEpad and camera! "YES!" he found himself saying aloud. Then again, why shouldn't they be where he had left them? He was confused. Immediately, he popped two pseudoephedrine and felt better. Certainly his MEphone and MEpad would have some answers to his strange experience. He could call Barb, investigate.

To his dismay, his MEphone was dead. He tried pressing the power switch several times to no avail. Not a flicker of light softened the cold black screen displaying greasy finger prints. He pulled his MEpad out of his briefcase and hit the power belly-button. The machine remained silent and dark.

He cursed aloud. He almost felt like weeping. He was overreacting to low batteries. Perhaps he was just suffering from low blood sugar. He hadn't slept well and didn't remember having eaten breakfast.

He took a breath and remembered the spare charger in his desk drawer. He plugged it in, and tethered his MEphone to the pad with the emergency umbilical cord he had stored. Once charged, the wireless sync would kick in. To his delight an orange light glowed on the side of the MEpad power cord. Now he'd just have to wait. His stomach grumbled. His screen told him it was not yet lunch time. He couldn't call Barb for a couple of hours anyway, he realized.

He returned to his work, but presently found himself looking for a coworker in whom he might confide. Really, there were none with whom he felt at liberty to be candid. His eye began tearing, his head pounding.

Ian stumbled aimlessly over to the coffee machine. Just then, his coworker Robin approached with her stylish short gold and copper hair streaked with red. Ian tried to look as though he were too busy pouring coffee to admire her tall, trim figure.

She scanned her retina with the sensor to subtract the price of the coffee from her net worth. "How are you," she said plainly in greeting. It was not a question. Her voice was throaty and sexy, like that of Mae West, and she spoke with very little movement of her facial muscles. Consequently, her face was young and smooth.

Ian nodded in response, extending his coffee cup as though to toast to good health, but tried not to dwell too long on her gaze. No one burned him twice.

"Everything okay?" she inquired.

Ian peered at her through his leaky eye, hoping the tear would not release itself. Then it occurred to him: why not tell her? Her cynicism at work had set her apart from the rest in his mind. Unlike the mannequin-like cheer of his coworkers, Robin never masked her unhappiness in ingenuous smiles. Instead of cheerleading poorly-thought out ideas, she was always the first to happily throw a wrench of integrity into the machinery, to pour cold water on the upbeat, dishonest babbling of staff meetings, causing a sudden silent void. Other than these periodic bursts, she primarily kept to herself.

Ian had always marveled at how candid Robin could be without losing her job. Obviously Bear-TT knew the value of Robin's web wizardry.

"Actually a really strange thing happened to me on the way to the office," he said.

"Oh?" Robin gazed at him from behind her mug. He tried to stay focused on his story, instead of the green feline eyes.

"I... I." Suddenly Ian felt self-conscious.

Robin stared at him patiently, stirring her coffee with her index finger.

"Does this building house a prison on its top floors?"

"What makes you ask that?" Robin licked her finger and looked at Ian intently. Ian couldn't help flashing on his intimate experience of that tongue back in his Tiburon home. A year ago, she had grown extremely friendly at work, after a long hiatus.

Just then, Alice called Robin away to look at something on the website. Ian begrudgingly trudged back to his desk, thinking about Robin. Over the last several years, Robin had dropped by his home intermittently. She seemed to have only sex on her mind. A few times, she had spent the night, and she had worn him out.

They had wandered out onto the deck after making love and stared at the myriad stars together, listening to the creek of the masts on the yachts in the harbor, the lights of San Francisco as tantalizing as rubies and garnets, an occasional emerald. Breathing in the sea air, glimpsing occasional shooting stars and trying to identify the faint, fast moving satellites without the aid of his MEphone, as the boats slumbered in the harbor, always reminded Ian of faraway coastal towns and fantastic lifetimes. It was these random recollections of enviable moments that gave him the most pleasure in the present.

But their last encounter had not gone off as smoothly. It had been an atypically hot summer's night, almost a year ago. Ian hadn't felt like cooking so he had taken Robin to Sam's Anchor Café next to the Water's Edge Hotel. The deck, a floating dock, had been packed with a hundred or more people, reminding him of the summer nights along the water in Majorca. Tourists flocked to the spot like seagulls to the scraps they left behind on their plates.

For some reason, the conversation began to sour. She seemed to be growing bored. He hadn't been able to figure out whether it had been the conversation about their aspirations. Or whether she had thought him too forward when he asked her if she'd ever like to live in Tiburon. Probably she could tell he was starting to get attached, he figured.

In between all the awkward silences, he invited her to go on the Ferry Sunset Cruise around Richardson Bay, hoping Captain Maggie would help him rekindle the evening's spark.

"Not this time," Robin said, standing, to his amazement. "I have to head back."

"Was it something I said?" Ian scanned his retina without looking at the bill and rose to follow her.

"We're pretty different," Robin said bluntly. "I was hoping to keep things light."

"We'll both be light on the water," he laughed. "No? What about in the tub again? We'd also be light there...."

"There's no tub," Robin said with irritation.

Ian was perplexed. "Well, not here at Sam's, but in my home."

"Right, we're at Sam's," Robin muttered. "Look, Ian, I need to get going."

"At work we're not so different," he had offered.

"I hate Tiburon," she said.

"Can I walk you to your car?"

"I'll be fine. It's safe here, right? That's one of the things you love about it, isn't it? Millionaires only go after big stuff and poor people," Robin said, heading off without looking at him.

"You were saying about a jail above us?"

Robin's whispered voice startled Ian. As his gaze followed the thigh high black leather boots, cut-off shorts and spiky neon hair over his desk, he realized she would probably dig his jail story, this woman who hated gated communities. The fact that she was whispering gave him hope that she might not think him a nut.

"You're not going to believe this, but I woke up in some prison that might actually be in this building... because I just took the elevator and here I am. Or maybe it was just a dream."

Robin almost spilled her coffee. She didn't look skeptical, she was suddenly riveted.

"You're not on antidepressants, are you?" she asked.

Ian shook his head. "Just pseudoephedrine. But that makes no sense for this to be a prison, right?" Ian said pointing upward.

Robin nodded, slowly a grin spread over her face. "You mean you finally realized you felt confined like I do in Tiburon!" she laughed through her teeth, staring at him in her old risqué way.

For a second Ian was too stunned to respond. Then he said, "Really, Robin, it was weird." He began to let down his guard, fanning his longish brown hair with his fingers. "I mean I woke up in this weird prison with interactive multi-screens in the cells and—Today some guards came and—It does sound too weird. But they really made me put on this suit, which was in my cell, and escorted me to our elevator. Really, Robin, now that I'm remembering it all, maybe there really is a jail up there somewhere," Ian began whispering. "Come with me after work. I can show you."

"I've heard that line before," Robin laughed and headed back to her desk.

Ian in turn returned to his cubicle. He reflected. He had to be careful; she was smiling at him again.

He glanced at his phone. Certainly by now there'd be just a glimmer. He'd be able to use it as long as it was connected to the pad. It was high time he went to lunch and called Barb. She'd help him sort things out.

He pressed the power. An icon came on, and then a little thin white bar at the bottom. Nothing he did would change the image. At least it was on. Then he realized with horror the configuration belonged to the master reset. Something was erasing the contents of his phone, all his contacts, his notes, passwords to his accounts, directions. He caught himself and laughed aloud. All that data was safely backed up on the net! *I can just sync it on the net when it reboots*, he reminded himself.

The incoming email glass-tinking sound on his work pad compelled him to desist obsessing. It was his boss with some suggestions for the current ad campaign.

Ian grabbed his MEphone again. The thin little bar was now filled with a tiny corner of white. Ever since he quit smoking, Ian had taken to playing with his MEphone whenever he got fidgety or lonely. If there were no new messages to receive or send, nothing to text, he'd Ogle® his own name to monitor whether the links to his photographs and work had shrunk or expanded.

He felt fidgety, but alas, his mobile had gone a tenth of the way through its erasure and nothing he did could stop the progress of the white bar. "Oh well," he thought. He wiped his eye with a tissue and headed over to Robin's desk to invite her to the Atrium next door for lunch. There was too much work to take a longer break.

But her cubicle was empty. He rooted around his briefcase for his emergency power bar. There will be other chances now, he told himself, his mouth full of sugar-free protein-chocked cookie-dough flavor.

III

MIRACULOUSLY, WORK ENDED a bit early. Ian had been so swamped, he forgot to check on the status of his MEpad. He glanced at the MEphone. It had rebooted, but to his dismay, even the calling software must have been erased, he realized, because the phone would not receive nor place calls. Nor was it hooked up to the net, he soon found out; no access to his backups, then. Ian's heart sunk. Maybe once he synced his pad again, the access to his phone would somehow also be restored. At any rate, he'd have to wait until the pad was ready to trouble shoot some more, since his phone was clearly not talking to the net. Only when he examined the pad, it was still dead. Something had gone wrong with the connection. He'd charge it back home. Home?

An uneasy feeling overtook him. Was it the intermittent headache he had developed since his jailing or hallucination? Ian packed up his valuables and decided to relax with a drink and dinner in the revolving restaurant on the top floor. The panoramic view of the surrounding skyscrapers, bay and bridge was stunning as they revolved around the diners. That would help restore him to the mood he was in before his devices and mind began deceiving him. *Funny*, he thought, *it's as though some common fuse in all three has shorted.*

After washing in the restroom beyond the lobby fountain, he headed over to the glass elevators and waited for the express. He loved watching the restaurant and diners becoming miniatures, nearly disappearing as he floated upward in the lift.

This time, however, rather than sailing upward without interruption, the elevator stopped abruptly on the third floor. Three policemen entered. The doors closed. Ian tried to reassure himself, it was just a coincidence. After all, the ones in his nightmare had dark sunglasses.

The lobby became a toy model below and the view went dark. Ian turned to behold one of the officers staring at him. He was big without being overweight and had a large pink head, stubble for hair, a mustache the color and texture of a broom and cold blue eyes. After what seemed like an eternity—Ian's heart in his now cotton-dry mouth; eyes studying the lumps and uneven terrain of the officer's cranium, Ian's left eye watering for the first time all afternoon—the elevator stopped. It was the 84th floor.

"Out," said the officer with the lumpy, large head, putting his hand on his holster.

"Are you talking to me?" Ian inquired.

"Out!" bellowed the bald lumpy-headed guard, before putting on a pair of sunglasses. The other two officers followed suit. The doors opened onto a row of jail cells.

"Keep moving!"

Ian despaired. Many years ago, when he'd been depressed, he kept having recurring nightmares in which his torturers would pick up right where they left off in the previous dream, like a *Twilight Zone* episode. This was just one of those nightmares. It was time to wake up. Instead he felt himself going cold.

As they made their way onward, Ian noticed the cells were largely empty. Through the four-foot-high bars, which in his cell remained hidden from his view by the ivory glass balconies, Ian saw a couple of captives lying or sitting on their cots. Alas, there were too many real, concrete details for a dream: the texture of the nicely painted walls surrounding the bars, the wooden grain of the doors visible underneath the coat of mocha-colored paint. In fact, he felt more awake, his senses more alert, than they had since his youth.

"Could you please tell me why I am being held?" he pleaded, wiping his eye, the events of the morning suddenly a raw wound again.

"Why don't you ask your conscience that same question?" one slender guard offered, almost cordially, with a sympathetic smile.

No, this was no dream and with the realization came the burning of cheeks and back of his neck. It took him a second, but he recalled the feeling years ago, in his teens, during an Occupy-style protest, when a cop had asked him to hand over his red spray paint can as evidence of his defacing of the Civic Center.

The meaner-looking cop snorted.

"But I have a right to know the charges," Ian turned to him, his tone begging. The guard only shrugged. The lumpy-headed guard waved his ADS heat ray, as though to discourage conversation.

Had it been the graffiti? It had taken a week to sandblast his anti-war slogan from the heavily textured stone blocks he had inspected daily to gage the longevity of his message. While that day he had managed to skateboard to his freedom without having to dodge police bullets, perhaps the reporter who had interviewed him before the crime had turned him in, or his editor. Perhaps the badly-oxidized wheels of justice were only now catching up to him.

I'm just claiming my portion of public property to tell the side of the story the press overlooked. What I want to know is why the lives of the children killed by U.S. troops are worth less than this wall?

Of course his statement had never seen print. If he could delete that frame from the album of his life, would he now? He was suddenly dizzied by a wave of nostalgia for those days. There had really been nothing wrong with what he had done. On the contrary. How had he become....

He tripped, steadied himself, looked from side to side at the guards who suddenly stopped and regarded him with suspicion. They continued toward the bank of cells.

Yes, he had undergone a tremendous metamorphosis since those days. If not in ideals, in actions. True, his means to those ideals had been more extreme back then. But weren't all young people rebellious, drunk with delusions of grandeur and immortality? Wouldn't it be counterproductive to punish him for taking actions he now viewed as extreme? After all, wasn't jail supposed to be a deterrent?

He had dozens of colleagues who could attest to the fact that he was engaged in the betterment of society. Bear-TT was saving countless lives of patients who otherwise would have died of AIDS or cancer. Ian's photographs and collaboration on the ad slogans had certainly contributed to this, he reflected with some pride.

They passed another cell with a fellow who seemed immobile, his head in his hands. Surprisingly, they passed two women as well. Neither gender seemed to notice Ian. Particularly those staring at the color screens droning in their cells. Of these, half were engaged with their interactive sets, laughing, conversing, nodding as though deep in conversation with the three-dimensional images. One tall woman with midriff exposed was involved in an interactive game of tennis, but the top of the cells decapitated her. Perhaps this was the reason for the balconies and short bars—to give the inmates in this co-ed setup some privacy, sort of like blurring their face, since one could not really see into the cells very well except when passing them, and even then, those standing were not there from the neck up. Or perhaps it was to foster the sense of isolation that had been festering in Ian.

They came upon a cell with an elderly couple. Ian wondered if the two had met in the jail and were allowed to marry, or had been incarcerated for a crime they had both committed. Failing to pay a mortgage? Homelessness? At least they had been allowed to be housed together Ian thought. Whether this sort of humane treatment of inmates owed to his being in a low-security prison, or to a new trend, it was a good sign.

The thinner guard pulled out a card and waved it at a tiny red light that unlocked the door to Ian's cell. He held the door for Ian.

"I have a right to an attorney!" Ian said. "Will you arrange a call for me?"

"You expect us to pay for minutes? You got a MEphone, don't you?" the bald guard laughed.

"It's not working."

"Why's that our problem?" The thinner guard shrugged.

"So no one's going to fix my set either?" Ian grumbled. The salt in the corner of his eye was beginning to sting, the tears welling up like poison, making it difficult to see. He used his cuff to wipe them.

"He thinks this is some kind of hotel," the slender guard said to his colleague before the door slammed on its spring.

The meaner-looking, bald guard just stared at Ian through the bars. "Now, tomorrow at work, no hanky panky. No MEphones, no MEpads, no trying to leave to go to lunch or you'll come right back here," he cautioned, picking a piece of food from his teeth.

"But what am I to tell my coworkers if they invite me? That I'm in jail?"

"You try that!" the guard laughed. "Better yet, why not find out what happens when you attempt an escape?"

The thought of interrogation by this official was more than Ian could bare. He sank down into his cot, his head pounding. He felt like breaking down crying, but everything was too absurd. He was dreaming; certainly, one of those dreams where he thought he was awake. It was like some nightmare by Franz Kafka, Ian thought to himself, though maybe what his left eye needed was a good flushing out.

A few visitors marched past Ian's cell. They looked like commuting refugees from the financial District, some with their wires dangling, others with dark GPS mobile glasses and pale blue or white buttoned shirts with ties and neatly ironed slacks. They all seemed to be distracted by conversations on their devices or the scenery or ads on their GPS bifocals.

More clumps of commuters emerged, the women in work skirts and heels, most of them attached to wires or mobile glasses. Then came several women with children, a male here or there with a child. Probably a tour, Ian thought. He stood and craned his neck. More marched by obstructing his view, some on the balcony opposite. Ian noticed one with a briefcase and scooter remove a card from his breast pocket and wave it to open a cell door. Up and down the corridor and across the way, other doors were opening. Soon the sound of sets or pads starting up began to drone out the noise of opening and closing doors. The floor came to life as inmates began interacting with their sets, pads, music or other electronic devices, moving back and forth in their cells. Ian saw only the tops of the heads—some removing clothes and putting on night clothes or lounging attire.

"Thank frickingod it's Friday!" came a male voice from the cell next to his. To his surprise, a woman called out to him from what seemed like the same cell, then the sound of two children.

"Turn that screen off! It's dinner time!" the woman shrieked at them.

So the hotel in which he worked also housed a co-ed prison which allowed families. Obviously it was a low-security, luxury prison, perhaps where corrupt politicians and millionaires ended up. Perhaps some Bear-TT employees?

Judging from the hubbub, which seemed to issue from the floors below and above, there seemed to be a great number of these returning inmates. Ian knew prisoners were farmed out to various corporations, but he had never fathomed the scope of the phenomenon.

Ian scolded himself. How could he have not realized he had been working along side prisoners? What a fool his coworkers would think him for being so naïve! He wondered how many at work were in his predicament. Did his boss know about his new situation? Would he fire him if he didn't and were to find out? What had Ian done to wind up here anyway?

The answers to these questions obviously would find no response until morning, Ian realized. One thought was reassuring, however. Regardless of the details, the prisoners were obviously allowed use of their electronic gadgets.

Anxiously, Ian fumbled in his briefcase for his devices and charger. He set the docking station that was left there for him on the desk and placed his MEphone inside. A sliver of green lit up the phone's battery icon denoting that the battery was charging properly. The sense of relief made him feel giddy. Soon, he told himself, things would begin looking better. He'd sync his phone, get back in touch with his friends, who'd connect him to a lawyer. He could use the time anyway to organize his photographs and docs, tackle his budget, check out some music and apps, why not?

He decided to busy himself with a photo series on the jail. He could imagine himself during a campaign deadline at work, looking back on these moments of leisure with fondness at some distant future time.

After about an hour of shooting with his Canon, the already-loaded card was full. Ian checked the MEpad. The orange ember had burned out. He cursed and jiggled it until it turned on again. Another hour wasted, he thought.

He thought of how dismal his events calendar would become, army green for distasteful events, no more Caribbean aqua fun calendar. Recalling his stay-positive podcasts, he reassured himself that his turquoise photography calendar would brighten things.

Ian tried the power switch on his pad without success. *Give it a good hour,* he told himself. Directly opposite, a woman with a child entered a cell into which Ian had already witnessed a man enter. Some time later, Ian noticed some prisoners leaving; one cute woman with a blonde pony tail in grey, three-quarters running tights and white tennis shoes, adjusting a tunes pod on her hip. It seemed as though some of the prisoners were on the honor system, he mused, baffled.

By seven o'clock at night, at least according to the time on his MEphone, most of the cell doors remained shut, with few exceptions. Ian kept checking his useless MEphone for messages, out of habit. He tried the pad's power button to no avail. The little orange ember was no more. He cursed and wiggled it and it came back on. The phone was now fully charged, so it had to be the power cord. This explained the problem at work as well. Only what if he were denied a new cord? The thought of enduring jail without his beloved devices seemed too much to bear. He had no idea how attached he'd become.

I'm going through withdrawal, he told himself. Perhaps this explained his headache when he first arrived. Absentmindedly, he wiped his eye on his cuff.

Ian didn't hear the cell doors open much for two days, though occasionally a senior or family member would wander out or in with a shopping bag. Every time they left the cells, an alarm would sound and a cell number would be announced. Were these escapees? Or just under heavy surveillance.

Of course, he realized, *it's the weekend; we're let out of here mostly to work. Only why would the chap next door be so happy it was Friday, then? He must have been one of the ones they let out to go shopping.* Ian knew the society had been jailing criminals at record proportions, but he had no idea it had come to this.

Over the course of the next two days, with no devices and nothing to do, Ian's feelings of panic only increased. It was the music he was missing most now. And texting. And selfing. He was also vexed by the idea of his email piling up, unanswered and unfiled. He still could not shake the habit of checking his pocket for his MEphone. Several occasions of staring at his own reflection in the dark glass sped his cure. Now all his obsessive tendencies were focused on one sole goal: freedom. He had decided that in order to figure out how to accomplish this, it was imperative to understand the motive behind his imprisonment. When he tired of tinkering with his pad charger, Ian would pace on his treadmill and review what he could remember of the year, searching for clues besides the spray paint episode.

He stopped in the middle of his sixty-fourth sit-up. He had forgotten to return the magazine he had borrowed from Helbert when he'd left town and asked Ian to retrieve his mail. Ian had read somewhere that tampering with mail was a federal offense with a minimum five-year sentence. Had Helbert complained? He was such a whiner. Or that other psycho neighbor across the street with the body of a pear who, in spite of disliking dogs, had purchased one when the house up the hill had been broken into and was baffled when the burglar who hit her house befriended the dog by offering it treats. Perhaps she had seen Ian reading Helbert's magazine and had called that terrorist hotline she was always sending tips to.

Or was it when he raced through the Fast Track lane behind the Mercedes after his balance had run to zero and he had forgotten to update his new banking profile?

No. How foolish of him. He'd been in denial and had really hit a bicyclist the time he thought it was a tree branch or his neighbor's side-view mirror and he had sped off without looking back.

He wiped his eye and a cold wave of panic overtook him. He was shaking. It was all the pseudoephedrine he'd been buying; more than the allowed three boxes a month. That was a Federal offense as well!

That was absurd. He wouldn't be in this situation over cold

medicine, a magazine or a hit and run, would he? Misdemeanors, weren't they? Unless he'd hit a person. But he'd know, wouldn't he? Surely, they would have informed him.

No, clearly, they thought him a terrorist. There was that Marsec warning on the ferry. Had he done something on Federal waters to trigger that? He knew penalties were stiffer in certain maritime zones.

Absentmindedly, he pulled his MEphone from his shirt pocket and checked it. He congratulated himself for only having checked a few times this hour. The behavior was clearly diminishing. *Self-control*, he told himself, thinking of his mother.

Suddenly he remembered that the weekend would soon be over and he hadn't called her! She was expecting him Monday evening to rearrange the furniture to accommodate her new walker. It wasn't really that the walker wouldn't fit into her elegant one bedroom, he reflected, but rather she wanted help with her apprehensions about her new dependence on such a contraption. Though she was ninety, the expectations she held for herself were of a fifty-year old, he smiled, recalling her fussing with her eyeliner and lipstick in the mirror before he last took her out to Scott's Seafood. She had maintained her good looks well.

His faint smile faded to a grimace as he imagined her calling his home. She'd keep calling and grow frantic with worry with each subsequent call. Ian seized the bars in disbelief, searching for a guard to allow him his one phone call. Presently, he gave up and sat back down on his cot. At work tomorrow, first thing, he'd call Pleasant Gardens and arrange for one of the workmen to help her out. Then, he'd tell his mother—*What?* he realized.

Aside from the time he had almost burned down the house with his chemistry set and she mistook the burn for his having spilled soil repotting house plants, he had never kept a secret from her. He thought about the time he had been busted for smoking pot in the high school bathroom, then for underage drinking. Now they just laughed about it.

A chill went through him. Had these prior crimes counted in some way? Three offenses had locked people up indefinitely.

You're never going to believe this, Mom, but, I'm in jail.

She'd blame him. That would be the end of her heart. He couldn't tell her until he had more information.

He wiped his eye again. It was getting increasingly difficult to see, to think. If only he had hot water and a washcloth. First thing at work tomorrow, he'd get hold of a phone and charger. Robin would probably help. This thought cheered him.

His head. He got up and lapped up some water from the sink, washed his face, brushed his teeth and prepared himself for bed.

For the first time in months, he didn't chase the image of Robin's Cheshire cat smile and feline eyes from his thoughts, instead allowing more and more memories of her to flood his mind. Presently, he was asleep.

IV

MONDAY, ALICE HEAPED on the work when Ian arrived. A new supervisor named Neil had apparently replaced Pat. The other change was that his work phone had been disconnected to "minimize interruptions." And Alice never stayed off hers long enough for him to borrow it. Eventually, Ian gave up on the calls; all his numbers were on his dead devices. He cursed himself for having placed his mother on speed dial instead of having memorized the number.

But soon, lost in returning emails and prioritizing his to-do list, Ian gave up on calling Pleasant Gardens for his mom. Funny, he thought with some resentment, how the most trivial aspects of work, had such a way of overriding the most urgent personal emergencies. Ian didn't have a chance to speak to anyone about his myriad questions until mid-afternoon when he snuck into the bathroom to wash out his handkerchief and bathe his eyelid in warm water. All morning, he had scrutinized his coworkers and none behaved as though he or she were an inmate. Then again, why should they? He wondered whether he himself was truly imprisoned. It was difficult to believe this at work.

Finally, Ian's thirst drove him to the bottled water station at the same time as Richard, "the Walking Encyclopedia," was retrieving a cup of coffee. Richard and Ian had often gone out for a drink at Vesuvio's saloon in North Beach. He was one of the few coworkers Ian could tolerate: friendly with a great sense of humor.

"When are you getting out?" Ian asked, jovially, scanning his retina to deduct the cost of a bottle of water.

"Five, like everyone else."

"Not 'off,' 'out.' I mean, your release date?"

Richard peered down at him almost coldly through his good looks.

Ian almost regretted having asked the question. What if some folks were inmates but kept their identity private?

"December, before the Christmas rush," Richard responded politely. The date was the deadline for the ad campaign.

"No, I mean, *your* personal release date. They haven't really told me mine and—"

"Excuse me?"

Ian stared hard at Richard. He debated telling him what was happening to him. Chances were he'd just think him daft and that would be the end of their tenuous collegiality. After all, wasn't he going nuts? "Nothing," Ian mumbled almost stumbling back to his desk. He was glad for the privacy of his cubicle walls when he arrived.

Several hours later, when Ian's eyes felt as though they were congealing from working on his inbox, he gave a furtive glance around the office and pulled up his personal web account. He had been warned by the guards not to use his pad or phone and he imagined the ban extended to this site. He had protested that he was allowed one phone call. "Besides everyone has those devices in their cells."

"You waive all your rights the second you enter your work place," the meaner, lumpy-headed guard had said. "Rights-free zone, remember?"

When he was satisfied that no eyes were upon him, Ian logged into his account. A yellow and black hazardous waste icon popped up on the screen with red letters: "ACCESS DENIED." Ian shuddered and scanned the office again for potential guards or informers. He wiped his eye. Then he checked the caps lock key and typed his password again. The red letters flashed once more. His work pad moaned with more incoming mail on his work account. Ian jumped as Alice dropped another pile of documents and photographs on his desk. He covered up by bolting toward the coffee machine.

Robin looked up, fluttering her lashes, after the retinal scan for her coffee. Her pupils dilated as Ian came into focus. Without much introduction, he got right to the point.

"Would I be able to borrow your MEphone?"

"Yours is broken too?" Her gaze was intense. Ian felt a part of something sink inside him, while another bubbled to the surface.

He nodded. "My Pad too."

Robin took a pensive sip of coffee. "Mine too," she muttered.

Ian looked into her eyes. Was this a clue of inmate status? He stirred some powdered chemicals into his coffee and took a sip. "Hey Robin, where you living these days? Still the Mission?"

"Here," she said plainly, smiling. Was she just toying with him because of their previous conversation?

"Funny." He half snickered and took a step closer to her. "Me too," he continued.

"I know," she responded, looking him over a little too intimately for comfort.

"So when do you expect we can retire?" Ian tested the waters.

"Never." Robin shrugged.

Ian gazed into transparent emerald eyes. Robin didn't flinch or meet his gaze with judgment. "Do you ever feel like you're an indentured servant... like you're in jail?" he challenged.

"How'd you guess?" she laughed. She cocked her head in an almost overly-flirtatious manner. "You in jail too?"

"Yeah, baby. It's right upstairs. Care to see it? Or is it against regulations. Do you know?" He looked at her, almost pleading.

"You're funny. But I don't have to see your cell to know what one is like," Robin gestured at their cubicles. She laughed, cupping her thermos in her hands and taking a loud slurp of black liquid. He could not see her eyes through her hair. "Seen any good movies?"

"None. Absolutely none," Ian said with irritation, wiping his eye absentmindedly. "Like I told you, I've just been stuck living in this weird prison up there."

"I just saw *Avatar* at a friend's who lives a few floors up," Robin said, still not looking up.

"Another fellow prisoner? Would you mind introducing me?" Ian tested the waters.

She ignored him and nattered on about the film's virtuous anti-colonialist perspective. Perhaps she thought the office bugged. Everyone had MEphones, after all.

"*Avatar,* huh. Wayback machine," he said finally. "Wasn't that before GPS bifocals?"

While the bifocals were part-clear lens and part-GPS, most people relied on their GPS scenery simulator to guide them as they walked, instead of actual scenery. It was especially helpful for directions as holographic arrows would light the way. The bifocals also enabled various stores to advertise through the earphones attached to the glasses, as one passed them. It always startled Ian how only the stores that contained items or packages he might actually purchase would call out to him, merely based on his purchasing profile.

"Hey good-looking." Richard had sidled up to Robin and was peering down at her, grinning.

"Hey, how are you?" Robin's discreet smile hinted far too much familiarity for Ian's comfort. "I'd better get back to it," she said, her temple throbbing slightly and face showing some strain as she departed for her desk.

"Guess, I'd better—" Ian began. It was well past time to wash out the handkerchief with which he'd been wiping his eye.

Richard's hand on his shoulder stopped him. "Hey, buddy. I couldn't really understand what you were asking me earlier," he said. "I was sort of distracted."

"Sure, Richard," Ian agreed. "Hey, I have a favor to ask. Could you plug my pad in at your station? I'm trying to troubleshoot why it's not charging."

"No prob," Richard led Ian back to his desk and plugged the pad in. Within minutes it lit up.

"Now why wasn't it turning on before? Can we wait a sec?" Ian asked, leaning over the machine.

"Sure," Richard said politely. "If you'll excuse me. Be right back." He headed toward the rest room. When he returned, Ian was fiddling with his pad and wiping his eye in an agitated state.

"My files have all been erased! This is the weirdest thing! My desktop looks like the default, yet some things, like this note I wrote, are still here! How do you explain that? If this was reformatted.... This shouldn't be here..."

"May I?"

"Be my guest!" Ian stood up and pulled over another chair, while Richard explored his MEpad. "Oh, this is all that's wrong my friend. Here, type in your password."

Ian obliged. "It says this is not my password, but I've used it for a decade."

"Your password's been reset," offered Richard. "You use all your applications on line?"

Ian nodded.

"That's all it is. Technically, because you used their software, they own the copyright to your work, so you can't access it without your password. Did you forget to pay a bill?"

"Oh, shit!" Ian stood and pounded his hand with his fist. Thursday! The day he woke up in jail, he had been planning to deposit some money in his new account. Somehow, the merger had screwed up his auto-pay. By now, all his accounts would have been in default. Without his email or phone working, he wouldn't have been able to receive any warnings.

He began pacing. Still, they shouldn't have terminated his account without some kind of grace period. It made no sense.

"Take it easy, bud. Once you straighten your accounts out, everything should snap back into place."

How convenient, thought Ian, wiping his eye. So really they, not he, owned even the music he had paid for, all his documents, all his photographs. It was an outrage! How could things have come to this?

The orange light glowed and died.

"Looks like something's wrong on the pad end of your plug," Richard observed. "Maybe it's time to ask Mr. White for a new pad."

"Great," Ian choked, since only Bear-TT employers were authorized to issue ME products and Ian had a terrible feeling this was not a case of unpaid bills. Probably, whoever had jailed him had also removed his device privileges. What had he been thinking? His heart dropped to his stomach at the thought of all his photographs. A lifetime of developing art, gone like that! The movies that were his life, his peak moments—and his music! *Erase a person's music and you erase the pathway to their personal history, their chronology, the feelings and sensations the movies didn't capture! Erase an artist's art and if the artist can't produce any more, you might just erase the artist and all the history he or she represents!*

But, why then, Ian puzzled, did the other inmates seem to have these devices? Were theirs as bereft of real data as his—or was he simply a higher security risk? If only someone would answer his questions!

V

WEDNESDAY, IAN FOUND an envelope on his desk, marked "urgent." Inside, was a piece of toilet paper with blue felt tip ink scrawled on it:

"YOU'RE RIGHT ABOUT ME, BUT WE HAVE TO BE CAREFUL. PLEASE FLUSH."

Ian lit up. He wadded up the paper, stuck it in his pocket and headed straight for the john. Watching it swirl down the pipe, it occurred to him that the note might be from someone other than Robin. He regretted not having hung on to it longer. The ink had been blue, hadn't it? The color pen Richard always used. The print had been all caps. Very male. *We have to be careful.* There was a hint of intimacy there, like an affair. Had he evidence that Richard was attracted to him? Then again, why would Richard be in the closet?

His thoughts snapped back to Robin. At first a distraction, his growing obsession with her was becoming proportionate to his anxiety about not being able to communicate with his mother. At times, he'd startle awake worrying about his mother, her walker and what must have been her own anxiety about the whereabouts of her son.

Unfortunately, over the next few days, Ian did not cross paths with Robin. His repeated trips to the coffee machine were in vain. And with the passing of each day, he became increasingly agitated about remaining completely *incommunicado* with the rest of the world.

A few times he managed to make eye contact with Richard, who grunted a greeting here and there and resumed his trajectory. Somewhat to Ian's relief, when he mustered the courage to ask Richard to lunch, the latter complained that his work load wouldn't allow it.

Thursday, at 4:47, at long last, Ian cornered Robin at the coffee machine.

"Hey, didn't you quit coffee several years back?"

"Sometimes one needs a drug to cope, no?" She looked at him coquettishly.

He took the opportunity to ask her to lunch the following day.

She declined, taking all the buoyancy out of his step again.

Friday, at half-past five, Robin brushed by Ian's desk.

"Dinner plans?" she asked casually.

"Actually, no," Ian answered beaming, beginning to rise from his seat.

"Follow me," she whispered striding out of the office.

Ian wiped his eye on his handkerchief, hit "send," slung his camera bag over his shoulder, and with his long strides, easily caught up with her.

Robin approached the complex doorway. Ian was overcome with a feeling of dread as he recalled the guards' admonition about leaving the building. "Hey, why don't we just have lunch inside in the atrium?" he called out. "My treat."

"Hold on a sec," Robin reached into her purse. Ian's spirits soared at the sight of her phone.

"It's working again?" Ian bubbled, temporarily forgetting his worries.

He could see Robin's temple throbbing as she smiled. "It doesn't call out, if that's what you mean. "Wait," she whispered, fiddling with her screen and key pad. She aimed her camera, fidgeted with her screen some more and looked around furtively, brows knit. Ian noticed an unmistakable trace of fear in her eyes and mannerisms. "Okay," she exhaled finally, then smiled broadly at him, all apprehension gone. "Quickly, follow me," she urged, striding out the door.

"I can't, Robin... I mean, I forgot something...."

"It's O.K., really! Trust me," Robin whispered, almost desperately.

Against his better judgment, like an addict, Ian followed. He glanced over his shoulder as he kept up with her. They proceeded up Drumm Street.

Relieved that no one was after him, Ian began to relax. They exchanged small talk about the heaviness of their work load and the speed with which the cotton bursts of fog were sweeping into the brilliant autumnal sky.

"Your ME," Ian persisted once satisfied that he had spent enough time on pleasantries. "You say you can't call out, but you can still text? Send email?"

Robin shook her head.

Ian frowned. Why didn't she want him to use her phone?

Robin forced a smile. "What's the name of that place in North Beach you like?"

The fog had already begun to erase the tops of skyscrapers as Robin and Ian made their way down Market Street's brick pavement, toward

North Beach. Robin stopped under one of the sycamores, the wind adhering some discarded dirty napkins to its base. She began fiddling with her MEphone to shut it down.

"Robin, why don't you want me to use your phone? Short on minutes?"

"Here you go. Try it."

Hungrily, Ian punched in a few different versions of what he recalled of his mother's number. Nothing happened. He repeated the action several times. The band indicating service was blanked out.

After a while, Robin held out her palm. Ian blinked, then handed over the phone. Robin shut the device down and stored it in her purse. She glanced up at him, nervously fluffing the reds and copper streaks in her stylish short gold hair.

"So you're right. We are both in jail. We're not allowed calls. We jailbroke my phone, so it can talk to some wireless networks."

Ian spun around and started walking. They passed a prone figure in a boarded-up doorway, blanketed like a hastily wrapped corpse in a war zone. "But it makes no sense. Jail—" Ian muttered, after a while.

Robin laughed, "Come on, Ian. Haven't you noticed how strange the cubicle is you go home to every night?"

Ian recalled his tiny cell with the stained toilet, chipped walls and bars. "Yeah, I know we're in jail. I mean..." His mind flashed on the odd treadmill, interactive set, his desk and few clothes. The procession each morning to work. "I don't know—" Ian conceded, rifling his fingers through his hair, then glancing sadly down at his shoes. Finally, he summonsed the courage to stop and look intensely into Robin's green feline eyes. "Okay, Robin. But why?"

"Why no calls?"

"Why are we in jail?!" Ian hissed with irritation.

A grin spread across her face. "Oh, nothing in particular. Why were serfs indentured?"

"Funny."

"Not really. OK, then. You first. Tell me, Ian. What's your crime?"

"I don't—that's what I mean," Ian stumbled. "I'm still trying to figure it out. They've never informed me, formally."

"Right," Robin said skeptically.

"Isn't there a law against that?" Ian vaguely remembered.

"Aren't there laws against lots of things that aren't enforced?" Robin laughed. Then she smiled, though it was difficult to tell if her smile was genuine, or really more of a grimace.

"What if it didn't just happen to you Ian? What if you've been in jail for years? What if we've both been in jail forever?" Robin began to laugh.

They turned up Montgomery and immediately were engulfed by a marching army of suited men, their shirts and slacks perfectly pressed and creased; the women uniformed in heels, short skirts and tight tops revealing no cleavage. The throng herded past them en route to the BART train or parking lots. The wind made Ian's eye tear uncontrollably.

"So see that phenomenon, Ian?"

Ian stopped, wiped his eye, blinked, scanning his surroundings. A thin man with grey hair and tie bumped into Ian from behind and apologized before dashing uphill toward North Beach.

Robin laughed, shaking her head imperceptibly at the commuter. She continued.

"Haven't you ever wondered about this herd phenomenon at rush hour? I mean, do you think this looks normal?—grown people rushing down sidewalks in the same direction at the same time like lemmings, without thinking that they're on some kind of team?"

"Go 99ers," Ian snickered. They both began laughing uncontrollably again, evidently tipsy on each other's presence.

"What if we're not the only prisoners at work? What if we're all prisoners in this society? The workers anyway," Robin stated.

"Plausible," Ian said, still smiling.

"I mean, look at them! They're so automated. Like the guy who ran into you. That you should suddenly stop wasn't in his program. What if he has a chip implanted in his brain? What if they all do? What if thanks to these chips, this society's 'owners'—AKA the 1%—allow them out of their jail cells to go to work each morning. Then around five p.m., they're led back to the jails en masse, thanks to their mobile phones, wireless devices, whatever, that trigger their REM, creating the rush hour phenomenon?"

"Cute," Ian smiled, somewhat amused. He found himself focusing more on the intricate patterns in her jade eyes, her lips, the mole on her neck, than on her words. "But don't you mean, 'we?'"

"Well exactly. Haven't you noticed you get this weird impulse to use some kind of device the second you get off work?"

Ian laughed.

Robin attempted to suppress a smile. "What if it's no coincidence? What if prolonged use of these electronic devices triggers our brain-enhancer chips which, in turn, activates our you know, hyper-REM sleep states—you know, our utopian illusory worlds, built from images and sounds from, uh, interactive screens.

"But no one realizes all this," she continued, momentarily composing herself, holding back a giggle. "We simply think we have to make a call or hear some tunes or check messages and presto... we're beamed into some pseudo-reality. Taking the BART back to the East Bay or Marin. You thought you were taking the ferry back home to Tiburon, right? Arriving in your Tiburon mansion, seeing me at Sam's. Leading a fulfilling life. Ha!" Robin cackled, almost maniacally. "But all along, you were sitting in your jail cell. Little did you and I suspect, when we switched on our MEphones, that those sexy little white wires were our tethers, our umbilical cords to our imprisonment."

They turned left onto Columbus Avenue. "You've certainly given this a lot of thought," Ian said.

"Like you, I have a lot of time on my hands to think," Robin said flatly. Was her paradigm a shell game to mask some terrible crime, or was she just nuts, he began to wonder. *Shame*, he thought.

"Robin," Ian interjected. "Don't you remember from our Bear-TT anxiety workshop: 'What if' thinking is just Worrier negative self-talk."

"Ha ha," Robin laughed sarcastically.

Ian knit his brows. "You're not really serious. You're speaking metaphorically, right?"

She stopped and stared at him for several seconds. Then her deadpan face broke out into convulsive peals of laughter. "Absolutely. What are you thinking? You can't blame me for wanting to infiltrate reality with subversive imagination every now and then, right?..."

Ian flashed on his life in Tiburon: piles of dirty dishes and laundry; his empty refrigerator, endless supermarket shelves boasting too many confusing choices; the long lines; his desk piled high; his mailbox jammed with nasty notices and junk mail; his boss's diatribe at the last meeting; the ticket and late notices he hadn't followed up.

"Right," Ian mumbled.

Caffé Puccini was one of the only North Beach venues that had preserved its original style. While seeming cozy back at the turn of the century, it now seemed expansive and authentic, given that most restaurants and cafes were a third their size compared to the previous century. This change was acceptable to the general public due to the increasing popularity of wall-size picture frames, allowing restaurants to project virtual views through false windows of scenery like the Venice canals, Greek windmills or other exotic locals.

The quality of the cuisine and charisma of its generous owner, Graciano Lucchesi, who refused to raise prices, kept it from going under.

"Look, your favorite table." Graciano's cousin, Dolores, smiled broadly at Ian and tucked a lock of gold hair into the bun piled high on her head. She and her coworker, Areli, always seemed pleased to see Ian, though at times he'd occupy the table for hours, working on his photographs. Gracefully, Dolores bent her hour-glass figure over them to close the ceiling-high windows.

"The hotter it gets in the day, just make more fog at night. Free air-conditioning," she smiled. She fed an old-fashioned bill in the adjacent jukebox and selected Patty Prado.

Robin reclined back into the window seat facing the green awning of Café Trieste. She gazed at a trolley full of tourists rolling by Calzone's red awnings on inauthentic rubber wheels. "Great choice," she added. "Off the radar. They even still accept cash."

Ian had a hard time chuckling. He was preoccupied with his current predicament, his coworkers' reactions, were they to learn the truth about it, and the temptation to attempt a jail break after dinner with Robin.

"Seriously, though. Are we the only ones at work who are in jail?" he inquired.

Robin fiercely shook her head. "Everyone's in jail." She glanced up and caught his expression. "Don't you think? But this system depends on each inmate blaming him or herself. You think: *I'm the only one, the only closet inmate, the only loser. There's something wrong with me and everyone else is doing things right. And if I only could get along as well as the rest, I'd make it.*"

Was she back onto her parable? "But our coworkers don't seem to think they are in jail. And they don't look like it," Ian said, now beginning to feel genuine concern for Robin.

"That's because they're not in REM when they're at work," Robin joked.

"And remind me why they're in REM?"

Robin read his expression. "I knew you wouldn't believe me. The absurdity of it, is what enables the system to survive," Robin teased with overly-dramatic emphasis.

Areli set down their plates. Robin took a bite of clam linguini and closed her eyes as though she'd never experienced such a feast.

Ian admired her sensuality. "That good?" He was trying to recall the time when she reached climax with that same expression. Had it been the morning they had greeted the dawn then gone out to breakfast at seaside bakery? Or in the alley on the way to the movies?

"Especially compared to prison food," Robin winked, changing the subject to the charming view from the window, then his photographs, then his most recent trip.

What had become evident was Robin's refusal to reveal her crime if she knew it; worse was the possibility that she didn't know it and he'd never learn his either.

In either case, her REM fantasy was probably how she avoided responsibility for either having committed some heinous crime, or the horror of being held without knowledge of her crime.

He wondered how long she had been imprisoned. And what he would be like in the same number of years. When he asked her she only evaded the question again.

When they had finished their meal, Areli brought Ian's *doppio cappuccino*, so frothy it looked like a cake: "Ah, here's my 'cap-Puccini,'" Ian winked. Areli smiled at him. He got up to powder it with chocolate.

When he returned he met Robin's gaze and leaned in close so that his near whisper was audible. "Robin, what keeps you going back to the jail? I mean, why should we return?"

He took a sip of his cappuccino, that was so charged with taste he felt drugged. *No one makes a cap' like Puccini*, he thought to himself.

Fear flickered in Robin's eyes. "What do you mean?" she asked.

"I mean, why not rent a room somewhere and stay there?"

"You mean together? Nice, try," Robin joked through her teeth.

"I think it's time for me to get going," Ian said. He scanned his retina to pay the bill, then rose.

Robin stood to meet him. Gently, with both hands, she grasped either side of his jacket collar, as though she were leaning in for a kiss. "Ian, are you deserting me?" she asked, gazing into his eyes seductively. "I was hoping for an escort back to the complex."

They started back up Columbus. Robin took Ian's hand in hers. Ian assessed Robin skeptically. Why was she so sexy? Why were all the women he liked so unstable? Soon, they blended with the commuter stream, en route back to the prison.

VI

IAN LAY ON his cot, his mind reeling, recalling the feel of Robin's hand in his, reviewing the days' events. Still groggy, he recollected Robin's bizarre metaphor. For amusement, he reflected on his idyllic daily routine, attempting to see it through her sci-fi lens. Each day, he used to walk down to the dock and catch the ferry to Fisherman's Wharf, then skip over the Powell-Mason cable car, take it to the California Line and disembark at the Embarcadero next to his work. According to Robin, this experience would be manufactured by a combination of his implant and REM. Here, the metaphor fell apart. The journey seemed no less real than his lunchtime jaunt through the intricate towering marble and brownstone buildings of the financial District, past the tourists, through bustling Chinatown, up Columbus into North Beach, when, according to the metaphor, he sometimes would have been fully awake, since workers were awake during working hours, she had said. His cheek pressed against the bars. Obviously, her game was not going to let him off the hook, allow him to rationalize his imprisonment.

For that, apparently what was required was a more thorough self-inquiry. The Thursday he had been arrested—his day off—had begun like all the other Thursdays, with breakfast and the *New York Times* on his third floor terrace. He distinctly remembered the crystalline view of San Francisco on his left, dissipating dreamlike white puffs of fog softening the panorama spanning from the Ferry Building and TransAmerica pyramid downtown, to the towering, Gothic spires of Grace Cathedral on Knob Hill. Yet somehow, it seemed more alive now in retrospect than it had at the time. According to Robin's silly metaphor, he would have been in his jail cell, in REM sleep the entire time.

Directly across Richardson Bay, framed by the oversized red geraniums he planted in terracotta pots, stood Belvedere with houses poking out of the lush hillside like on Capri Island in Italy, their window boxes dripping with more hanging flowers. The morning had been exquisite, but not unusual in any other way, nothing which corresponded to his current surroundings.

He vividly remembered racing to catch the special 11:45 ferry to San Francisco's Ferry Building to meet his friend Barb. As usual, upon boarding, he had turned to the right, avoiding the hordes, and sat on the secluded bench in the nook behind the gangplank. Robin's paradigm didn't account for the fact that details such as these were far too real. If someone was indeed manufacturing a reality, they would have rendered it more utopian, sans the crowds.

He tried to recall every detail of the trip. The water below had looked like cut green glass, the foamy wake conjuring images of Grecian voyages, ferries through the Caribbean. He had enjoyed the view of Angel Island, then Alcatraz. He got to the bow in time to see the Golden Gate Bridge on the right, the Bay Bridge on the left and the San Francisco skyline straight ahead with its Ferry Building clock tower. There he was, dreaming, spray tinting his sunglasses, the taste of the Indian summer in his mouth—at least now, as he thought about it. Had it been as real at the time?

The city had loomed up with its beautiful brick seaside skyline, Coit Tower like an upright Tower of Pisa and illogical palm trees ruining the ambiance of brownstone buildings yearning for sycamore and walnut. He had walked over to Market Street, hopped on the California cable car and enjoyed the brisk hike to Union Square to meet Barb.

Thanks to her looks, she had secured one of the best tables on Macy's rooftop. She looked magnificent with the sun catching her blonde hair, high cheekbones and the tight, metallic fabric covering her breasts.

He'd have to tell Robin that there were far too many details for her dream story to work. It had been a flawless afternoon; twenty degrees hotter in that sun than in the rest of the city. Ian couldn't really remember what Barb and he had talked about, only that he had taken some fabulous pictures: of Barb, of the French angel in the center of the landscaped square holding Neptune's fork, her copper oxidized to green. The beautifully-crafted brownstones and marble buildings surrounding Union Square, with their textures and flourishes: green marble, copper, awnings, gold gilt, chandeliers glistening, surrounded by sycamores and church spires.

He remembered feeling like the Greek gods on Mount Olympus looking down upon Barbie dolls relaxing on the benches or sipping their cappuccinos at the polished metal tables of Il Caffè—one of his favorite haunts. His camera had recorded the diorama quality of the square, the toy taxis, toy open-air Big Bus tour buses, toy children with a balloon, a model of an elderly woman walking a dog, miniature motorcycle, a child's red and gold cable car passing. From that height, even the homeless were transformed into contented dolls. From that height, it seemed as though everyone else was having a good time too, which made it far easier to enjoy oneself.

He thought about Barb. Imagine he had indeed been in a jail cell on his day off. How would Robin justify Barb? How would she explain their conversation?

He shook his head. Her metaphor was ill-conceived. The details of reality were far too numerous to be manufactured. Why would REMtime include such unpleasant details as sewer smells and litter on his way to the square? He'd have to remember to tell her.

He was seized by a wave of humiliation. Why was he giving a second thought to her cockamamie idea? It was just a joke. He was allowing his attraction to Robin to override his rationality. Obviously, Robin's REM paradigm, joke, whatever, was how she coped with her own imprisonment. Perhaps she had never learned the reasons behind her own imprisonment, and this had driven her insane, prompted her to toy with manufacturing her own reality.

Ian lay back on his cot, with his hands behind his head, a feeling of dread in his gut. How long ago had Robin been imprisoned? And what mental state would Ian find himself in a decade from now if this continued?

Regardless of the degree of Robin's sanity, this year had started out badly and was just getting worse. *Year of the Tiger*, Ian hissed through his teeth, remembering what his Chinese friend, Carmence Gao, had told him the Monday preceding his arrest. *Arrest?* he mused, for he didn't remember ever being apprehended.

Monday had been unusually hot for the city. During lunch, when, according to Robin's paradigm, Ian would have still been awake in Realtime, instead of REMtime, he had stopped for his suits at Ko & Company. Carmence, who owned the dry-clean business, often worked past seven and took only Sundays off—the day Robin would say was her full day in the jail, Ian reflected.

Carmence's husband did all Ian's mending. Over the years, Ian had learned that Carmence's son had an immune disorder which required all her free time and much of her revenue. To help Carmence, Ian bought all his nieces and nephews some of the extra toys Carmence sold as well.

"Look, the orchid you gave me is growing another row of blooms!"

Carmence said, motioning toward the window, her smile lighting up her dimples. Her black short styled hair was cut in angles and points around her pretty face, accentuating her almond eyes.

"It really likes that spot," Ian had commented.

"Yup, every year, this time," Carmence said. "Going to work on your photographs now?" Carmence had inquired.

The two often exchanged stories about interesting occurrences. Ian remembered having complained that day to Carmence about a series of parking and speeding tickets, as well as being put through an hour of tests for a DUI which resulted in 0.0 on the breath-a-lator. "And I don't understand," he had said. "It's my year! I'm a tiger."

"But this, year of the tiger," Carmence had said. "Very bad for tigers. Not good."

Ian let a laugh of amusement escape.

"Oh, Ian. Excuse me," Carmence said suddenly. She rushed into the next room, opened a small icebox and brought out a sandwich wrapped in a napkin. She dashed out the door and handed it to an elderly homeless woman who was struggling down the sidewalk with a discarded baby stroller piled with garbage bags full of belongings.

Carmence popped back in. "I'm sorry, Ian. It's just that I thought of Bertha when I made my sandwich this morning and—" She shook her head. "It's not right. Someone that old. Some people in this country have everything and they don't care that they leave nothing for others."

Ian nodded sadly. He handed Carmence a bill. "Give her this next time you see her."

"You're very generous," Carmence smiled. "What were we saying? Oh yes. I'm sorry. Very bad year for tigers. Stay home. Don't take risks."

Stay home. If only he had been able to follow that advice. Ian ran his fingers along the bars. He had a sinking sensation. Was his odd imprisonment more of the same bad luck with the authorities. "Absurd," he said aloud. For the woman whose old age had brought homelessness, every year now was unlucky.

He did notice that his sporadic headache, which he was learning to live with, subsided when he was daydreaming. Even his eye seemed to be tearing less often.

After talking to Carmence, he had wandered into Molinari's for a custom-made Italian sandwich. Franco, the older, rounder butcher with a mustache and gold spectacles, was busy singing opera with a customer from Puccini's, while Vince, the handsome butcher with streaked hair who'd grown up in the Bronx, served out a taste of Italian syrup to an Italian man in a suit.

According to Robin's fiction, that would have been Realtime, Ian reminded himself, *since it was my lunch break.*

"Pretty early to be hitting the bottle, isn't it?" Ian had joked.

"It's never too early. That hits the spot." The Italian business man played along. "Another shot of *Cuervo*, please."

Ian walked over to Washington Square Park and sat down to enjoy his feast on a bench directly across from Saints Peter and Paul's Parish with its ornate castle spires that, at night, lit up in pale blue light. He noticed a homeless man, who had been napping in the sun, eyeing the half sandwich he was carefully wrapping to take home.

"Would you share this with me? Shame if it goes to waste...." Ian had said, handing the parcel to the man, who got to his feet eagerly to receive it.

Ian's pacing on the treadmill stopped. He used to think that the homeless problem had greatly improved over the last decade. He had assumed the wealth was being distributed a little more equitably, as in Europe. Now as he thought about his own predicament, he wondered whether or not the diminishing number of homeless wasn't owing to increasing incarceration.

The absurdity of it, is what enables the system to survive, Robin had joked.

Shame, he reminded himself, wiping his eye and recalling her finely-chiseled features, graceful figure. *This is simply how she copes with her imprisonment.*

Ian rose and mounted the treadmill, trying to recall more clues to justify his own predicament. Up until his imprisonment, there really hadn't been anything out of the ordinary to justify his confinement. In the days preceding his apprehension, his work had been light and he had been able to take two-hour lunches. He had brought his MEpad so he could work on his photos. He had stopped at one of the last independent stores that still sold books made of paper, City Lights Bookstore, purchased a book of photographs by David Bacon and headed up to Puccini.

Certainly there had been nothing criminal in any of his jaunts, he mused. Had he miscalculated on his Federal Income tax forms the year he did his taxes himself? Ian found himself pacing back and forth on the treadmill. Or was it that time he didn't tell the sales clerk when she forgot to ring up the artificial log for his fireplace? Or the fact that the artificial log company had recently been cited for destroying a rain forest.... What if he had been jailed for something or someone he had photographed? His head began to throb.

What if the next time he had a chance, he were to check into a hotel? Would they come after him? What could they do? For all he knew, he was never getting out anyway. And the death penalty seemed extreme. The next time he had the chance, maybe tomorrow after work, he'd check into a hotel.

Robin's flirtatious smile and feline green eyes penetrated his thoughts. Too bad about her, he reflected. Why was he always attracted to unstable people? Alcoholics, drug addicts, this time a criminal. Except Barb of course. But she was unavailable. And who, after all, would dream of coming between Barbie and Ken?

VII

THE NEXT DAY at work, Ian found himself avoiding Robin. He kept primarily to his cubicle. This only increased his sense of isolation. Now who could he trust enough to help him figure out the motive behind his incarceration? His coworkers would think him insane or the criminal he likely was.

At lunchtime, he caught sight of Richard's hair, floating above the cubicle walls, on the way out of the office. Ian bounded after him.

"Richard! Hey! Got any lunch plans?"

Richard backtracked to Ian's cubicle. "What did you have in mind?'

"Where were you headed?"

"Mijita's."

Suddenly Ian had a craving. "I sure could go for one of those puffy quesadilla things. All that guac—"

"You buying?" Richard prodded.

"Sure!" Ian followed Richard toward the building's entrance. Then he noticed the elegant panther-like officer he'd seen before, peering at him through his square-framed dark glasses, arms crossed.

They started outside. Ian's eye beginning to tear more with the cold, sun and wind.

Panther followed, caught up to Ian. "Excuse me. Can I have a word with you, sir," he inquired, reaching for his heat ray.

"Certainly." He turned to Richard, his heart in his throat, coughed. "Why don't you go on without me. I forgot I volunteered to provide some information," Ian lied, wiping his eye.

The guard escorted Ian to the elevator, up a tremendous number of floors and down a desolate cement corridor stripped of carpet, where the doors were closer together. He opened one and Ian was seized by a foul odor. There was no light inside.

"In the corner, you'll find a bucket for your needs. Food will be dropped off twice a day," the man offered. "After some time here, folks usually remember not to walk out of this compound with coworkers and such."

Ian demanded to know on what grounds he was being held. When he was denied any information, he kept at the guard: why didn't his devices work? What was his new password? The guard snickered and shook his head as he closed Ian's cell door.

For the first hour, Ian pounded on the walls and what felt, oddly, like a wooden door.

He recalled his conversation with the pink, lumpy-headed mean guard.

What am I to tell my coworkers if they invite me to lunch? That I'm in jail?

'You try that! ...why not find out what happens when you attempt an escape?'

He screamed. He whimpered. Finally he settled down in a heap. There, he found a scratchy wool blanket that smelled of mildew. He hoped his eye wouldn't get infected. He curled up without the blanket, and tried to makes sense of what was happening to him and what he would tell his coworkers upon his return. He assumed he'd return. Of course he'd return.

It was Thursday. His one-week anniversary of being in jail. Three days from now would be Sunday. If he was released Sunday night, he wouldn't be late for the staff meeting Monday and folks might just forget he had been missing prior.

For some reason, his thoughts drifted off toward Robin. *Face it,* he thought. *An adolescent who can't accept responsibility for her own actions.* The realization filled him with a weighty and boundless sadness. Why hadn't he checked into a hotel after she had escorted him to Puccini. Somehow she must have helped him evade detection by the guards. Would he ever have the chance again? He fell into a fitful, long sleep.

When he awoke and managed to unglue his left eye, there was a tray of odorless glop. While it had the consistency of dog food, it didn't really taste offensive. He was grateful for the clean water and napkin and used them to bathe his eye. Next he lapped up the food hungrily and ruminated on what he'd tell his boss and coworkers upon his return.

Devoid of most other distractions, including his truncated crush on Robin, his thoughts returned to the most compelling problem. What was his crime? He tried to think, focus his eyes, but the darkness bore down upon them. He yearned for light.

He remembered the flashlight app on his MEphone. It cheered him immensely, until he realized all his apps were tied to his password. Sure enough, when he turned the phone on, the flashlight was not there. But the screen light was enough to be able to see. While there was not much there save for the four corners and bucket, it was somehow reassuring, instead of the feeling of floating in endless space. Unfortunately, within a few hours of high screen use, the entire device went black.

After this, he began to lose track of time and grew increasingly dependent on his meals to help him distinguish night from day. Once he woke up and found that his meal had already been delivered and this threw his count off entirely. Added to this, he became increasingly depressed and began taking long naps, which made it impossible to sleep the equivalent of a night. Interspersed with these long fitful spells of sleep, were hours spent turning over every detail of his life in the vain attempt to find a skeleton worthy of his sentence. Most of his adult life, he had been responsible to a fault. Especially when it came to work.

"It's a mistake!" he kept calling out, at times crying.

A realization came to him. Maybe the movie company had caught up to him for mailing back a lousy movie he had purchased elsewhere instead of the classic they had sent him, which he still enjoyed from time to time. Or for copying the movies he downloaded onto his hard drive with the aid of Pirate freeware. This in itself was considered a Federal crime punishable by a quarter million dollar fine and a decade in jail. A sinking feeling took hold of him. He had heard that under the "Three Strikes" laws, which locked people up for life, the last crime didn't have to be a felony. It could be something petty, like buying too much pseudoephedrine. This could account for the low-security prison.

He began to panic: What if he was to finish out his term in solitary like this? What if he was never getting out, but instead was going to be left to live out his days buried alive like in Edgar Allan Poe's *Cask of Amontillado?*

He gave a second thought to the cases of some whistleblowers in the government's top echelons earlier that century. The first legendary soldier had been held in solitary, forced to sleep naked without sheets or pillows and plied with antidepressants to keep him alive. This, for having disseminated classified information about the government's war crimes, which followers argued actually led to the withdrawal of the nation's imperialist troops. Some argued it was the soldier's contribution that put whistle-blowing websites on the map. These in turn inspired much outrage in an impoverished Tunisian vendor that he set himself ablaze in protest. This ignited a growing movement of leaderless, un-hierarchical, consensus-driven, anti-owner protests world-wide. Ian thought for a moment. While he had briefly partaken in a similar movement as a teen, he had assumed the movement had fizzled out. Perhaps this was not the case and his activism had been regarded with more apprehension. Was this guilt by association, then, the true motivation for the society's jailing? It had happened at least twice before in the country's history: the red menace, then the terrorist menace.

He was filled with a terror he had never known. He screamed and cried out, pounded on the door until his hand felt as though it were broken. He thought of his mother. Clutching his hand, he sank into a heap and cried uncontrollably for what seemed like hours. Eventually he fell asleep.

VIII

WHEN IAN AWOKE, the room smelled like the cat glop version of the prison food, fortunately, the swordfish-smelling kind that vaguely reminded him of one of his favorite meals at Sam's Chowder House in Half Moon Bay. He wiped his eye with the back of his hand. He advanced toward the door and felt for the tin. The wetness of the food around the edge surprised him and he licked his fingers hungrily, like an animal. He felt for a spoon, but could find none. He groped up and down his cell, combing every inch. At last he gave in and ate with his fingers, licking and sucking them, since there was no napkin or cloth. His eye began tearing at the thought that it would not be bathed.

Still, after the meal, he felt less desperate, though he was still quite hungry. He tried to meditate. He remembered what a legendary author named Piri Thomas had written about his own imprisonment: "There is nothing worse than the prison of the mind. In jail, I learned to free myself, to travel, dance... *bailar* with my imagination...." It was a practice he was determined to develop, one of life's tests or lessons, he tried to console himself. The inspiration brought hope. He imagined himself in the tepid aqua water of Playa Del Carmen, saw the storm clouds reflected in the surface, heard the water slapping his torso, looked up and down the coast, spotted seaweed tangled in the bright teal fishing nets. He could feel himself relaxing, his anxiety level evaporating.

Suddenly, as though in a dream, his cell lit up with an aqua hue. A screen projecting clear, refreshing aqua water lit up. The camera entered a cabaña on stilts above some placid neon water, one of the dreamscapes Ian had Ogled®. The camera focused on a plate of grilled crab, lobster, pancetta-wrapped prawns, a Caesar salad, side of mashed potatoes, and a tall, frosty glass of milk—his absolute favorite combination. Ian stood, walked toward the screen, tried to reach and put the lobster in his mouth. Instead only the cat-glop smell of prison food prevailed. How had they known his most recent preferences at the restaurants he frequented? He remembered scanning his retina multiple times to pay various e-bills that must have recorded all his selections. Somehow these were being filed and saved under his name.

Just then an Armani add appeared. How Ian longed for his cologne to eradicate the cat food smell. Suddenly, he realized how filthy he had become. The stench of his own body odor and urine became dizzying.

For the next hour, he could do nothing but plot ways to obtain Armani Cologne.

The screen went black, the room turned back into an abyss. Ian moaned and threw his cat food plate against the wall and began sobbing. For hours after the ordeal, all he could think about was lobster and mashed potatoes. Mashed potatoes and milk. With the images of what he'd seen flashing before his mind's eye, against his will, he felt like Tantalus. "Miiiiiilk!" he cried piteously aloud like a child. Milk, if only he could have some *miiiiilk* coating the sides of his stomach, easing the nausea, calming his nerves. He thought back to his mother bringing him milk in his bed and reading him a bed-time story. He always felt satisfied and contented drinking it and could never seem to get enough of it. His mother always blamed him for drinking it all up! A milk-thief, she called him. And she'd been right.

A wave of guilt suddenly swept over him. Then like an intrusive, unexpected jellyfish, his thoughts returned to the motivation for his incarceration. Was his present circumstance his own doing or due to something beyond his control? Was he guilty of something after all?

A thought struck him. Bear-TT had some enemies. Someone somewhere always had an ax to grind about a poor relative who died because of their inability to pay for a Bear-TT drug or some fluke accident. These were the people in the predictable margin of error, beyond the statistics accounting for the saved or improved lives.

It was never the CEOs who took the rap in situations like this; it was always the poor lowly fools slaving away in the company, simply following orders who took the rap. Just like soldiers who paid with their lives for the poor orders of their superiors. Vaguely now Ian recalled several lawsuits filed overseas claiming that a monopoly by Bear-TT had driven out inferior, cheaper products. Well, perhaps not inferior, but produced by companies who were inferior when it came to competing.

Ian recalled that in the largest class action suit with a few thousand claimants, a couple of Americans living abroad had died, supposedly because they could no longer afford their medication. The judges had ruled that no anti-trust laws had been violated. There was just no solid case there.

Perhaps some nut fringe group had finally won a class action suit arguing the company's liability in the soaring cost of medical care. In the near decade Ian had worked for Bear-TT, it had managed to buy up most of the pharmaceutical market. They had undercut local competition and once they had gone under, Bear-TT prices and profits soared. It was just smart business. If not Bear-TT, then some other company would have done the same. If there was any fault, it lay with the system, not Bear-TT.

The ads Ian had put together had certainly contributed, he realized, especially when his images and slogans began airing regularly on the screen. Could this be why they were after him?

There were certainly a lot of angry people looking to blame some pharmaceutical company for driving up the price of health care, making universal health care an utter implausibility and driving thousands to financial ruin and homelessness.

Ian pulled out his dead MEphone, expecting to check the time. Suddenly he glared at the device with abhorrence, for inadvertently, if BEAR-TT was at fault for his imprisonment, and actually ruining thousands of lives, then it was his MEphone that was ultimately at the root of his woes, not to mention BEAR-TT's financial power. He had fallen in love with the device, then gone after the job that issued it, since that was the only way to obtain a ME.

He remembered his obsession with his first MEphone and dismay at learning that not only did he have to land a job with Bear-TT to obtain one, but he couldn't buy insurance for it; if it was stolen, if he accidentally cracked the glass or dropped it in water, he was entirely at the mercy of his boss for another—just like his health insurance! He remembered joking with his colleagues that over the years he had become so addicted to all his prized electronic Bear-TT vices, he was virtually indentured to his company to retain possession of them. Fortunately, he was able to joke—he did so love his job in those days, he thought sadly.

Could people have really died as a result of Bear-TT? he wondered. Perhaps overseas, yes. Here? Okay, but the company had saved so many lives as well. Certainly more than it helped terminate! By far!

The screen in his room lit up again—a child stuffing Nutella-covered cookies into her mouth, then chasing it with a creamy glass of milk. The milk poured down from on high, morphing into an aqua waterfall from the Mexican jungle... one of Ian's favorite vacation spots. He ran over to the screen, tried to dive into the pool of water, drink it. He found himself licking the walls and sobbing violently again.

The solitary confinement was breaking down his ability to reason.

The door opened, and light flooded in, confusing Ian, since usually, by the time food came, he was so hungry, he didn't think twice about eating it. His eye began tearing like crazy. He could make out the bald head, small elegant nose of the guard he called Panther. Panther motioned him outside. Ian stood, stretched the pins and needles from his right leg.

"What day is it?" he asked apprehensively. It would be the end of his job, certainly.

"Sunday."

"Sunday?" Ian shook his head.

Panther smirked. "You prefer more?"

"How long was I in? Ten days? Seventeen?" Ian inquired.

"Three."

"Three?" Ian squeaked.

"Look, buddy, don't push me. Policy is not to disclose duration. But I took pity on you."

IX

AS THE ELEVATOR descended, Ian felt as though he was riding down a waterfall of lights. Spanning the entire lobby, dazzling sheets of tiny snowflake lights hung down from the fiftieth floor, reminiscent of Niagara Falls. He used to love Christmas time at the Embarcadero Multiplex and would often take the elevator up to the revolving restaurant and down just for the rush of lights.

During his work breaks, Ian would often walk to the east wing of the lobby and stand at the window overlooking the elegant Ferry Building clock tower and steely bay beyond. On the brick pavilion, with the Bay Bridge and palm trees in the backdrop, stood the Embarcadero Center's fountain sculpture. Though it did not snow in San Francisco, at holiday time, the pavilion would be turned into an ice-skating rink, giving the appearance of snow. A couple of times, Ian had brought a date to the rink. It was a great way to get close quickly, helping her dodge all the overly-confident skaters who had not been on ice since their childhoods and hadn't updated the perceptions of their abilities accordingly.

Now, out of the elevator, Ian lingered with some other tourists at the tremendous lobby fountain that spanned a city block, before heading into work. A miniature winterscape stood atop the endless marble platform. Mysteriously originating under the platform, sheets of cascading water fell so uniformly, they gave the appearance of cellophane. He tried not to think of the year they closed the fountain because of a toddler drowning.

Walking around the exhibit's perimeter, Ian imagined himself strolling along the snow-covered village chalets and shops, riding on the musical carousel, then rushing with a pair of friends over to the gondolas and taking one to the top of their favorite ski slope before catapulting down. Where had he actually done this? This was Tahoe, or Lake Arrowhead or Cambridge; someplace he'd spent a lot of time as a kid. Where was that?

But the copper sign attached to the exhibit, only referred to the 3,000 piece exhibit as "imaginary," stating that the Embarcadero Multiplex inherited the collection from a deceased local artist the previous century named Len Connacher.

It was at times like this that Ian nearly forgot he was in jail. It was like those moments when he forgot his eye was constantly tearing.

Aside from the huge turn-over at work, not much had changed in his work life, Ian reflected, as he meandered toward his cubicle. He was fortunate that he loved his job. And that was most of his life anyway, so really things weren't that dire, he argued with himself. He was even beginning to enjoy moments like this without his music or MEphone. He'd actually forgotten to check it for long stretches of hours at a time.

At times, Ian would be overcome by a heightened sense of liberation he had experienced once or twice in his lifetime, when he had emerged from the other side after quitting smoking, before the addiction to his devices. Although, he had to admit, most of the time, he was still miserable without the devices. Absent the image-boosting enhancements of his electronic persona, his self-esteem was taking a blow. But the thought of more enlightened moments helped him endure withdrawal.

At work, Ian replaced personal message or image-checking moments with observing his coworkers, whom he noticed growing increasingly impatient with him for some reason. Although he was always looking for signs that they shared his situation, he had failed to find any. Ian had seen most of his coworkers either enter or leave the building at some point from the outside, with the possible exception of Robin, who kept mostly to herself and never seemed to leave the office to go to lunch.

Probably, we're the only imprisoned ones, he reflected. Because of this, Ian had come to consider himself fortunate to work among all the other free citizens. He had known that both the need for more prisons and the popularity of prison labor had expanded exponentially, but he hadn't had the slightest inkling that jails were now being situated inside everyday plants and companies—or was it vice versa? He had been naïve not to notice all the security guards at his job before.

From his cubicle, Ian had a perfect view of the ten story Christmas tree with the ornate, giant blown-glass ornaments and long, glass icicles ejaculating aqua light. He did have one of the best views from his cubicle.

He sighed and wiped his eye. His breathing had grown shallow, his stomach muscles, knotted. He was thinking of his mother again. The thought of what Christmas would be for her without him was too much to bare. She must have worried herself sick. Surely by now she would have called and gotten no response. He tried to recall the longest period they had gone without talking; perhaps a month when he was abroad. Countless times, he had tried to borrow mobiles during the period corresponding to his mother's exercise class or weekly lab tests, but something always interfered—almost as though his coworkers had been instructed that Ian's phone privileges had been revoked. All he wanted was to leave a little message, like, *just wanted to let you know things are going good at work. Hope you're well.*

In his nearly two months in prison, he had still never learned what his crime was nor his release date. Because of this, he had resigned himself to the possibility that his crime was terrorist-related and his location, for security purposes, kept secret. After all, he reasoned, what wasn't terrorist-related these days? Even the White House had an interrogation chamber in its basement, beyond the corridor of the West Wing. Were his crime not terrorist-related, surely by now his mother would have learned of his imprisonment and visited.

Ian absentmindedly checked his shirt pocket, and pulled out one of the mints that were ever-present at work. He was eating so many of these now, his stomach had begun to develop burning sensations. He put the mint back and logged into his email for a distraction. The fact that he was being held without knowledge of the accusation infuriated him to the point of sheer panic and he could not let one of these panic attacks manifest themselves at work.

More than ever, he was concerned with doing a good job, for fear that the only island of sanity in his life might be taken from him.

He tried to recall whether he had ever seen anyone else suffer from similar panic attacks or odd behavior at work, but only wound up feeling more alienated.

Just then Robin approached on her way back to Design from a meeting with the boss.

"Mr. White wants you to stop by his office." She looked at Ian and shrugged, as though wanting to be an ally, but not having enough information.

Ian's face flushed; his forearms and nape of the neck burned and his eye began tearing. Why did he keep harkening back to Poe? Why was he terrified his boss would notice his heart pounding in his chest as loudly as the Tell-Tale Heart? For months, he had been desperate to ask Mr. White for a new MEpad, but the thought of being confronted about his imprisonment filled him with a terror akin to—there it was again, that fear of being buried alive—stuck in a cell without access to the world or virtual e-world.

"Please shut the door," Ian's boss instructed, motioning with his head of thick grey and black hair, parted on the side. His short legs barely rested comfortably on the top of his desk. Ian felt his throat constrict and his nerves slide to the pit of his stomach.

Neil White coughed into his fist. "Some of your colleagues have come to me asking for help. It seems they are concerned we are going to lose clients. More than one has complained about some inappropriate comments they overheard coming from your desk when they were interfacing with Alice. Perhaps we should move your cubicle. Tracie said she'd be willing to trade. "

"How generous of her," Ian muttered. Tracie, everyone knew, hated her cubicle, which faced the corner. It was probably she who had come to Mr. White. He wiped his eye and became self-conscious that Mr. White might misconstrue his malady as an emotional outburst. "Only—I'm afraid I'd be unable to do my work because of the light. That's why Pat put me there…"

"Oh right, the light. I'll have to think some more about this… Meanwhile, please watch what you say. Your coworkers are concerned."

"I'm so sorry, Mr. White. I've been under a lot of pressure at home. It won't happen again," Ian mumbled.

The statement only seemed to irritate his boss. He stood.

He knew. *Employers must know*, Ian realized.

"Another thing," Ian forced the words out. Bad timing, but he was like a heroine addict and it was his last chance. Then he'd know where he stood. "Mr. White, it seems I need a new MEpad."

"Oh?" his employer's demeanor was stern.

"To work on the campaign at home. Mine's not charging." Ian could feel his ears burning up.

"I'm afraid that's not possible at this time," Mr. White responded, escorting Ian to the door almost forcefully.

"My password has been reset and the tech—,"

"Isn't he doing his job?" Mr. White raised his eyebrows, almost threateningly.

"Oh, certainly. It's just me—" Ian felt like breaking down sobbing as he closed the door to Mr. White's office, though he had predicted the response.

He put his earphones in and tinkered with his MEphone, though nothing came out.

No relief from the withdrawal. No vices. I knew that, Ian stewed. He knew his boss was cognizant of his imprisonment. "So what," he said aloud. Probably the others didn't realize he was only talking to himself. "So what," Ian said again and submerged himself in his work, though his insides were twisted with worry about being forever barred access to MEpads, his files and life's work, since only Bear-TT employers were authorized to issue the devices.

Back in his cell that evening, Ian had trouble eating or sleeping. All he could do was obsess about his files and ME devices and which coworkers had conspired to help Tracie try to steal his desk. From his bed, he could not help fixating on the scratch marks in the wall, which included a bit of someone's nail, it seemed to him, in plain sight, in the most private place he'd sit whenever he was having a panic attack.

At least, he realized, he had not checked his MEphone since he'd returned! He had really been trying.

Finally, at 4:42 in the morning, after much back and forth about his enemies, after having narrowed it down to two main adversaries, he fell asleep.

This obsessing about work and his mother continued for the next couple of weeks. Presently, he convinced himself that his mother had learned of his imprisonment and had disowned him. Around his coworkers, he increasingly felt like a leper. He constantly dreaded that they would learn about his terrible secret and further isolate him. He hardly ever smiled or laughed on the job anymore… unless he was interacting with Robin. The more unstable he felt, the more forgiving he was of her defects. And the more insecure Ian felt at work, the more important it was to him to perform well. In the cell, work was almost never off Ian's mind. He began to think his life had always been nothing but work and wondered how he ever had time to work on his photographs. Now it was as though he never left his job. But wasn't this better than dwelling on his imprisonment? he consoled himself. After all he liked his job, right?

X

DURING THE NEXT weeks in jail, Ian did not glean any more information about the exact nature of the crime for which he was being held, nor his release date.

Then one day, when they were both working late and there was almost no one else around, Robin turned around after retrieving some coffee and found Ian admiring her backside. Perhaps because the office was nearly empty, Robin threw her head over her shoulder and laughed, then she walked backwards toward Ian, still watching him. He broke out into a grin as well.

"You stopped avoiding me?" Robin muttered.

Ian could feel his face flushing, his eye tearing again.

"So Ian, you've been in jail a while now. You never told me what exactly you did to end up there."

"Excuse me?" Ian coughed.

"I get the feeling you didn't go for the Realtime vs. REMtime paradigm of why we're imprisoned," Robin laughed. "So tell me why you're in jail," she added flatly.

Ian stammered, started to formulate a response. Stopped himself, began again. What he'd give to know the answer. If anyone could help him, he felt, it was Robin, the only other soul who had admitted to him that their imprisonment was real.

"Robin," Ian began. He looked around to make sure no one was watching, then grasped her firmly by the shoulders. His voice was gentle as he looked deeply into her eyes. "I know this reality is harsh for you, right? But you have to remember. Why were you originally imprisoned. I mean, how did you first end up in jail? I mean, you couldn't have been born there, right?"

"Here," she clarified. "Petty little things, I suppose, like everyone else: speeding, jaywalking, tossing out a jury duty notice; forgetting to pay for something stuck in the shopping cart or that I ordered in a restaurant that the waitress forgot to charge me for. Ever since the campaign to crack down on crime at home—"

"Come on. I know there are things wrong with our society, but things haven't gone that fascist yet."

Robin smirked. "O.K.," she said finally. "You're not ready for the truth."

"Come on Robin. Stop with the games."

"Bear-TT."

"What do you mean?" he demanded. At times during his increasing frustration with the lack of information about his incarceration, it had been almost merciful to convince himself that the not-guilty ruling to Bear-TT's anti-trust law violations had been reversed and he was just one of the fall guys. "The overseas companies we drove into bankruptcy?"

"They should be held accountable for all those deaths too. Remember the Morpho campaign?"

"The flu vaccines?" Suddenly Ian had trouble seeing through his tears and fumbled for his handkerchief.

"You were the one who came up with the symbol, didn't you? Blue Butterfly?"

Ian nodded, but he was absorbed in tending to his eye.

"Why that butterfly, Ian? It's not even African?"

Ian looked up. "I don't know. Catchy image. Like a blue flower. Seems impossible. Like the image we wanted to get across about cheating death and disease." He paused. "So that's why they got me. Only, I'm confused. What about that campaign actually got Bear-TT in hot water?"

"The flu itself wasn't deadly. But did you know our vaccine had something like a 10% mortality rate?"

"So the high margin of error? What, did people overseas file some kind of suit?'

"Negligent homicide. It's still supposedly illegal to test vaccines on human subjects." Robin's tone became almost diabolical.

"But they all signed releases, didn't they?" At the time Ian had been dumbstruck by the naïveté of the population that had deigned to stand in six-hour lines in 104-degree heat for the vaccine.

"Didn't you wonder why both your boss and supervisor have been replaced since your incarceration? Can you recall any that have lasted for more than six months?"

Ian reflected. He never came into contact with the engines of the machine. It was quite possible that they had all been placed in jail.

"You be the judge," Robin smirked and walked back to her cubicle.

Increasingly, Ian found his thoughts meandering toward Robin again. He kept finding excuses to bump into her and engage her in snatches of conversation. As long as they discussed Bear-TT's culpability, they had common ground.

Thanks to Robin's input, over the next months, Ian began to believe with increasing conviction that his company had indeed been responsible for the deaths of thousands of people. This obviously outweighed the company's good deeds... and perhaps placed the crimes of Bear-TT employees in the category of "terrorist." "Maybe," was all Robin would commit to saying on this topic, perhaps, in denial of her own culpability.

Slowly, as Ian began to come to terms with the permanence of his incarceration, he found himself relying more on Robin for solace. He began to convince himself that once she gained his trust, she might feel confident enough to confide in him about the motives for her incarceration.

During his darkest moments, Ian would wonder what kind of suffering his own ad campaigns had inadvertently caused. Whether someone somewhere would not have died had he selected a different career. He began obsessing about this, attempting to put a face to the victims. Some nights he was haunted by the images he recalled his boss having dismissed as propaganda, submitted to a judge in a case against Bear-TT a few years prior: an infant trying to nurse at his dying mother's breast, who couldn't afford cancer treatment.

Other nights, he felt directly responsible for the recurring memory of a family weeping over what they denounced as the senseless death of their son, proudly showing the camera photos of him taking his first steps, then the medicine cabinet with his empty medicine bottles—images Ian had initially dismissed as nonsense.

Had Ian caused the death of a child? More than one? How many would have still been alive if Ian had never taken the Job? If collectively the company, through its workers, had been responsible for thousands of deaths, how many was he directly responsible for?

At these times of excruciating guilt, Ian's incarceration seemed fitting, almost a relief. His remorse for having accepted the job in the first place grew to the point of being almost unbearable.

Why, he berated himself, had he not settled for a job that provided the b-phone with the blue b-tab available from City-Chased Bank Group; the clear ones from Wolf News; the black devices and wires from Black-RAW; neon lime green wires from Chev-GT Energy or red ones from Alianz Axa? Weren't those companies a bit more moral? He would have adapted to their devices eventually. Better yet, why hadn't he learned to use a second-rate device that didn't require a specific employer at all? Of what use were the Bear-TT devices now?

Then there were times after a day's work that Ian just felt like a nut. This usually occurred after he'd probed an employee about the company's practices; whether they were indeed causing harm; whether the company had changed. These inquiries were usually met with indignation or patronizing shrugs that left Ian feeling as though the coworker thought him unstable, and Robin was simply engaging in some conspiratorial lunacy… and that the coworkers were right.

One evening, just as Ian was getting ready to leave, he had such a conversation with a blonde coworker whose name he could never recall, because it was a common name, and he was more preoccupied with her resembling a horse, her bone structure, facial features and nose particularly, especially the nostrils. He made the mistake of bringing up the usual suspicions about BEAR-TT. She had looked at him with abhorrence, and began scrolling through her ME. He was almost certain she was going to turn him into Fatherland Security.

"Don't leave, Ian. Wait," she said.

He contemplated running and decided it wouldn't be wise.

"I'm going to bump you a number?"

"NO!" he felt like screaming, but obediently got out his ME.

"You're supposed to call. I mean we. When we… feel… you need someone to listen…."

"Thanks! Mmmm—" he beamed. It started with "M," her name.

He thought hard about what she had said.

That's when reality came pouring in like megabytes loading an image. He was mad. Of course. He and Robin were the only ones who were in "jail" in their workplace because they were the only mad workers, the ones committed to the asylum. They were having a psychotic break and were in some kind of mental institution. That would explain all the other mental patients returning at rush hour to— not the jail, where he slept, but the asylum—after mainstreaming into society in regular jobs.

Had his asylum-mates been talking through mobiles and radio- wave ear devices or to themselves? Ian had once read in a paper he had bought from a homeless man that mental institutions were increasingly becoming more jail like. This would neatly explain Robin's bizarre sci-fi REMtime idea, as well as her Bear-TT conspiracy.

Robin was indeed mad.

Unfortunately, so, then, was he.

XI

ONE EVENING AFTER work, Ian's heart leapt at something he saw in the cell across from him, three cells to the right. The chamber had been recently vacated by an older man who had suffered a heart attack. Now a cart piled with belongings was being emptied into the vacant cell. Then, Ian's tall coworker, Richard, was shown into the cell by two guards. One of the guards turned on the interactive set. Richard tuned in attentively, gesturing and speaking as though to the set itself. One of the guards tipped his hat in a gesture of polite farewell, as if he were a porter after a tip. The other smiled his goodbye. Why were they so good natured with Richard and not Ian? He was used to being on everyone's good side. Yet Ian was so overcome with gladness, he didn't allow this irritation to bother him.

By gum! I knew it! Ian thought to himself, restraining himself from leaping with glee. *Yesss! I knew it! I knew it!*

"Richard!" he shouted. "Richard," but the man was too absorbed in his conversation with his screen to hear.

So that settled the question. Robin had been right—he was in a jail, not in a mental institution after all! The fact that he was overjoyed at this realization surprised him. *When they jail you, at least they don't take away your sense of self, your pride....* What was it? He couldn't explain it, but anything seemed preferable to not being able to trust one's own mind, than to lose one's core. Although, perhaps that was the goal of terrorist prisons as well—

So Bear-TT employees were being arrested after all, he reflected. Only Richard was not particularly high up on the food chain. He was just a copy editor for the ads that went out. Were they arresting everyone now?

Poor Richard, Ian thought: *giving up his nice house in Marin.* Although, finally Ian would be able to talk to someone about what had happened to him. "Richard!" he kept shouting, before realizing he'd have to wait until Richard turned the set off.

Ian fell asleep waiting.

The next morning, Ian was up before dawn. It seemed to take forever for the light to stream into his cell. He schemed about walking over to Richard's cell on the way to work, but the cell was on the other side of the chasm and the guards escorting him to work every day would not grant him this opportunity.

When he arrived at work, Ian was a half-an-hour early. He thought Richard would never arrive. Finally at 9:45, Richard walked in apologizing to Alice about oversleeping because of a headache.

Screen hangover, Ian snickered to himself. As soon as Richard sat down, Ian sauntered over to his cubicle with a few slogans for the latest campaign.

"Richard, have a minute?"

"What's up?"

"What do you think of these?"

"Can you give me a moment to think about them?" Richard asked. "I'm not myself this morning."

"Sure," Ian began to walk awkwardly back to his desk. "Hey Richard,"

"Yeah?"

"Want to grab a bite at lunch?"

"Puccini?" Richard asked naïvely.

"They didn't tell you? We have to eat here in the restaurant."

"A little pricey. I'd rather not. Anyway, since when can they tell us where to eat? Bear-TT paying for it?"

Ian shook his head.

"I'd rather do Puccini," Richard insisted.

Ian gave up trying to convince Richard. He'd learn soon enough when the guards came around for him, he reasoned.

When lunch time came around, Ian shadowed Richard until he walked straight out the Embarcadero Multiplex doors.

"Something wrong, Ian?"

"I forgot something. Why don't you go ahead. I think I have to skip lunch today," Ian said, starting away. "Hey can you get me a Turkey sandwich with provolone, hold the mustard?" A guard in dark glasses started toward him. He glanced around, but there were no other guards on their way to apprehend Richard. Richard's long legs carried him away down Drumm Street with the ease of a gazelle.

Later Richard dropped by Ian's cubicle with a paper bag containing his sandwich. "Thanks, buddy," Ian hesitated. "Still living in Marin?" he inquired.

"Yeah, why?"

"They're expecting some winds this evening, no?"

"Yeah, thanks for reminding me. I'd better move the begonias off the deck railing when I get home tonight. We just moved and... Veronica will cry if the pot she made breaks..."

"You're going right home tonight?"

"Yeah, why?"

"Nothing. I'm working late's all."

Ian repaid Richard for the sandwich and absorbed himself in his work. His heart sank. Apparently, he had mistaken Richard's identity. Was this more proof of his insanity then?

He stared at the pile of work before him. He never seemed to be able to keep up now. He glanced around at his coworkers. His closest friends had been replaced. He wondered whether they had also been arrested or if he was just nuts. Regardless, the fact was that now there were so few colleagues to whom he could relate, really. In fact, the opposite, increasingly there were more unpleasant exchanges among him and the rest.

That evening, Ian strained to see the man he was certain was Richard inside his cell. He only saw the top of his head, for the man was mostly sitting this evening, probably in front of the screen. At last, the lights in the mystery cell went out and Ian was left lying alone on his cot with his thoughts. He was flooded with memories. As the months had worn on, Ian had become more resigned to his confinement and his uncertainty about its end. Without a light at the end of the tunnel, his only recourse was to hold onto what he had of himself and what was left of his sanity, by reviewing, reliving his memories to the greatest extent possible.

The next day, the burden of these memories nearly broke his spirit. In the prison's rooftop courtyard during the exercise period, the air was chilly, the asphalt wet with a recent rain. The weak sunlight through the snow-like clouds felt so good on his cheek, the smell of the rain on the patches of gold and green grass. At the periphery of the yard, some bamboo that looked eerily identical to the patch in his patio, rustled in the wind. Ian bumped into the branch of a tall willow, which dumped water on him as he passed by, the way his plum trees would after a rain back home. It was dusk and the cheerful chatter of finches and soothing sound of water dripping from a faucet into a barrel of water reminded him of the sound of his fountains from his balcony back home.

When would he ever sit on that back bedroom balcony again

listening to his buddies Eric Robertson and Clifton Ross spin their stories, as they watched the finches bathing their yellow chests in the angel fountain, or the squirrels foraging for the peanuts Ian had scattered in the garden? He had taken a photograph of the duo in the weak, fall late-afternoon sun, enveloped in the lava and orange embers of the Chinese maples, their fire echoed in the red geraniums in the balcony flowerboxes. That afternoon, the sky above the crimson leaves had been a piercing autumnal blue. The setting sun caught the trunk of the pine three levels below in the garden, turning the fern and bamboo an iridescent yellow-green. The cherub hiding under the rose arbor glowed with celestial light. Above, on the patio, lavender impatiens framed the Italian fountain, the water falling in tears down the three levels of shells reminiscent of Botticelli's Venus. Hopscotch for the eyes. With the breeze massaging his cheeks, the sound of the bamboo rustling in the breeze and the fountain trickling directly below, he remembered feeling drugged. He recalled all this with longing that seemed unbearable and began to sob.

Several mornings later, Ian noticed that Richard showed up with a knick from shaving. Ian slaved diligently at his desk, trying to speed up time to go back to the cell, where he'd be able to see if the new inmate also had a bandage on his chin as well.

Ian left work early on an excuse to make sure he arrived before the Richard look-a-like.

Eventually, the man entered. Ian craned his neck. There was the bandage! There was no question that the two men were one and the same.

The following day at work, Ian cornered Richard by the coffee machine. "So why'd they move your cell?"

"I didn't move cubicles," Richard replied, stirring some white waxy powder into his coffee.

"Not cubicles. Jail cells."

"Huh?"

"Jail cells." Ian crossed his arms and looked Richard straight in the eye. "We're in jail together."

"What's going on, buddy? I thought you loved your job!" Richard looked concerned.

"Richard, you don't have to hide the fact. I go back to a cell each night too, dude!"

"I'm happy about my home life. Forgive me for saying so, bro, but sounds like you're depressed."

"Really, Richard, you don't have to be ashamed that I know. We're both in jail together. Your cell is right across from mine. Haven't you noticed?"

Richard put down his mug on the light laminate table. "We've had this conversation before, bro. I think I've said this to you before, but maybe you'll really act on it now. We've all been under a lot of new deadline stress with all the changes in management. Bear-TT offers counseling and other help for people in crisis. I'd be happy to get you the number again."

"No wait!" Ian called out, but it was too late, Richard had already approached Alice for the hotline number.

Ian's eye began leaking uncontrollably. He slammed his fist down on the table and walked back to his cubicle.

By the time Richard approached him with the hotline number after lunch, Ian had cooled off. He had spent the break at his cubicle, picking at the Caesar salad from the Atrium restaurant next door, contemplating Richard's theory about losing his mind. Of course he was. No sane person would think they were living in a jail and going to work every day. What had he been thinking?! He was obviously psychotic, like some of the people he'd seen on the streets who heard voices and saw things that weren't really there. At best, the jail did exist and he was in jail for the criminally insane. Perhaps that's why Robin made no sense. She was nuts too.

Ian barely had the strength to thank Richard for the number. As soon as his colleague walked away, Ian put his head in his hands. Tears came, in spite of the will to suppress them. He punched in the numbers on the slip of paper.

"I'm cracking up. I'm cracking up," he whispered into the phone.

XII

IAN'S BRAIN SURGERY was scheduled for the following month. He anticipated this time with hope; something had gone terribly wrong in his brain and nothing was making sense anymore. At work he searched for internet articles on the subject of brain damage and memory loss and the findings restored in him much optimism. In turn, his coworkers seemed more cheerful toward him. At last, there seemed to be light at the end of the tunnel… until Robin cornered him late one evening at his cubicle, as he was getting ready to head out.

"So I hear you may have to go to the hospital," she said, cracking her voice a bit in what Ian recognized as feigned empathy.

"Yeah, Robin," Ian said recalling his malady again. He brightened. "But it's not what you think. I'm actually looking forward to it."

"Ian, there's something I have to tell you," Robin almost whispered. "Want to have a drink at your favorite bar?" She seemed to be pleading.

Ian knew Robin was referring to Vesuvio. He smiled at the fact that she remembered the bar was one of his favorite spots to photograph.

He considered the proposition, his heart racing. Then he took a deep breath which ended in a sigh as he came to his senses. "Thanks, Robin, but it's not worth another trip to solitary—er or whatever that is."

"Don't worry about that. Really," Robin's voice gained an octave and she sidled up to Ian like a cat. "Remember how easily I got us out last time?"

Ian shook his head. "We were lucky."

"Believe me, there's nothing to worry about there, babe. Now the operation, that's something to worry about. Not a good idea—" Robin looked at Ian seductively. It was the fact that she had called him "babe" that made him acquiesce. She hadn't used that endearment since they had last slept together. Besides, he had been dying to get out of the jail to buy a memory card for his camera. Though he could do without her opinions about his operation.

"You know how much I dig Vesuvio," he conceded.

"I remember." Robin looked at Ian provocatively.

Another refuge from the wall-size digital scenery of other restaurants, Vesuvio had worn antique wood, Tiffany lamps and old-time photos of James Joyce, Beat Poets and patrons from the previous

century. On the way they had stopped to pick up a memory card for
Ian. When they had emerged from their fluorescent daze, the fog had
blanketed the streets. The misty tendrils accentuated the flashing gold,
red, green and purple lights of stripper joints along Broadway,
reminding Ian of New York playhouses or Mexico City movie theaters.
He flashed his camera.

Once at Vesuvio, they sat upstairs on the balcony at a table
overlooking the Broadway neon. Using his elbows to form a tripod, Ian
slowed the shutter speed to capture the juxtaposition of a gargantuan
flower arrangement hanging from a lamp post; the pink fuchsias, red
geraniums and cascading yellow and white flowers echoing vibrant
colors of a mural in the alley, along the wall of City Lights Bookstore.

"You know who did that mural?" Robin inquired, sipping an Irish
coffee.

Ian shook his head without looking up from his screen.

"Trish Trip. What a name. And the owner of this bar was named
Janet Planet, believe it or not," Robin chuckled. "It's a recreation of an
indigenous Zapatista mural in Taniperla, Chiapas. The government
burned it down the previous millennium and artists like Trish repainted
it in cities throughout the world," Robin beamed. Ian paused to capture
her smile with his camera.

"You seem to love that," Ian laughed, snapping more pictures of
Robin laughing.

She nodded. "I do. When they try to crush us, and instead we
multiply. Like bamboo."

Ian's smile faded. He stirred his martini, savored an olive. "Who's
'we?' Robin? The inmates? The patients?" he said finally. "If we're all
inmates, as you implied, then what am I doing here? Them—" He
pointed to the other hipsters around the bar. "Are any of them in our
shoes?"

Robin sighed and raised her glass. "Salud," she said, taking a sip.
"Do you have a couple of days?"

Ian skeptically took a sip of his martini.

"How's your martini?" Robin asked, her tone growing sweet again.

"Strong. Is that what you want to hear?"

"Have another sip," she laughed, waving her long fingers at him.

"We're inmates, according to your parable. But we're here. It
makes no sense," Ian repeated. "How come every time I'm with you, I
can leave the jail or whatever it is, but when I'm not—"

Robin took a sip of her Irish Coffee and wiped the whipped cream mustache from her upper lip with her tongue and bottom lip. "Okay, Ian, remember my joke about the rush hour phenomenon?" she began.

"The herd going back to the jails after work, that one?"

"It's no joke. I'm serious, Ian. Our brains have been deliberately jail-broken by the movement. So our chips stopped triggering our REM states. That's why you are aware that you are in jail and others are not. Those hipsters could be owners, but more likely they are also inmates taking a break before heading back to the jail—"

Ian choked. Was it possible that Robin was nuts and he was not?

She bolted ahead with her argument, utterly oblivious to his skepticism—a characteristic of unstable minds, Ian thought to himself.

Middle-class worker inmates—like Robin, Ian and most of the Vesuvio hipsters—were given much more freedom to frequent the outside world, to come and go at their leisure, Robin explained. This was contrary to the situation of impoverished prisoners, who were jailed without the relief of REM sleep brain implants. Owners were not too worried about people going astray since the advent of tethering workers to the jails through the implants and wires. It was possible to control them as long as they stuck to a dozen or so haunts each. They were programmed through their wires to repeat these haunts like hamsters running the same confined treadmills and paths over and over.

"Think about it, Ian," Robin challenged Ian. "Think about all the places you go to on a regular basis. Are there more than a dozen?"

Ian thought hard. Shook his head. There had to be a logic to her madness, a way for her to rationalize to herself that she was indeed sane.

Robin proceeded. After commute hours, inmates were not limited in their comings and goings, just closely monitored, she explained. This freedom enjoyed by the inmates—insofar as it could be considered freedom—made it possible for couples to meet each other, then raise families inside their cells. Of course they would be in REM—sleepwalking during this time, so to speak.

Ian was impressed with Robin's ingenuity. Funny how her talents as a web architect could become so warped as to construct such an elaborate fiction.

"Robin, so tell me this. The joggers that go running down by the Embarcadero after work? How would you explain them? They're not in jail. Owners?"

"Could be. But more likely, inmates," Robin said. "They're in

REM. Either that's part of their commute or they've gone back to the jails to change after work."

There was a method to her madness. Ian probed further. "Okay, Robin. So if I've been in REM all this time, explain the fact that my work situation has remained the same even though my reality suddenly shifted to a jail. I mean, I didn't suddenly wake up and find myself doing this job for the first time. I've been doing it consciously all along."

"They want us alert at work. That's the only time we're really awake."

"And the rest of the time we're asleep?"

"In REM."

"So when I'm in my house in Tiburon. When we went to breakfast at—"

"I keep trying to tell you, Ian. You've never lived in Tiburon. You've been in a cell all those years. In a rights-free zone, Ian! It's all a fiction created by that chip and the images on your interactive set. The bakery conversation was taking place with me in your cell."

Ian's head was bobbing up and down in agreement, though his smile had evaporated.

"Fine Robin. Remind me why. Why, then?" he demanded. "What for?"

It had been a mistake to rekindle feelings for her, he thought sadly, as she jumped into her warped analysis.

It took another round of drinks to swallow, but from what Ian could gather, Robin divided the society into two major classes: *inmates* like himself, who largely inhabited rights-free zones and *owners*, whose rights were still intact. There were also *outsiders*, free citizens who were not in the owning class, who had somehow escaped imprisonment, but these lived precariously on the fringe, she explained.

The wealthy owners, Robin explained, were the ones Ian saw glimpses of on the screen, particularly in reality and travel shows. They actually lived out the lives upon which Ian's and so many other inmates' lives were based. These were the hyper-consumers of Realtime products with many over-stocked Realtime mansions each. The lives of owners were relatively stress free. Competition for their preferred haunts and places of leisure was slim—there was only a rush at lunch hour and right after work for the restaurants and shops they frequented. Except in what Robin called "owner" or "tourist magnets"—

picturesque cities like San Francisco, New Orleans, Paris, New York, Florence and the like, which attracted gluts of owners from all over the globe, creating long lines of owners forced to behave in demeaning ways, such as in Disneyland.

The owners had at their disposal an army of what Robin cynically defined as their slaves: inmates who looked after their every need and whim; who gave their lives to build their bridges, house and clothe them and grow their food; who flew their jets and drove their limos; pampered them on their vacations; who designed, built and transported their favorite toys and gadgets; who fixed their rotting teeth and cleaned their bums when they took ill; who listened to their inexhaustible narcissistic natter about every solipsistic neuroses, desire and imperfection in their near-idyllic lives—lives shared by less than one percent of the planet.

The owners—the only citizens who regularly inhabited zones with constitutional guarantees—were well aware of the compromised position of the rest of the society, but argued that the ends outweighed the means, since inmates were leading far more fulfilled lives than had the generation of workers in the old order. The owners took great pride in their own ingenuity—the advent of interactive screen implants—for having improved the overall quality of life. If the old order had been democratic, they reasoned, the new one was far more so, for more of the population not only were able to carry out the pursuit of happiness, but a greater majority were able to achieve it.

The toiling recipients of the owners' generosity—the majority of workers, known as working citizens in the previous order—were almost all entangled in the criminal system until their dying breath, either imprisoned, under probation or as ex-cons, all mostly within rights-free zones. Policemen and guards belonged to this class as well.

The underclass, defined as merely criminals in the old order— robbers, petty thieves, addicts and dangerous offenders—were in traditional jails without the relief of illusory REM sleep nor the ability to leave. They were the only inmates who really understood that they were in jail.

Except for immigrants and the working poor. "But that gets too complicated," Robin had interjected, returning to the general paradigm.

The more fortunate group of inmates, the productive working class, though aware of the crimes leading to imprisonment, was able to remain in denial of their imprisonment. Even though they spent most of their lives in rights-free zones, most felt as though they'd gotten away with something, and in fact had received a promotion, since once imprisoned without waking knowledge—but all made legal through consent waivers—their lives would suddenly take a turn for the better as they began living out their REM sleep television fantasies from within their jail cells. Thus the working class of prisoners was afforded the illusion of a contented, even luxurious life through radio chip implants in their inner ear and behind their retinas.

The drink was starting to take effect and Ian stumbled slightly on his words. He realized he had not consumed alcohol since his confinement. "So you're saying, Robin, that except for an occasional group of owners, most of the folks here belong to the inmate class, since this is real time—er... whatever?"

But before Robin could answer, Ian began to tune out and shake his head in disappointment. Suddenly, it all seemed too absurd. His sleeve had become wet with the discharge from his eye during the conversation.

"Ian!" Robin pleaded, reading his expression. "Look, if you doubt that we have implants, explain your eye condition. It's caused by too much pressure from the implant along your tear duct. It's a sign that your body is rejecting yours! It stopped working. That's why your Tiburon illusion turned off and you woke up and realized you were in a jail cell one afternoon!"

Ian stopped. His heart sank suddenly. He blinked hard at Robin. He took a sip of his martini and choked, then began gulping his water.

"I want to believe you. And I don't want to believe you," he said, finally. "Suppose I did believe you. You still haven't explained why we are here and not in jail."

Robin lowered her voice. She took a last, hungry sip of her drink. "We escaped. I used this to hack into the guards' access codes." Robin flashed her MEphone.

Ian laughed. "Group access codes?"

Robin looked around the bar and began whispering. "See, the guards also have censors implanted. Screens send out different codes corresponding to different groups of users to trigger them into REM at various times," she explained. "Some colleagues showed me how to jailbreak my phone. Then we hacked into the system and found where the user groups and access codes are stored and how to shorten or lengthen a group's REM sleep cycle. Guards have a certain group number in common. You and I and all our coworkers belong to another group."

"What, like work shifts?"

"Exactly," Robin smiled with relief. "You can think of it like this. I used my phone to trigger the guards' REM. So they were sleeping on the job. So we were able to get out."

Ian listened to all this, picking at his olives. Of course, the crazier she sounded, the more rational his own commitment to a psych ward and the operation seemed.

Robin noticed Ian's expression. "See. I know. I sound crazy. That's how the regime survives," she sighed. She stirred her drink listlessly.

Ian flagged down the waitress, signaled her to bring the bill. "We should get back," he said, sadly. The operation would probably reset his brain... but her? He'd have to resign himself to bidding her farewell.

"What's the rush?" Robin inquired.

"Don't we? I mean, if we're really inmates."

"It doesn't work like that." Robin said.

They were silent.

The waitress came and Ian scanned his retina despite Robin's protests.

"Thank you," Robin said sweetly. She spoke up, looking intently into Ian's eyes. "Babe, just imagine for a minute I was telling you the truth. You understand my theory about REM?"

"Sure," Ian said, stretching his shoulders and rolling the kinks out of his neck.

"So you understand, my concern about your operation, then—"

"Let's see. You think my chip malfunctioned and so the operation—"

"The operation is to restore it. It's to launch you back into REM, back into your illusory reality."

"Mmmhmmmm. What would it look like to you—er me—if this operation is a success from your viewpoint?"

"Ian," Robin took his hand. "It would mean you'd lose touch with reality again. It would mean you'd think you were in Tiburon, not jail again."

"Wait a minute. That sounds pretty good," Ian laughed. "You mean I'd get out of jail free, so to speak? Why would you be against that?"

"Why would I be against your staying awake and conscious?"

Robin stood, the previous restraint in her voice gave way. "Why wouldn't I want you asleep, brainwashed and deluded?" she shouted over the bar noise. "Why wouldn't I want you to be the same boring, shallow guy I dumped in Tiburon?"

They walked down most of Columbus Avenue in silence.

"Robin." Ian stopped in his tracks, stared at the glitter in the sidewalk reflecting the street lights. He shook his head. Suddenly he grabbed Robin's shoulders, shook her. "Robin, look me in the eye."

Robin met his gaze.

"My house. Where we made love. So you're saying it didn't exist? Think about this Robin!"

"It didn't exist," she said, holding her gaze fast.

"Where were we then?"

"Your jail cell. When we were at Sam's, we were actually in your jail cell. I had to keep reminding myself that you thought we were at Sam's."

"Right," Ian said glumly, staring at the pavement.

They walked another block in silence. As they approached the Embarcadero building Robin stopped. "So did I talk you out of the operation?"

"I'll think about it."

XIII

THE OPERATION WENT well; the hospital workers were kind and Ian was grateful for the time to rest without thinking of anything in particular. As usual, he missed his devices, but soon grew to appreciate the luxury of being able to laze in bed and read, watch the screen and escape on the Bear-TT Vicodin they gave him for the pain. He definitely felt less anxious, less stressed, less confused, and to that extent, he assumed the operation had been a success.

His first day back at work did not go as smoothly. To begin with, he was released, not to his home to rest, but to his cubicle to work. Next, he found Tracie sitting at his cubicle. Alice came running over to escort him to his new spot.

Habitually, Ian got his handkerchief out to wipe his eye, though he realized it hadn't been leaking. Not since the operation.

"Guess what? Tracie volunteered her cubicle for you so the light won't bother you, nor all the distractions. So now you have the cubicle you wanted! White approved the move!" Alice beamed.

"The operation seems to have fixed my eye," Ian mumbled at Alice's back. He furiously took a seat at the corner cubicle and stared at the joining walls. His terrible headache left him too weak to react, and instead, he summonsed his energy to attack the mountain of work on his desk. The only bright side was that now, perhaps because they had taken his primo view, or perhaps because news had circulated about his illness, everyone was treating him as nicely as they used to in the old days, before his incarceration.

He thought about the possibility that the operation had indeed cured his eye and for a moment harkened to Robin's brain implant theory, then waved it off as he would the intrusion of a noisy horse-fly.

If only, he thought to himself, unable to quite chase the idea from his mind. If only Robin and he weren't mad. If only he had a chip in his brain that would start working again and take him back to Tiburon.

After work, he decided he'd try to get back to Tiburon. He'd just stroll right out, catch the California cable car line, to the Powell-Mason line to the pier and catch the ferry, like in the old days. The guard he thought of as "Panther," inquired if he was lost and whether he needed an escort back to his room.

"That's very kind of you—" Ian paused so the guard could insert his name, but it didn't work.

"I'm Ian and you?"

"Yes, W. Let me help you back to your room." Panther gently took Ian's elbow to lead him.

"That won't be necessary. I'm headed out—"

"Really?" Panther inquired, patting his heat ray.

Ian felt like a rapidly-deflating balloon. Too bad. Robin was indeed mad after all.

"On second thought. I think I forgot something."

"I'm sure you forgot something," Panther shook his head.

At night, back in his cell, the good news was that the multi-screen finally worked, transforming half his cell into 3-D seductive scenery. His headache left him with little energy for anything else. The aqua-colored images of Lake Sirmione in Italy below, framed by the arches of some ruins entwined in bougainvillea above him were making him drowse as they evoked memories of his own journey there. It was as though lying on his cot, he was on the beach, staring down at the neon aqua water. Why had he bothered spending money to travel anymore, he wondered. This was paradise without all the packing, inconvenience, expense and misfortune.

Then, he caught sight of the next travel episode. The program's focus was San Francisco and after a 3-D ride in a cable car, the camera stopped at Union Square and drifted up the Macy's façade to the Cheesecake factory. He startled. Suddenly, there was Barb, life-size, right before his eyes, having lunch with a good looking blond fellow in mirrored sun glasses! And she was wearing the skin-tight shirt Ian loved so!

"How about that! Barb on the screen!" Ian said aloud. He wanted to call her, but his phone privileges had obviously been taken. Barb smiled, as though at Ian and offered him a chair. Ian sat up on the edge of his cot.

"How have you been?" Barb flicked her blonde hair behind her shoulder and smiled again at him, waiting for an answer.

"Barb!" Ian said aloud, reaching over to hug her, and hugging only himself.

"Mmmm hmmmm," Barb said, cocking her head coquettishly to the side and resting her cleft chin on her knuckle as though listening. "What else have you been up to?" she said after a while.

Ian peered at a cell in which he could see the top of a male's head engaged in a conversation with the talking heads on his interactive set. *That's crazy*, he thought to himself. *It just looks as though Barb's talking to me; it's not real. Is it?*

"Terrible! Barb, Terrible!" he shouted at the set. "I'm crazy. Or I really am in jail and I'm innocent. Get me out of here!"

At once he felt terrible for lying to her about his innocence, for part of him had begun to come to terms with his own guilt.

"That's nice," Barb flicked her hair, which had fallen over one of her eyes, to the other side of her head, creating a breaking wave of golden hair.

She got a job working for the station? Ian puzzled. *No, she just happened to be filmed in a reality show.*

Ian noticed a guard without dark glasses pass by his cell. They made eye contact for an instant, in the gap of the bars. The guard quickly turned away, as though embarrassed for having invaded Ian's privacy—quite different behavior from the guards with the glasses who would stare right through the walls at Ian, if they could.

The cable car proceeded on a tour of North Beach, including Puccini. The reality camera dipped and rose with the slope of the San Francisco hills, giving the viewer the feeling that they were right on the cable car, enjoying the tour first hand. The conductor rang the bell and they proceeded down Columbus to the Embarcadero, admired the clock tower at the Ferry Building, fashioned after a Spanish tower, then doubled back toward Fisherman's Wharf, where the camera took viewers onto the Tiburon Ferry.

Ian enjoyed the slow ride out of the San Francisco Harbor, then the speed-up on the open waters. He unrolled his shirt sleeves and buttoned his top button, bracing himself for the cold. He could almost feel the foam on his face, taste the salt on his lips. For a good twenty minutes, Ian felt as though he were right aboard the ferry. Maybe this is where things went wrong, he thought to himself. I'm going to get back on and continue the ride home—"

The ferry stopped and everyone, including Ian, disembarked onto the dock in front of Guaymas restaurant. The blonde narrator of the reality show stepped off the boat and removed his sunglasses. "And now we'll take a stroll along Main street and historic Arc Row," he said. After scanning the elegant, open air Mexican restaurant patio overlooking the water, the camera crew paused in front of the window of the Candy Store on Main Street. Toy trains hauled candy around

Sugar Mountain and a neighborhood built of candy and gingerbread houses.

Ian was thoroughly absorbed. *I'm almost home!* he beamed inwardly. *The operation worked! I'm not crazy anymore! I'm not a criminal! I'm going home!*

He could feel the sun on his face, the wind, and for the first time in nearly a year, his eye wasn't tearing when exposed to strident elements! Almost delirious with happiness, he spotted the familiar brick walk, then the stairs leading up to his house. He opened the door, and made his way to his terrace. Everything was just as he left it; perfectly neat and clean as well. Elsa must have come yesterday, he thought to himself as he made his way to the deck. The view was stunning. How he had missed it.

Only... helping themselves to his marble deck table, and sunning themselves on his patio furniture, were four absolute strangers. A very stacked brunette with long wavy hair adjusted her recliner, then took the hand of her well-built bronzed blonde husband, while an elderly couple talked to the show's narrator, who had just joined them at the table.

Damn it! Ian stood and slammed his fist against the mansion wall. *They've taken my house while I've been away!*

Ian sank back down into his cot, took his head in his hands and shook it, back and forth. *What did I expect while I was here?* He began to sob. He had lived the life most people would envy; the quintessential American Dream for which half the world sweated blood, shed tears, and sacrificed lives; he'd held the whole world in his palm at one time and somehow had allowed it to slip through his fingers.... "What happened?!" he cried.

His artistic gift amounted to this?

Whether he had been committed for being unable to withstand the pressure from his job or jailed for aiding Bear-TT in illicit campaigns, one thing was certain; he bore the responsibility for his present circumstances.

Perhaps if he hadn't been so selfish and had tuned in a little more to other points of view, then maybe he wouldn't have broken the law. Had that been it? Or was it that he had tuned those points of view out in order to be better liked?

"What, are you siding with the hippies and kooks?" he could hear Richard saying when he had caught Ian wincing at the photographs from the lawsuit against Bear-TT.

Was it cowardice or ignorance? he chastised himself. Perhaps if he had stayed a little more alert and better informed, he might not have been complicit in Bear-TT's unconscionable practices. Instead, his eyes always glazed over whenever figures and statistics were rattled off on the screen. If he had only paid a little more attention to the criticisms of his company, perhaps he'd still be sitting on his patio instead of that family. The real thing. Not watching his life flash before him on the screen.

Suddenly, he noticed a grey-haired guard with a mustache and black leather boots standing very close to his cell, observing him through some mirrored glasses. Probably getting off on his misery, he thought, like one of the vultures that preyed on Tantalus' liver.

"Cruel and unusual punishment is illegal!" he yelled at him. But the guard didn't flinch,

"How long have you lived in your beautiful home?" the narrator was asking the elderly couple.

"Almost thirty, no, Martha? Right?"

The man looked very familiar to Ian.

"Thirty years next month!" she said, revealing a mouth full of implants and gold bridges. "Just before Jacob was born." Her son turned from his girlfriend to smile at his mother.

"Liars!" Ian shouted. "You have some nerve to just bury my legal right to my house like that! Liars!"

Ian fought the treadmill over to the bars. "Enough! I need a lawyer!" The grey-headed guard reached for his heat ray. He seemed to be talking into his wire. Ian backed up on the treadmill, falling backward on his cot.

The elegant bald, ebony-headed guard with square-rimmed dark glasses appeared and said something to the first.

The camera panned back to what the announcer said was older footage of the family, fifteen years prior in their home, focused on the elderly man seated at Ian's desk in his bedroom, looking over his photographs.

This was clearly Ian's Federal-style secretary, just small enough to fit inside the nook by the French doors. How Ian missed sitting there with the French doors open to the balcony, listening to the water trickling from the fountains enveloped in the fragile green leaves of the Chinese maples.

This had been where Ian had liked to do the more creative, intimate work on his photographs. This had also been where he had brainstormed the slogan and had combined his photos for the ad which helped Bear-TT launch the campaign leading to the takeover of most of the pharmaceutical market, he recalled, with a mixture of old pride and new shame. His shares in the company had soared, allowing him to consider retiring within the next decade. And now? he thought sadly.

But then, how could he be seeing footage of another family occupying the same house with the same furnishings?

He continued watching the footage of the man at Ian's desk, examining what appeared to be Ian's photographs. The man and his family looked fifteen years younger—something stage make-up could have solved. All of the footage could have been fabricated, except for one glaring fact. Ian had seen this man before, and the more he thought about it, the more he was certain that he had seen all this footage before as well, many years ago, before he moved into the Tiburon house. He knew this because he recalled watching the footage and wishing he were that man living in that house, and being grateful that his wish had been fulfilled once he moved in.

Ian experienced a chilling sensation at the nape of his neck. His arms broke out in goose flesh.

This is how I learned about Tiburon in the first place. I know that man, that family has lived there a long time. I've always known it. Ian was baffled. *How could this be?*

Well, he thought, *suppose I wasn't living in that house, where would I have been living?*

The chilling sensation overcame his entire body. It was an awful sensation, like falling off a cliff into an endless abyss.

He saw Robin's face talking at him from behind her cappuccino at Caffé Puccini.

I keep trying to tell you, Ian. You've never lived in Tiburon. You've been in a cell all those years. It's all a fiction created by that chip and the images on your interactive set.

No, he thought. *That's absurd. Isn't it?*

Ian battled his way back to the bars and peered at the other inmates. They spent most of their time at work or interacting with their screen shows. Yet take a worker like Richard. He was in jail, yet claimed to be leading his regular life in Marin. Was this a nut house, or was something really creepy going on, as Robin had insinuated.

"Hey, Sirs!" he walked toward the guards and called out through the bars, "How many years have I been here? You can tell me that can't you?"

The graying guy looked at the Panther-like guard. "This guy gets on my nerves," he said.

"How many years? One? Five? Ten?"

Panther mumbled something into the older one's ear. The older one shrugged and shook his head.

"You can't remember?" Panther asked Ian.

"I can't." Ian insisted.

Panther rocked back and forth on his heels, hands on his gun belt.

"Told you this guy gets on my nerves. Denial." The older guard was shaking his head in disdain. "Let's see, I was hired eleven years ago next month, Derek? Oh, right you weren't here. But you," the guard pointed at Ian, "came the year after I did."

"I knew it!" Ian spun around. "What on earth did I do?"

"You tell us. The fact that you're in denial of such a terrible— That's a crime in itself!" the older guard was yelling.

Ian took the treadmill back to his cot and sat down, shaking his head.

"You're just trying to make me go nuts, aren't you?"

Both guards stared at him, stone faced.

"This is a nut house, isn't it? I'm in a nut house. Why won't you ever tell me? This is a nut house, isn't it?" Ian inquired.

Panther's face finally showed some emotion. He laughed. "Absolutely. Folks have to be sick in the head to end up here."

XIV

AT WORK, IAN had little time to dwell on the feelings of self loathing stirred up by the guards, nor to ponder the philosophical questions they posed. The bright side of staying so busy was that it also minimized the unpleasant interactions with his colleagues... and his contemplations about the futility of the operation he had undergone.

If he allowed himself any time to think of personal matters, he tried to conjure excuses to talk to Robin, whose cubicle was now at the opposite end. He was no longer near Alice, and people didn't pass him very often anymore. Robin seemed to pick up the cue, because whenever he got up and idly made his way to the coffee maker, she'd be there shortly thereafter. This, despite her one glaring shortcoming, he realized, cheered him immensely.

"We have to stop meeting like this," he told her one late afternoon. "How's it going?"

"As well as can be expected. You? You still feeling good after your operation? Any change of heart about what it accomplished?" This was the first time Robin had referenced her REM theory. Up until now, they had only engaged in small talk.

"Well, actually, now that you should ask, the guards informed me I've been in jail a decade."

"Really?" Robin stopped cold. Her entire demeanor changed and she began to speak rapidly, in the higher-pitched voice she used when she was excited or happy. "You're not still living in Tiburon, then?"

"If only," Ian responded sadly.

"I'm sorry the operation wasn't a total success," she said, almost giddily.

"Thanks for your sympathies," Ian said with some sarcasm.

"So you been here a decade?" Robin pondered.

"Not here. It's the home life."

"Wife and kids that bad?"

"Single."

"Maybe that's your problem," Robin said through her teeth, flashing a flirtatious sideways smile before heading back to her cubicle, thoroughly confusing Ian.

As the days went by, Ian found himself thinking about her incessantly again—that is, when he was not watching the screen or obsessing about his Tiburon home, previous life and the plausibility of returning to it. One thing was certain; the divide between Ian's sanity and Robin's was becoming increasingly insignificant.

Scenario one: Both he and Robin were nuts, so why not give in to the attraction? Obviously doctors had recommended the operation to find a cure for his insanity, but it didn't seem to have come off. Had the operation been a success, wouldn't he have less confusion about reality and less anxiety? Clearly this was not the case.

In support of his insanity, his idea that he'd been in jail a decade was delusionary, as may have been his notion that he had actually lived in Tiburon. This would indicate Richard was nuts too, for believing he lived in Marin. All three had probably cracked up from work pressures and were in a nut house for workers of Bear-TT. Maybe there was a class action suit there. Ian always envied Richard's relaxed work pace. But maybe he had a false impression. They had both cracked up.

His thoughts wandered to his mother. Had she consented to his admission in this low security nut house, wanting to make sure he didn't loose his job? But his mother was too devoted to his happiness to do something this deceitful without coming to see him. This scenario didn't make sense, since surely his mother would have visited. Something must have happened to her or she had never learned of his whereabouts. Moreover, he didn't feel like he was nuts. He could function and work. Wouldn't he have noticed?

Scenario two: The trio was not in a nut house, but in jail. Of course he was in jail. He grabbled hold of the bars. The problem was for what and for how long? In the second scenario, he had been jailed because of his complicity in Bear-TT crimes, and a family had taken possession of his home, and the government was involved in a cover-up. For whatever reason, the state was collaborating to drive him insane with the help of the guards who had lied to him about his date of imprisonment, perhaps so the state could lay claim to his terribly-appreciated home with more legitimacy, though wouldn't it revert to his mother? How could they get away with this?

Scenario three—and this was the one which most intrigued him. Robin was not crazy and her paradigm was true. He thought of Robin's sea-green eyes, lanky legs. How he wanted to believe her. The guards were not playing a sadistic prank. He really had been in jail ten of his thirty-four years. He had never lived in his Tiburon home; it belonged to the family he had seen prior footage of living in it. But he had memories of living in his Tiburon house all those years... This could explain why an operation to cure his insanity failed, since he had never been insane. But it would not explain Robin's insistence that the operation was to correct a malfunctioning implant, since nothing had changed in his perceptions...

At this point in his reasoning, he would flip on the screen. He realized he now watched it with the same frequency as the other inmates. He'd stay up late, pouring through the programs, as if they would offer him more clues to his existence. He was barraged with images of his previous life: the boat cafes along the Seine in Paris; the dreamlike teal and sapphire coves in Majorca's Calo Vicente and Mykonos; Paros windmills; Hotel Lagunitas in Yelapa with its artificial aqua lagoon pool overlooking the beach; Pink Las Rosas in Baja; the Pink Montecarlo Hotel in Mexico City; the pink flamingos at Casino de la Selva; the pink jeeps winding down pink paths to the beach with pink shells at Hotel Las Brisas in Acapulco where he'd wake to *pan dulce*, coffee and pink hibiscus strewn in his private pool; the lavish home-made breakfasts at Calistoga's Eurospa; the nation's best omelets at Café Sarafornia, aaah the just the sight of the Palisades omelet would trigger that Tantalus feeling again.... It seemed as though the screen was playing a tribute to the life of Ian W. Or was it merely a concerted attempt at psychological torture?

Somehow his screen-watching seemed to reassure the guards, it seemed to Ian. Ever since his operation, the guards had been allowing him to walk to work with the rest of the herd of inmates, instead of directly under their supervision. The guards he interacted with occasionally now wore no dark glasses. For some reason that Ian could not figure out, they belonged to a kinder, more humble breed, like regular security guards. At times, they were polite, helpful, almost willing to please, like hotel or club concierges, the way they had been with Richard.

"Ohhhhh! How bout that shot!" One evening, Ian recognized Richard's excited voice across the chasm. Regardless of other evidence to the contrary, there could be no more denying that it was Richard, he concluded. Richard was absorbed in a game of interactive golf on the screen. Richard must have marched home from work with the other commuting inmates, who mostly interacted with their sets or electronic devices. Countless times, Ian had felt such pity for the other prisoners: their lives consisted of nothing but interactive screens and pad screens at work, mobile screens at work, b-tabs or listening devices at work, e-pad screens at work, then the interactive screen at home, the interactive screen on vacation, then the screen at work again and the screen, the screen, the screen, and now he was just one more of them.

Richard insisted at work that he still lived in Marin, but this was clearly Richard in jail. *Which is why this could be a nut house,* Ian thought. *This is a nut house.*

For hours, Ian would pace back and forth and up imaginary hills on the treadmill obsessing about his future, hands riffling his head, making his hair greasier than it need be by morning. Would he ever recover his sanity? And why did the asylum look like a jail? Was it a prison for the criminally insane? Had he been responsible for more deaths than he admitted working for Bear-TT—actually killed people without acknowledging this fact, like a sociopath? Maybe that's what it was. He couldn't feel remorse or guilt for his crimes because he didn't admit to himself that he had committed them.

This obsessing was the worst on weekends, when Ian had not much else to do but obsess about work. The work week was kinder.

After much observation of Richard at work, the nut house hypothesis seemed less plausible. Instead, Ian began to modify his third hypothesis slightly. He had come to the conclusion that nothing else about Richard seemed unstable. Just his claim about his living situation. Which was Ian's problem, if the family who claimed to have been living in his house all these years were telling the truth. True, Richard and Ian could be in a nut house for this very reason, only this did not explain the bars and jail-like aspect of their imprisonment.

We both have in common that we thought we were living in idyllic situations but were really in jail, as Robin has stated, Ian tried to comprehend. *But the memories of our idyllic lives just seem too real to be fabricated.*

One Friday after a work reception celebrating a successful new campaign, during which Ian made sure to polish off the equivalent of a bottle of champagne on mostly an empty stomach, the answer came to him. It had seemed a year that he had not been allowed a drink. Now that the kinder guards overseeing him no longer forbid his indulgence in this area, the alcohol went straight to his head.

Once home, Ian began to long for company, especially Robin's. He stood at his bars and called out to Richard, but Richard was busy on his MEphone. He must have had it fixed, because when Ian had tried to borrow it at work, it had been broken. Ian didn't understand why Richard was allowed to keep his. Ian felt a pang of longing for his old MEphone. Maybe Richard's didn't really work. Maybe it was an illusion, like Richard's life in Marin.

"Richard, dude!" he yelled again.

We're so isolated here, Ian thought. Not that he spent much time after work with people in Tiburon. He mostly went to work and puttered around alone at night as well. But in a situation like this, he could have called people before—at least left a long rambling message or text or blip and felt better.

As usual, when he began feeling lonely, angry or frustrated, Ian flicked on the tube. This time, the program focus was a stay at Rio Villa resort in the Russian River, ironically the last vacation he had taken before his imprisonment. He stood and glanced at the other inmates. *How can our memories really come from screens?* his drunken mind mused. His last vacation to Rio Villa had been so real. He could recall being seated on the patio shaded by the lovely pastel lavender and aqua umbrellas, the gurgle of a fountain behind him and the river framed by graceful tendrils of the aspen and willow blowing in the breeze. How could he have imagined everything so vividly from screen images?

The screen focused on a child smelling honeysuckle hanging down from one of the balconies. *We stayed in that room!* He thought. Only he didn't remember the scent of the honeysuckle.

"Say Robin's right and I've been in jail nearly a decade. Then my memories of the outside would have only taken place in the years I had on the outside, between the ages of 18 and 24," Ian said aloud, to an imaginary listener. This was probably where Ian had built up his store of sensory information for his phony memories. "If I were always in jail, I never would have lived in Tiburon. "

Yet, oddly, the only scents he seemed to be able to recall were the roses and jasmine in his Tiburon garden. This could have also been memories from his teenage job in the flower store. There was no honeysuckle. He tried to recall other smells—chocolate, for example—and began to panic. "U.S. chocolate is nothing but wax," he remembered a European friend once having commented. Perhaps U.S. chocolate has no smell, he reflected.

His mind returned to his Río Villa vacation. It had been so tangible. He could see the redwoods on the far bank and colonial-style pale yellow clapboard houses with white picket fences. One of the guests had been playing guitar on the lawn, the music gently sailing in and out on the wind. After three days there, he vividly recalled he had developed a way of life, as though this were his summer villa and the river, his back yard. He remembered taking his breakfast on the patio under the umbrella until it became too hot, then the little hop, skip and jump down to the beach, relaxing in the sun, then sitting in the low river, a shower of sunlight playing on the surface, the little minnows darting around at the bank, and his feeding Cheerios to the ducks. He recalled gazing upstream at the river winding its way down from the mountains where there was nothing but redwoods... staring at that pristine view all the way back to Neolithic consciousness... the ripples taking him back to the lazy, endless summer days of childhood.

No doubt that it was a genuine memory. How could he have been in jail?

He remembered the feel of water evaporating from his skin in the sunlight. The temperature of the water was— He traced his steps to the water. Imagined swimming to the other bank. The water was—-warm. It had no temperature because it felt like his own skin. Or had it been icy? It would have had to have been cold in the mountains, he realized. Would one necessarily remember the temperature of the water?

Ian turned off the screen and sat on his cot, riffling his hair with his fingers. His thoughts raced to the temperature of the lake-size pool at Indian Springs that doubled as both a jacuzzi and pool. All he could remember was its expanse and heavenly color, the hue shifting from green aqua to a more heavenly neon Caribbean aqua as the water deepened. He remembered floating for what seemed like days under the stars on luxurious white floating mats, but for the life of him he couldn't remember the temperature of the water. It had to have been as refreshing as a pool, but hot as a jacuzzi. Had there been jets? Ah yes, they had said the water was body temperature or a bit more. Perhaps that's why he had no memory of it. He could remember the warm breeze on his skin, the feel of evaporating water as he lazed in the sun on the thick cushions of the recliners, but if Robin were right, this could just have been the open air locker in the jail where the sun and wind came in on a few rare hot days.

At Indian Springs, the pool was flanked by long rows of lounge chairs under tropical canopies framed in palms. On the deep side of the pool, the lounge chairs were open to the sun, a cloud of steam rising from the natural springs just beyond. So the pool must have been warm. He remembered seeing his shadow as he swam, feeling free, as though he were flying. It seemed he had stayed under water indefinitely. And this is when the realization knocked him down onto his bed like a brick.

He couldn't remember ever having learned to swim. He had grown up with constant admonitions from his mother about this fact. And he had no recollection whatsoever of any lessons ever rectifying the situation.

Ian, you don't believe me, but if you sift through the details of your life, you'll find little clues that you were not really alive in that moment, that you were in fact imprisoned at that time.

He decided to think of a more recent memory. The heat wave the weekend before his imprisonment. He had spent an afternoon with Eric at McKnee's Ranch beach. He remembered lying on his fluffy Egyptian towel on the coarse grains of primo sand and looking at the cotton wisps of fog clouds teasing out the sun… the glitter on the piercing blue-green grey water, water the color of Robin's eyes.

Because the beach was tucked into Devil's slide, it was forgotten by rangers and time and the hordes. It was also hidden from the fog bank. It reminded Ian of a secluded beach he once stumbled upon in the French Riviera… yet the cliffs were as dramatic as those he had once seen in Rabat, Morocco. A beach to dream, imagine…. Everything always seemed alright there.

He remembered having removed his shoes. He had been chilled by the freezing water, but that was expected from screen images of anyone entering the ocean. But he could not remember details a director might have overlooked: like if the coarse white sand had clung to his feet and clothes, or if it had easily been shaken off. Had they brought a lunch? The more he probed into his memories, the more he realized he didn't know.

He had been living his life half asleep without really being aware of the details.

"Wait a minute!" he protested aloud. He thought about his morning at work the week before the beach. To his horror, he could recall everything about it, from the bitter black coffee, to the trouble he had untangling paperclips that morning.

That settled it.

Increasingly more panicked, he combed through his mind for reassurance like a swimmer scrambling to grab onto a root or boulder to avoid being swept down the rapids. At last he thought of his photographs. Ah yes, he had a photograph of his time at Indian Springs, and another of Eric at McKnee's Ranch. Wasn't that proof of the existence of the real memory? He clung to the idea like a lifesaver, referring back to it each time he began to doubt again, but still he could not seem to fall asleep.

XV

IAN NEVER SLEPT that night. Unfortunately, a little past midnight he had recalled old documentary footage of a time when people wore full, instead of partial, GPS bifocals that gave the viewer the feeling they were in alternate idyllic places. For some reason, they had fallen out of favor. Could it have been with the advent of the sleep chip? Regardless, a society capable of this level of technology, he realized, was probably capable of altering digital photographs.

He poured through all his memories for evidence that they were not fabricated—by some combination of the screen and his childhood memories, most likely—but he found little. Robin's paradigm seemed to make increasingly more sense. Richard, the other inmates, and he were imprisoned with fabricated memories of a life they had never lived.

In the morning, not a guard was in sight as Ian boarded the elevator alone. He hardly ever saw any guards in dark glasses anymore. Ian laughed aloud. *Could it be because I've been watching the screen so much ever since my operation?*

A chill surged under the surface of his skin, raising the flesh. What then, had they attempted to do in the hospital? If, as Robin said, inmates had implants installed, his had obviously malfunctioned or been overridden by repeated awakenings? That could have explained the headache of his first day in prison. Perhaps it was after a failed operation. Nothing had happened on the ferry. He had never been on the ferry. Just dreamed it somehow. Something in the implant projected this false reality. He had been living in the jail for quite some time and had merely woken up there by accident. Or, rather, he had been woken deliberately, according to Robin.

As he marched off the elevator with the rest of the inmates, off to their jobs somewhere else in the building, he realized that he used to be under the illusion of a long journey home to Tiburon every night. How did this work if he was just going upstairs? And how could Richard maintain his illusion. Clearly he was lucid at work, but once outside the office doors—of course, that was where the illusion took place.

Ian had once read about experiments conducted with REM sleep: subjects could even perform complicated tasks like preparing a meal or riding a bike while sleepwalking and dreaming that they were somewhere else. They didn't appear to be sleeping; they just seemed robot-like. *Like commuters on the BART, walking down Montgomery, or texting in the driver's seat of driverless cars,* Ian thought.

Robin claimed various devices triggered the workers' REM sleep as they left work. Sure, Ian would always plug into his tunes. Or his GPS bifocals. If an RFID chip had also been implanted with whatever chip triggered REM, that would account for the consumer purchasing profile triggering advertisements by certain venues as he walked past.

Sometimes after work, Ian thought he was going to Puccini for dinner. Perhaps he did walk there without being in REM, then back to the cell… He had to ask Robin for more information.

Ian looked up from what was now Tracie's cubicle before proceeding to his own. The inverted Escher-like pyramid architecture of the jail served a purpose. From the cubicles, no cell door or bar was visible. The tinted elevators and special balcony glass projecting white opaqueness prevented workers from seeing that they were really working inside a jail. So that's why the bars were only as high as the balcony line as seen from the lobby!

The workers or inmates or whatever we are, he thought, *feel as though we're the only ones in the whole building. Same goes for the inmates when we're in our cells. They would not have taken the trouble to hide the fact that we are in jail,* Ian reflected, *if we were in REM sleep during work. Besides,* he recalled, *REM sleep is triggered by electrical impulses and must be expensive.*

As Robin's paradigm began to amass more weight throughout the day, he found himself increasingly desperate to talk to her. Yet it was difficult to find time away from the other coworkers. In the past, when he had tried to invite her to the restaurant next door for lunch, she would grumble about having too much work and ate at her cubicle. Inviting her to lunch in the restaurant would have been risky, anyway, Ian thought. At the behest of an official, management could easily turn all the MEphones into listening devices through the net, Ian realized. This is probably why in the past he'd never heard from other inmates in his situation.

At lunch time, Alice backed away from Ian when she approached with some mail, making him realize he still stank of alcohol. He chewed a few mints and headed to the coffee machine. Within minutes Robin was there. A cleaning technician was vacuuming a coffee spill.

"O.K. So we've been in jail most of our lives, right?" Ian was whispering, yet trying to be heard above the sound of the vacuum.

"What?"

"What you told me. You're right." He was barely audible over the noise and too tired to preface what he was saying. He took a sip of coffee.

Robin looked puzzled for a fraction of a second, then a grin swept across her face.

Ian sidled up next to Robin and whispered in her ear. There was urgency in his voice. "Only a couple of things don't add up about what you told me. I have photographic evidence of memories you say never existed."

"You have it exactly backwards, Ian. Your memories were created by the scenery in the photographs. The photographs came from screen images that triggered the sensors of your brain-enhancer chip. The people are superimposed, sometimes before, sometimes later."

Ian took a step back as if he'd had the wind knocked out. "No. This is getting too weird again. I'll have to think about that one," Ian said. "But wait. Here's something you probably can't explain away. We've been jailed for what we did here, only I've been in jail since I was 24. Maybe even before I came to work for Bear-TT!"

Robin shook her head almost violently. "No!" she said. "Ian, we were not imprisoned for our work at Bear-TT."

"Excuse me," he almost choked on his coffee. "But that's what you told me."

"We should all be locked up for what we've done here, particularly Bear-TT's shareholders and CEOs Ian, but that's not why we've been imprisoned."

"But you said—"

"You weren't ready for the truth then." Robin smiled and walked away casually.

XVI

IN RESPONSE TO his questions about the nature of their imprisonment, Robin said very little. Her behavior indicated that she thought they were being watched. Now, when Ian left the office, Ian would glance around the tremendous lobby, searching for a place where he and Robin might converse in private. Glancing furtively from the restrooms near the far window overlooking the Ferry Building, back toward the entrance one evening, he came to the conclusion that if the entire structure was a covert prison, there was obviously no privacy anywhere within its walls.

For the time being, he acknowledged, he'd have to be content to piece together her responses to his questions. Robin said he was not in prison for his crimes at Bear-TT, though they probably deserved it. That made sense. If indeed he had been jailed for some wrongdoing at Bear-TT, he probably wouldn't still be working at the company. But as Robin pointed out, this didn't mean Bear-TT or its employees were not without culpability. He could no longer deny he had been complicit in committing more harm than good.

Slowly, Ian began to accept that workers like himself had always been imprisoned, leading a life of pure illusion, though he could not figure out exactly the motive nor what had woken him nor why. Ian continued to allow the screen to run in his cell in order to deceive the guards, but he now spent most of his free time on his cot, thinking about Robin and his life. He had remembered that shortly before his awakening—what he used to call his recent imprisonment—he had just come up with the concept of "work think," and was cautioning his coworkers not to engage in it after work, but to enjoy themselves instead. Had this been the beginning of the malfunction of some implant inside him?

As usual, he tried to search out clues in the other inmates or coworkers, signs that there were other inmates who knew they were in jail or coworkers who might be imprisoned like Richard, but who were aware of it. Except for Robin, all of these clues and signs had turned out to be false leads.

His growing sense of isolation caused him to become increasingly depressed. The more depressed he became, the more he put his hopes in Robin, his potential ally. He'd dwell on her sexy slanted smile, almond green eyes, and half swallowed words. She had the cutest, petite ass, what he'd give to.... Only it almost seemed that since he had come to believe her, she had begun to avoid him.

He longed to stroll with her in Berkeley—where spring arrived sooner—as he had seen so many other lovers do, through the gardens at the University museum beyond Café Babette. In May, the scattered fog clouds hung like small dreams here and there on the satin blue horizon behind the poplars, now in their full verdant splendor. How he hungered for some of Joan and Patrick's gourmet cuisine and small talk. Robin and he could eat out in the garden, shaded by a canvas umbrella, in one of those Alice in Wonderland astro-bright green and orange heart-shaped chairs and chat about films and the latest art show. Then they'd walk through the Eden-like grass, up through the institutional bronze sculpture terraces, where he would kiss Robin under the graceful plum trees' auburn leaves... whether or not it was all illusory.

One day, Ian and Robin had to work late together again to prepare for another ad shoot. When the others were out of ear shot, Robin turned up the MEtunes on her work pad, then pulling up a chair for Ian, whispered into his ear.

Ian broke into gooseflesh.

"Tomorrow after work, meet me near the entrance. I got a car share."

XVII

IAN HAD FORGOTTEN how nice May was in the Bay Area, and how much warmer Oakland was than San Francisco. As they drove up from the foothills toward the redwoods in Roberts Regional Park, the car was filled with the nutty summer scent of fallen cedar and redwood needles heated by the sun. *Ah, summer in the Bay Area hills*, Ian thought. Oakland and its redwoods was the Bay's best-kept secret.

"Quick, that cute little white house there," Robin urged, pointing to the perimeter of a park beyond her self-driving driver's side. "It belonged to Joaquin Miller, a crazy poet who owned this land."

"Ever been to his park?" Robin gestured to some stone stairs leading up the hillside. Water cascaded down from a tremendous waterfall at the apex to a second fall that ran over shale and fern to a pool, with a view of three bridges, then a faux river that finished in a reflecting pool, she elaborated.

"Reminds me of the pyramid of the sun in Teotihuacan," Ian commented.

"Joaquin Miller actually did build a pyramid up there somewhere, around the back. Not as big as the falls—"

"No way. A pyramid? Why haven't I heard of it?"

"It's pretty small really. But it's there. All stone."

A little farther on, a large, noisy herd of goats was munching on the tall hillside grasses.

Ian laughed in amusement.

"Aren't they cute?" Robin exclaimed. "They're brought in every summer to consume the brush that poses a fire-danger."

As they continued up into the redwoods, they passed a stunning panoramic view of Oakland and Alameda off to the right, then they drove up and down a couple of small hills enveloped by rolling waves of tall, golden grass and turned right down a steep driveway.

"We have arrived," Robin laughed. "Once I figured how to hack my way out of the jail, club scanners like this were small potatoes. Just stick close behind me."

She stopped Ian from proceeding. "Let's make sure Paul stays busy talking to that disapprover. They all know everyone by name and I don't want them registering you as a guest."

An old woman was nattering on to the handsome front desk receptionist about a long-haired seven-year old who was under-age to be in the jacuzzi.

"I heard his mother calling him Rafael. In Spanish!" the disapprover tattled.

Robin allowed the scanner to read her ME. It beeped twice for both her and Ian. "Look," she whispered, laughing, as she pointed to the desk monitor displaying her image with an alias. "I created two fake memberships, one for a guest, but you don't resemble the picture I scanned in."

Robin grabbed two towels and led Ian to the pool area. They found two shaded recliners sequestered along one of the terraces, the stone walls dripping with rosemary and lavender reminding Ian of Indian Springs. Beyond, a picket fence, a gentle breeze swept the tall grasses on the hillside, recalling summers on the Cape. The sound of summer was embodied in the splashing and frolicking of children, evoking in Ian memories of California beachside summers and luxurious pools, his mother enveloping him in a warm, fluffy towel and offering him a sparkle ice cream bar. Then he realized these memories were mostly fictitious.

"My memories of summer at the Cape, California beaches and Mom—In fact, where really was our house? What jail is she in?"

"Let's just enjoy here now," Robin said sadly.

"So tell me more about these implants. What's going on?" Ian demanded.

Robin adjusted her recliner to sitting position and stared through a gap in the trees to the bay.

"Our implants...." she started. A family arrived and began to make themselves comfortable on the recliners next to them. "Actually, before I get started on that, we should probably get some dinner. Have I shown you the deck?" Robin asked, standing. "Just bring your jacket."

After ordering at the grill from a Gaorean couple Robin addressed informally as Soo and David, they walked onto a stunning deck that spanned the length of the building. "Take your pick," Robin said, referring to the ten or so empty tables with umbrellas. The expansive view spanning Alameda to Marin nearly knocked the wind out of Ian.

Ian took a seat at a table with a perfect view of the Transamerica building—and Puccini he imagined—blanketed by a dreamy layer of fog rolling in from the Golden Gate.

The neighboring hillside was golden with the pendulous sun. It was comforting to know that while his other memories of ecstatic moments were perhaps fictitious, there was assurance that here he was not dreaming.

"We're not in REM now, right. This is real, right?" he asked Robin.

"This is reality," she smiled. "Stolen, but real."

"So why is no one out here?" Ian asked finally.

"It's not in their program. Remember I told you they have only so many haunts where they're allowed to go. This isn't even on their radar. That's why we can talk. Ask away..."

"The one clue to my former life that I can't shake... Okay, the photographs I have of my buddies in my Tiburon home seem like proof that I lived there. You said my memories came from these photos, with the people superimposed, but I just can't believe—"

"Wait, Ian. They have WiFi here. I can show you. I have to get something from my locker."

Ian reflected on the sound of birds and few stray tennis balls in the courts far below. If he had his ME, he would have played Gypsy Kings *A Mi Manera*, but instead he contented himself by playing what he recalled of it in his head. *Yo quiero ser (estar) ahi nada más...*

Robin returned with an apparently clandestine MEpad and two paper cups of what Ian assumed was water. He seized it immediately. "Wait!" Robin put her hand on his arm. "That's an ouzo-gin martini. I keep a flask of it in this locker I hacked for special occasions."

They toasted to escapes and dined and inhaled the sunset, descending like a royal orange curtain on an unusually warm May day over the gold-plated bay. Little embers of lights began to come to life, ignite. Wisps of fog poured in from the Golden Gate lending a dreamy misty quality to the landscape framed by the three bridges.

This was *Xanadu, Lost Horizon, Shangrila* Ian thought ecstatically to himself. *Some people fall in love over and over,* he thought lazily, picturing Robin's green eyes. *They obsess, dream, email, photograph and phone over and over and over. I fall in love with landscapes too, with places. I play sappy music over and over and think of the place.*

He realized it was the first time he had been out of jail in months, his first release from his isolation, his depression. *So this is how people feel when they're released from jail,* he reflected.

"Look Ian," Robin said, pulling out the ME and flipping back the red accordion cover.

"I thought you didn't have a MEpad."

"You didn't see this," she giggled. " Look. You posted that picture you took of Clif and Eric on your balcony. See, here it is in your history. Now…" Robin began clicking, zooming, pasting. See, now I'm looking up the code. Wait a sec. There. Suddenly the backdrop changed to a balcony Ian had enjoyed at Hotel Catalina in Zihuatanejo, only instead being framed by red maples, Eric and Clif were surrounded by palm fronds and hibiscus, the sea beyond mysteriously enclosed by mountains and an expansive white hammock on the right.

"I was there with my girlfriend, not them. Or—" Ian shook his head.

"You probably weren't there ever, I'm sorry to report," Robin noted sadly. "Look." She typed in a few more numbers and letters and suddenly the backdrop changed to Ian's cell. "According to this code you three were actually in your cell at one time. That's probably when this was taken. Whether your memory of the moment on your Tiburon balcony with them was occurring simultaneously as you were in REM or whether the image was used to create that memory is not evident from this data.

"By the way, just to confuse you some more," Robin continued, "some of my friends think that inmates are given two weeks vacation a year to co-mingle in owner-magnets, which could account for some of the long lines we see in San Francisco. This theory would also explain some of the sensory memories we all have. Unfortunately, it's pretty difficult to distinguish real memories from REM sleep memories."

Ian took another sip of the martini. "I'm having so much trouble with this," he said, looking out at the Bay. "Tell me more about these brain chips or whatever you call them."

"As I started saying at the pool…" she began again, and launched into a lengthy diatribe about the advent of brain-enhancing implants. Apparently, the implants had come on the heels of a discovery by psychiatrist Elena Nelson-Hines-Flores-Guillot-Rasmukian who found that human beings rarely inhabited their five senses in moving through the world, but instead muddled through much of it unaware in a semi-somnambulistic state, particularly after the extension of the working day. This led to her discovery that it was possible to activate REM without simultaneously paralyzing the major voluntary muscle groups.

Low voltage radio signals from electronic devices such as MEphones and tunes pods triggered the brain-enhancer chip's sensors in the inner ears into stimulating a certain sector of the brain which brought on and slightly modified REM sleep mode without muscular paralysis. The same could be achieved in the implant behind the retina, through a series of images on interactive screens, coupled with the radio waves, first known as Blue-Tooth in its most rudimentary form in the old order. From the inmates' point of view, the world which she would inhabit would be slightly more visually tangible if stimulated from the screens; more audibly tangible, if stimulated through the inner ear.

Now thanks to the implants, the workers transitioned into a desirable hyper-REM sleep state once they left work. They would remain in hyper-REM until they turned in for the night, at which point, they'd enter deep sleep, then surface to REM where they would remain until they entered the workplace. Here they would finally awake.

In other words, the only time workers were actually awake was to perform their jobs. Some, who commuted from their jail elsewhere, often began their waking states at some point during the commute, once they had exited the jails.

Given the dramatic increase over the years in responsibilities and the sixty-hour work week leading to a marked reduction in sleep among workers, the REM sleep arrangement worked out quite nicely to produce alert, awake and effective workers. It was generally agreed among the owning class that maintaining workers in constant REM would have been less cost-effective due to un-renewable energy demands, and would have made for too ineffectual a workforce. Thus, those in the service industry were really working those jobs in the outside world. When Ian was at Caffé Puccini, neither he nor the other workers—Dolores, Areli and so forth, were in REM. Those in the service industry simply returned to their cells like all the rest, via public transport, on foot or driverless autos.

"So the workers in this club, Paul—" Ian began.

"Omar, Jordan, Sasha, you're right. Are not in REM," Robin continued the thread.

By the time Robin was done talking, the Bay was a complicated tapestry of lights. The sky over the Bay Bridge looked green blue. Ian could make out the shape of the earth, see the moon. The crickets were so loud they sounded electronic. Only the light inside the exercise room at the far end of the deck remained on.

Suddenly a shooting star made an arc like the tail of a firework.

"Did you see that?" Ian said, putting his hand on Robin's thigh.

"I did," she said. She looked intently into his eyes, and Ian thought the star had somehow entered them.

He cupped her face in his hands and brought her lips to his. They began kissing gently at first. Without interruption, she slid onto his lap and melted into him. Their kissing became passionate, almost frenzied. They continued like this

"Let's go for a swim before they close," Robin suggested.

They floated on their backs looking up at the stars, kissed some more under the stars and swam and played like children. But when Robin tried to lead Ian to the deeper end, the laughter faded from his face.

"Come on, Ian. I brought you here because you wanted to know if you could swim. Let's find out. You seem to float all right."

Ian began by floating, the way he used to in his bathtub as a child. Then he flipped over. And sank and Robin had to bring him to the side of the pool. He was burping and coughing water.

"Well I guess that answers your question," she tried to lighten his mood. "Let's try the jacuzzi." She slid into the water as easily as a seal. Ian followed more cautiously from the steps and withdrew his foot immediately with a yelp of surprise.

"I forgot, this might be your first jacuzzi. It's usually hotter," Robin said.

Of course. Prison water wouldn't be warm. I've gotten used to cold showers, he reflected.

"I guess I am a virgin," Ian stammered, realizing this was his first encounter with the real thing. He noticed his ankles and feet had acclimated to the heat and lowered himself slowly into the swirling water. The motion of the jet surprised him.

"Relax into it," Robin suggested. "It can loosen knotted muscles."

The bubbling water seduced Ian into relaxing. Both Ian and Robin stared at the dark hillside, the shadow of a hawk passing overhead. The crickets were so loud, they could be heard over the sound of the jets. The alcohol seemed to triple in potency, and the anxiety he had felt after his pool mishap dissipated. His throat began to feel better.

"This is paradise," Ian said. "Can we do this often?"

Robin laughed. "You had some more questions I wanted to answer before this places closes. Let's take advantage that we're the only ones right now. Usually there's a couple more people."

"Okay, explain where I've been sending my mortgage payment

each month, Robin."

"All the payments we make while we're in REM are a big racket. They go to some owner or another. The system would all collapse without them. All those virtual trips you took around the world, all the virtual Bay Area vacations, all the meals you ate at virtual restaurants, they cost money. Embedded in each retinal scan payment is consent to pay for the virtual privilege you are enjoying."

"Down to the virtual furniture I purchased. So virtual payments—" Ian cupped some water in his hand and rinsed his face.

"Those were no virtual payments. Those were real payments for the privilege of believing you were living in a gated community, in an expensive house, with expensive furniture, taking exotic trips, sipping expensive lattés."

Ian was shaking his head.

Robin laughed. "Ever wonder where the money for your MEphone, utilities, cable connections goes?"

"Of course. How naïve of me. So the jail is charging the inmates for their own upkeep."

"How else do you think this economy was able to stay afloat after it farmed out all its labor and gross domestic product dwindled to almost nothing? After the resources and labor they'd been exploiting in developing countries dried up? After the citizens could no longer afford to be consumers?"

"After the pyramid scheme bottomed out," Ian offered.

"Exactly. Thus virtual products. Owners think they're being humane. They think it's 'green.' Part of the prisoner deal was designed to preserve our insanely wasteful economic system despite global warming. It cuts down on green house gas emissions, since the prison is a controlled solar environment. At least it helped save downtown from flooding. Originally, some animal rights and environmental groups were for the plan I think, though obviously, imprisoning the workforce isn't nearly as effective as imprisoning the perpetuators of this toxic economic system." Robin half-laughed, half-hissed through her teeth.

The economy depended on the inmates' illusory freedom, Robin elaborated. It would have taken a severe blow were it not for the inmates' dependency on their driverless autos and the electronic gismos. They paid for these things, as well as the prison's utilities, food and clothing bills. And moreover, they paid for the rights to live in their virtual homes, the rights to purchase their virtual possessions and other virtual privileges such as virtual travel. This, coupled with the owners' rampant consumption kept the latter class in its privilege.

Thus the virtual economy was built upon hyper-REM. It was through the REM that the workers agreed to fork over the fruits of their labor to the owners without anything tangible in return. It was through the REM that they were not only willing, but eager to spend most of their lives in cage-size spaces. They worked in such a cubicle, lived in a cubicle and dined in restaurants with such closed cubicle seating, they nearly resembled chickens whose beaks had to be hacked off so as not to peck each other from the duress of such close quarters. However contrary to the chickens—and there was a growing movement initiated by offspring in the owning class to subsidize REM implants for animals in order to reduce the horror of being farmed—through the REM, workers believed they were living rich, luxurious lives, once they left work. Of course those who loved their jobs—as Ian once had—were the happiest of the lot. Thus the entire basis for the economy, from the owner's point of view, was a benevolent one, as long as they were in charge to enforce it.

Robin and Ian treated themselves to a luxurious shower replete with body bath gel, lotion and Q-tips. Robin snuck into the male bathroom and escorted Ian to the dry sauna. They kissed and fondled on the bench of hot cedar. Robin wanted to take it farther, but Ian was worried someone might walk in.

When they emerged, an older trim gentleman in the lobby called Robin by her alias "Margot" and offered her decaf.

"I'm going to miss you when you're on vacation, Alex," Robin said.

"Alex is cool," she said to Ian on their way out, explaining that he had left Switzerland in his days to come to the U.S..

On their way back across the bridge, Robin began to laugh, as though she had been suppressing it in the club.

"What's so funny?"

"I always get a kick out of club personnel thinking I'm Margot Pepper."

"Why. Who was she?"

"A legendary Oakland author that lived in this parts decades ago."

"Never heard of her. Great name though. Was she a contemporary of Joaquin Whatshisname?"

"Miller. Joaquin Miller. No. Much later. She just happened to be one of the former members I was able to access. I just reactivated her

ID."

"OK, Robin," Ian grew serious. "Does anyone else know about this paradigm? I mean there has to be some kind of re—"

Robin squeezed Ian's lips shut affectionately with her right hand. "Shhhh," she said.

"What?" Ian inquired, listening.

"There is. But we'll have to talk about that at the conference." She pointed to the GPS.

"What?" Ian took a deep breath. Was her paranoia really justified? "What conference?"

"The conference on biotech copyright."

"Oh right." Ian hated conferences. Now they had a whole new meaning: escape, even romance. "You really think they'll let us attend that conference?" Ian said skeptically.

"Absolutely. They need us there. We'll have escorts though."

XVIII

THE INTERNATIONAL CONFERENCE on biotech copyright was set for late August in Half Moon Bay, weeks away and the wait weighed heavily on Ian. Robin avoided Ian for most of that seemingly-interminable period... perhaps to divert suspicion, Ian realized. There had to be some kind of resistance, and she was probably a part of it. His new memories of their romantic tryst at the Club kept him afloat for a while, but the monotony of work and his desire to talk to Robin tormented him.

Once, as though reading his mind, she looked him straight in the eye, put her finger over his lips and whispered in his ear, "Don't give up before your miracles."

Ian softened and smiled, fighting the temptation to kiss her index finger.

"We'll meet the deadline," she said aloud, throwing some doubt on his certainty.

Then she slipped him an envelope marked "Urgent." Inside was more toilet paper with black letters: "WE'RE BEING WATCHED. WAIT."

But as the days wore on without much contact, Ian began to doubt their participation in the conference at all. It made no sense for their jailers to allow it, he reasoned. And as he couldn't seem to find an appropriate time and place to discuss this nor any other matter with Robin, his apprehensions and anxiety only grew.

One Saturday morning, Ian was awakened by the strong scent of jasmine from his Tiburon garden. It must be mid-July, he thought, lazily, dreamily, luxuriating in its scent before opening his eyes. He imagined his balcony door open to a warm summer night, the air sweet with jasmine and French Lace roses. Only where was the gentle gurgle of water from the fountains? He could almost see the marble table in the garden below illuminated by tiny star-dust lights swirling in a cloud of crimson trumpet vine that entwined a tree in the garden's center; an angel bathing in the soft blues and greens illuminating the fountain and greenery beyond.

Then his lids darted open. It was morning and Tiburon was a long ago dream, he realized.

The scent from his garden wafted into his cell again. A few

moments later, a crew in tan jumpsuits backed out of the cell next door.

"That should take care of the problem. So just don't flush hair from your brush down the toilet," one of the men called out. "Oh, I hope you're not allergic. I used some of that air freshener."

How many flowers in his Tiburon garden had been manufactured by prison air fresheners, Ian wondered.

Ian recalled how his mother had loved to work in her garden. She obsessed and talked about it a lot to Ian. Had it been a prison garden? Children are impressionable, Ian thought. His mother's dreams would have helped form his own.

Once, during his teen years, he worked at a flower shop on Columbus Avenue—the same one which had employed his mother during the summers and school holidays. His mother was a school teacher by profession, but had to supplement her income after the divorce selling flowers. It had been she who had taught him to make arrangements. He remembered being so taken with their creations, he began photographing them. This is where his interest in photography had begun, he recalled. And this must have been how he had been able to amass the sensory material for his memories of his mother's garden and later his own in Tiburon, he realized.

Ian fell back on his cot, thinking of his mother, revisiting his childhood with his new eyes. He had grown up, an only child, in a family cell, which he believed had been a luxurious house, until his parents' divorce when he had been four. Their home after her divorce was small, according to Ian's recollection, but then again, he had been in REM sleep when they were together in the cell.

As far back as Ian could recall, from infancy probably coinciding with the end of his mother's maternity leave, Ian had been enrolled in childcare—what must have been prison foster care in a different wing of the jail. He recalled the privatization movement earlier that century, the move toward eliminating small schools and consolidating more and more schools in bigger buildings, then housed directly in the jails.

If most of the population was jailed to maximize profit and control for its elite as Robin had explained, then school was nothing more than indoctrination for leading a future life in prison. He tried to recall the exact details. In the name of meeting high testing standards, children were taught to obey authority, not to think for themselves, to open books at the same time, close books at the same time, write and line up and march to the jail yard for recess at the same time, just as their teachers were expected to teach the same scripted lessons at the same time, much like their commuting parents marched blindly like lemmings, back and forth from and to the jails. This mindless regurgitation of scripted lessons of course led to worse test scores, increasing the likelihood that the children would wind back up in the jails at an accelerated speed after their release from their parents' cells at age 18.

Robin had also explained that besides sleeping together in the family cells, the offspring of prisoners were allowed limited visits with their jailed parent: an hour before school and a couple of hours following their so-called after-school programs. In this way, the kids were under the illusion that they had parents, though the waking time they spent together was insignificant.

Ian remembered his resentment toward his own mother. How often, when he was upset with her, had he said to her or to his father, "You're not my parents." There had been more truth to that statement than he realized. At 18, the children were released from this situation, but within four or five years—once failure to participate meaningfully in the economy prompted them to commit the strikes necessary for life imprisonment, thanks in great part to the advent of high stakes testing and scripted programs—ended up back in jail permanently, what they believed to be studios or bachelor pads Robin had mentioned.

After the divorce, Ian's mother was never home and, during summer, away at a million conferences and workshops, if she was not selling flowers, so off he went to summer camp and all kinds of other programs which didn't require REM, but instead helped build up his store of sensory imagery for future REM fantasies.

Ian was now aware that the sensory images for his ecstatic memories, as well as those of all the other inmates, were largely derived from a combination of real experiences in the outside world in their jobs or post imprisonment teen years and the screen—which was mostly visual and auditory, not tactile nor culinary.

"In fact," Robin had explained, "That is how you can tell the source of the memory. If you can remember tasting or feeling something, it is probably based on reality, instead of the screen."

XIX

IAN CLEAVED TO his memories more than ever now, as though not
to do so would be to slowly erode them forever. Whether or not they
were real, they were all he had; to lose them was to lose his identity
beyond that of a prisoner.

He missed even the cold rain now, the cold spring clinging to Bay
Area skies and young trees that suddenly would shake their water onto
heads and bare necks if one happened to bump them getting into cars.
The ground would be soaked, cloaked in a delicate green mud clinging
to the soles of shoes, white calla lilies and azaleas fighting desperately to
stand tall under the weight of so much water.

In his old life, his mirage life, his garden was lovely but too chilly to
admire for more than a few minutes. Rainy days, he would head across
the Bridge to the Montclair Egg Shop in Oakland, a breakfast place
that was all brick and had trains running around a track on the walls,
miniature acrobats cycling on a tight rope and Henry Thoreau quotes
all over the slanted ceilings.

*"If a man does not keep pace with his companions, perhaps it is because
he hears a different drummer. Let him step to the music he hears, however
measured or far away."*

It had been started by an eccentric dreamer and sold to a cook
named Miguel Barrón.

The place must have existed, he realized; it must have been featured
on the tele, but he likely never set foot inside.

How he would have loved to make love to Robin on his bed
overlooking the Bay, then drive to the Egg Shop for breakfast the next
morning, and the Oakland Hills Tennis Club again, or at least live the
illusion. At least the Club was real, he consoled himself.

And what about February in the City. That particular month was
painfully beautiful, as he remembered it now, with the pink cherry and
plum trees looking so dramatic against the newly fixed up Victorians.
Their trim and molding so fastidiously painted in gold like historical
landmarks. There would be the slow pace of the elderly Chinese going
to market in Chinatown, that distinctly San Francisco smell of the
asphalt after the rain—or was that only the distinct smell of the jail yard
that he had grown to love?

When would he ever see the life he cherished so much again?—or,
rather, visit his haunts for the first time, since these were not real

memories, the water shaken on his head just the willow in the jail yard. When would he have illusions again, then? He missed his illusions! He wanted to share his illusions with Robin.

He was flooded with sadness at the realization of the impossibility of the fulfillment of his desires, of ever seeing his favorite spots again, or of ever having seen them to begin with. All this confused him terribly.

Yet what difference did it really make? How happy he had been all those years of illusion, regardless. Did it really make any difference whether he'd been sitting in a jail cell the whole time?

As the days wore on, the only thing Ian wanted more desperately than to make love to Robin was to make the illusions start up again.

Sometimes Ian would stand shaking the bars, calling out, "I give up. Give me the REM drug. I want the drug back." Sometimes he'd do this until he was hoarse; at other times he'd cry.

He tried to sleep and found that, increasingly, he could not. He tried to imagine bringing Robin into his former illusory life. But this only led to endless tossing and turning.

One early evening, mercifully, he fell asleep in a field he had never seen before, next to Robin. Sometime before he entered the dream state, he had realized it didn't matter where they were.

I'd give it all up, my old life, all of it, to sleep with her again, he laughed to himself. *We could build our own new reality.* He woke up counting the days to the conference, praying they'd really allow them to go.

XX

ABOUT A WEEK prior to the conference, Ian and Robin managed to leave work simultaneously.

"Mind if we step over to the fountain?" Ian hoped the sound of the water would make their conversation difficult to discern.

"Did you say you live in the same kind of studio I do?"

Robin let a chuckle escape from the side of her smile.

Ian persisted. "I'm on floor 84—"

I should get going," Robin suddenly cut him off.

"Wait!" Ian caught her shoulder. She spun around and looked up at him. They stood this way for a few seconds too long.

Ian cleared his throat. "I can't see them sending us to the conference—"

"They have to. The others wouldn't understand if they didn't send us. Last time, they just gave me a special room with special attention."

"Isn't that a little pricey? Your own guard?"

"I think they rotate them around. They're not paid much compared to what inmates like you and I bring in. Ian, listen, before I forget. Bring swim trunks to the first session. They sell them downstairs in the tourist boutique."

Ian was startled when Alice gave him his room assignment at the Beach House Hotel: a private two-room suite overlooking the sea. He could feel excitement bubbling up, bursting out of the top of his head.

"Why such a nice room?"

Alice shrugged and snapped her gum. "You tell me! Somebody likes your performance."

The hotel was packed with white collar Bear-TT employees. The first day of the conference, everyone was kept busy for nine hours listening to a consultant blather on about a new strategic plan. Food was catered and workers ate both lunch and an early supper on their laps, without moving from their seats. The eight hour stretch (ten if one counted the working lunch and dinner) was excruciating for Ian without a sign of Robin through the rows of heads and not so much as a MEphone to distract him from the nonsense. *I am, after all, in jail,* he kept reminding himself.

After they were released at last from the session at 7:10, he noticed her at the very back. She waited for him.

"Heading off to change in the restroom?" she smiled with some apprehension.

"Exactly," Ian assured her.

When they came to a pocket of space in the hallway without anyone else in earshot, Robin grabbed his arm.

"Straight to the jacuzzi, not your room, okay?" Robin looked at him intently, then headed for the restroom.

Just then, he noticed a young woman with long hair and green eyes assessing him. Her plump lips looked like the silicon job models had, the gold lipstick making them seem cartoonlike, like a Walt Disney goldfish. The girl smiled knowingly at Robin, who returned the grin.

"Do you know her or something?" Ian whispered.

"You don't know Angelina?" Robin looked around uneasily. "She works for Bear-TT."

Instead of heading back toward the elevators with the rest of the crowd to fuss with the personal luggage that had been deposited in each of their rooms, Ian approached the front desk to retrieve two towels and a bag to send clothes for cleaning. A guard with red hair approached, staring at him intently though brown eyes. With his red hair and freckles, he looked as though he had just come of drinking age. The guard followed Ian to the restroom, where Ian removed his clothes. The guard was posted outside when he exited. He followed Ian to the jacuzzi.

The jacuzzi was situated, like the hotel, atop a cliff, with the ocean steps away, below. Surfers sat like seals in dark wetsuits atop their boards, some zigzagging across the six-foot waves. To Ian's relief, a middle-aged couple and a graying woman were chattering away over the jets. Ian opened the circular gate. The guard put his hand on his heat ray and patted it. Ian smiled in acknowledgment at the hotel guests, then at the guard. He then removed his clothes, hung them on the gate and, remembering his jacuzzi experience at the Oakland Hills Tennis Club, stepped cautiously onto the first step.

The guard entered inside the gate and sat down on one of the lounge chairs.

The heavier of the two women looked at the guard with disapproval, then sank back down below the bubbles. The man noticed his wife's discomfort.

"Something wrong?" he asked the guard.

The young guard adjusted his hat and cleared his throat. He stepped over the water and stuck in his hand. "Just checking the temperature," he responded. All three guests stared at him expectantly, until he left the gated area. He took a seat on a bench not too far away, but to Ian's relief, out of earshot because of the roaring of the water jets.

Once Ian's limbs had adjusted to the high temperature of the water, he submerged the rest of his body, slicked back his hair with the water and sat up.

"Attending a conference?" he asked the male of the group.

"No, no. Thanks for the compliment but I'm retired," he laughed. "We're part of a wedding party—the outcast part," he snickered at the two women."

The prettier of the two women whose thick, layered brown hair had shrunk in size since it became increasingly wet, spoke up. "The rest of the group's staying at the Half Moon Bay Lodge."

"We procrastinated with the RSVPs," piped up the heavier woman.

"Good thing," her husband said under his breath.

"Shut up," his wife laughed. "They're a nice bunch!"

Ian was confused by all this. Clearly, they were not inmates, since this was no dream. Was this the real ruling class then?

Ian's body had acclimated to the new temperature. He reclined his head and wet his hair. Then he sank back into a jet, inviting it to work his knotted shoulder muscles as he took in the extraordinary view beyond the bars of the gate. At first these bars irritated him, for he felt once again like a caged animal.

Eventually, Ian stood and allowed himself to see beyond the bars. The low-lying pink and peach puffs of fog had caught fire over the horizon as a swollen sun sank into them, its embers lighting the water. The surfers sat still on their boards staring reverently at the tangerine orb as it sank. The three other guests had fallen silent as well as they admired the vanishing globe. Ian's eyes followed a boogie-boarder in a red suit, with long hair and what appeared to be breasts, knee boarding across a wave.

"Aahhhhhhh" he exhaled as he sank down again into the water, marveling at this fairly new sensation. He couldn't remember anything else feeling that good. Except making love, he smiled to himself. Certainly, that hadn't been a dream, or had it? Inmates had to be able to procreate or the workforce would die out. Though it would have had to take place during REM, since Realtime was reserved only for working, he corrected himself. So was he a virgin, then?

Ian thought of Robin. His sensual experience of her had taken place against a backdrop of illusion. He imagined inviting her into his luxurious room, kissing her as they sat on the edge of the bed, helping her to remove her clothes, then tumbling back with her, the windows open to the murmur of the waves just beyond. He looked over at the guard, still staring intently at him, and the feeling that was growing between his thighs subsided.

He glanced around for Robin and wondered if she had encountered an obstacle. It was then that he noticed a bouquet of flowers on the ground just outside the gate, their petals seemingly alive with the colors of the setting sun. He leapt out of the jacuzzi, startling the guard, who also stood and touched his heat ray. The male of the trio startled and stared at the guard. "Trigger happy, isn't he?" he smirked at Ian. "It's okay, that belongs to our party," the man spoke out. Ian withdrew the hand he had begun to reach under the gate toward the bouquet. "Son, go ahead. That was a bride's maid bouquet we brought back to give to one of the housekeepers we've grown fond of over the years, but she's off shift now." He looked at his wife.

"Yeah, she won't be back at work until they're wilted! Please take it!" his wife chimed, echoed by her friend.

"Thank you. Really," Ian said, rescuing the bouquet tied with a wet white satin ribbon.

Ian ran his fingers over the spongy, spiky galactic petals of the five flowers, round as blow fish. Together they looked like frozen fuchsia fireworks or a snowball melting into pastel and hot pinks, a warm hint of sunshine within.

Something about the feel and look of them was unbearably erotic. How he ached to touch Robin, possess her, stroke her, feel her breasts quiver beneath his open palm and tongue.

She appeared as though from his thoughts, tall and sleek in a black bikini with metal rings, the gold light beneath the horizon framing her red and gold hair, reflecting in her sea-green eyes. Ian felt himself turning the same color as one of the dahlias, as though she could read his mind. He adjusted the too-small trunks he had purchased. Fortunately he had positioned himself now so the guard was staring at the back of his head and could not see his expression as he grinned at Robin. She pretended not to acknowledge the guard's presence as she sat down next to Ian, staring straight ahead.

Ian suppressed his urge to greet Robin, instead playing along with feigned unfamiliarity until Robin made the next move.

"He just got a job in marketing at a subsidiary of Hewlett Bank." The prettier woman was chattering about her husband to her friend as her eyes glazed over.

Immediately, the guard approached the two. He leaned over, pretending to check the water again, glaring at both inmates.

"Oh, hey, glad you're still here," the trio's male addressed the guard. "Can you go tell them to turn up the temperature?"

"Well I don't—" the guard stammered. The three looked at him expectantly. "Be right back," he said, fingering the heat ray at his waist, scowling again at the inmates.

Robin stared down at the water, Ian straight ahead at the sea, until the guard disappeared behind the double glass doors.

"Yes!" Robin exclaimed in a low voice once the doors shut, holding her palm up in a high sign, which Ian enthusiastically met in mid air with his. He noticed how much like a man's her biceps were. They both laughed with relief. Ian handed her the flowers.

"Dahlias. How lovely! These two lemon bursts with orange peacock tips—the colors are so vivid. They look as though they were painted by Frida Kahlo or that Haitian artist what's-his-name—Look!"

Ian nodded enthusiastically, noticing she was as overwhelmed by the new sensory input as he.

"Jean-Edner Cadet. That's it! And this one! Lavender dragon flames! ...Doesn't it? And this one! Red and gold butterfly wings."

"Yes! Yes!" he was laughing. "You're quite a poet."

The prettier woman was nattering on about the details of her husband's job description and marketing schemes. Her friend, in turn, felt obliged to interject all the most boring details about having sold school and corrections officials on his company's school text books.

Confident that this chatter, along with the jets, was preventing anyone from hearing their conversation, Robin leaned her head on Ian's shoulder and explained in a low voice, very quickly:

"Charlie, who'll be back any sec, was my personal guardian last time. We'll meet ours eventually back in our rooms. One usually covers a bunch of us, but you're more problematic, so they may have ours with you mostly. More later, when we're alone."

"So that's why we were assigned doubles?"

"You got it. The fold-out couch is for the guard's convenience."

Ian's heart slid down the jacuzzi drain.

Look, he'll be back any second. "Come." Robin jumped out of the pool and grabbed her jacket from a chair. Drying her hands on the lining, she fumbled for something inside the pocket. Ian, stood dripping by her.

"Dry your hands and put this in your towel," she said, handing him the object. "You're going to tether this to the screen in your living area which sends code to your guard's infrared censor. You won't need to turn the phone off, since the prison removed our phone and internet privileges. I did manage to jailbreak the internet connection, though," Robin smiled parenthetically. "Just tap on Rawtooth, then type in the numbers I typed into the notepad." Robin hopped back into the jacuzzi. "Your guard won't be aware of our actions when I come in to see you."

Ian stared at the ordinary looking MEphone, then quizzically at Robin. He wrapped the object in his clothes, inside the plastic cleaning bag he had retrieved from the front desk. Shivering, he joined Robin back in the jacuzzi.

She noticed his brows. "I'm sorry. Remember the REM work-shifts we discussed at Vesuvio? Screens sending out different codes corresponding to different groups of users to trigger them into REM?" she prodded.

"Yeah, but—Robin, so much expense for us. A private room with a guard, even if he's shared?" The color was draining from Ian's face again.

"Like I said, we must be valuable chess pieces for Bear-TT. They've given up on me after five operations. Now they're just stuck with me as high security. Like for you, I guess. Ian, don't get distracted, there are a lot of steps to remember here—"

"Relax, I just tap on the Rawtooth setting and copy and paste the guard's access codes from the notepad. Then take aim. Anything else I need to know?"

"Make sure you enter the shift end-time as the current time. The code will allow you to reprogram their codes in the internet screens, which are transmitted simultaneously to the wires, to send them the signal which triggers their REM sleep." Robin was beaming. "They'll just behave as though their shift is over."

"So when I manage to hack into my guard's access code and trigger his REM, your guard will also slip into REM?"

"That's what I'm hoping," Robin smiled.

"So you've been on the net the whole time?" Ian's tone was accusatory.

"Yes, but since my password has been revoked, I've been denied access to any of my files or applications, including calls and email."

Wait a minute." Ian stood up, unable to take much more of the heat from the spa. "If both our guards are triggered by the same screen signals, why do I have to be the one—"

"Practice," Robin grinned, stepping out of the jacuzzi, followed by Ian.

"So elsewhere, a hundred more with the same group will—"

"Start to behave strangely," Robin tried to suppress a laugh, which only made more mirth bubble up, like a giddy teenager.

Ian was not laughing. "And if I don't pull it off?"

"You mean if it works on my guard, not yours?" Composing herself, Robin leaned in closer. "I'll come over at 9:30 tonight," she whispered. "Make sure you're naked. I'll knock. If your guard is still awake ask him to allow you to put on your robe. That'll give me a sec to get away. But, if he's asleep—"

"I'll come right to the door as is," Ian laughed.

Robin squeezed his shoulder, then said, "Shhh. Charlie!" She motioned toward the guard as he approached the guests with his news that the water would soon warm up.

"Good," Robin said, sinking back down into the water.

Ian took the opportunity to leave, the guard scowling at his back as Ian wrapped his towel about his waist and gathered his clothes. The guard patted his heat ray and sat down again to watch Robin.

XXI

IAN FELT AS though he were walking on the moon, strolling the carpeted hallways of the Beach House to his room. Two pretty young girls were working the desk.

"Good evening," the dark one with untamed curls and green eyes welcomed him, glancing at her blonde coworker. He smiled back his greeting and gave them his room number. The girls broke out into self-conscious giggles, perhaps at Ian's good looks, as they handed him his key.

Just past the desk, the lobby opened up with the light from the front entry doors. Ian glanced over his shoulder. Right now would be his chance, he thought to himself. He'd be in a better position to help Robin from the outside, he rationalized as he headed straight through the large glass doors.

"Lost?" he heard a woman call out after him as he began to sprint.

He stopped and turned to behold a beautiful female guard with blonde pony-tail, nodding in feigned interest. The subtle way she pointed her heat ray at Ian, reminded him of an intoxicating femme fatal from a James Bond flick.

"I just wanted to see if—" he began to explain. "If the ice machine—"

"ICE machine? As in Immigration and Customs Enforcement?" the woman wrinkled her cute, slightly upturned little nose at him. "It's in there," she motioned with her ray.

Ian walked toward the hotel.

"Room 207?"

"Just down the hall, right at the stairs, right at the last corridor. I'll be happy to show you," she said, motioning him to keep moving with her ray.

At the door, Ian waved the card he had received from the front desk A little light turned green with a click.

"I'll take that," the blonde female guard said, opening the door and snatching the card from his grip.

She motioned him to step inside and closed the door after him. He was greeted by the loud drone of a screen with a ball game in process.

With the female guard on other side of the door, Ian's reality shifted. The beauty of the view from the tremendous four pane bay windows overlooking Half Moon Bay was overwhelming. The middle two panes were actually sliding glass doors leading to a balcony. Beyond them, two long jetties that sealed out the rough ocean currents. Some sail boats drifted lazily on the sun-swept surface of the water, and the silhouettes of fisherman could be seen casting lines from the left jetty.

Ian noticed he was standing in a loft, at a large oak desk, overlooking the living room area that included the stunning bay windows. Behind him was a king-size bed with a white feather comforter. His small garment bag had been hung in the closet opposite a bathroom with double sinks, a shower and separate bath tub with view of a large screen inset into the wall at the foot.

Ian's eyes adjusted to the room, scanning it for signs of life, but saw none. On the right of the steps leading down a level to the living room area, was a tiny brass stove, refrigerator, oak cabinets, and stone fireplace. Directly across from the fireplace was a large coffee table, some comfortable chairs and what, from his vantage point at the desk by the stairs, looked like a long, convertible couch.

It was the most luxurious hotel room he could remember entering. And it was real, he thought, with some excitement. Ian stood, staring at the sun dancing on the sea as though sparks from a welding iron were perpetually falling upon it. But although the view and accommodations were stunning, Ian thought to himself that in the grand scope of his life, he would not be looking back at this time with fond memories. He was, however, immensely relieved that they had decided to guard him from outside the unit. He wondered how far the drop from the balcony to his freedom was, and whether there were guards outside.

But first, he thought, he had to turn off that screen to be able to think clearly. He set his bag of clothes concealing the MEphone Robin had given him onto the bed. His eyes scanned the desk area and found the master remote. He shut the screen off and stepped down toward the balcony.

"Hello, Ian."

Ian spun to face the relatively soft male voice that had addressed him. Suddenly, he felt self-conscious in just his trunks and towel. The man sat upright on the far left of the couch, previously hidden from Ian's view by the room's partition. He looked to be in his mid-to-late fifties, with coarse streaks of thick grey hair, parted on the side, that resembled a toupee. He was lean and tall, with angular long facial features; long chin, a beak of a nose, thin lips. His smile boasted a perfect set of teeth, which contrasted sharply with his red skin, marked by pockmarks and age-spots. His icy-cold blue eyes stared directly at Ian's. Something about the combination of his teeth and eyes reminded Ian of a calculating rat. There was an unsettling, but casual air of authority about the man, like a bureaucrat in charge of massive lay-offs, or genocide. Perhaps it was the grey wolf-like wool suit.

"I hear the screen doesn't do much for you," he smiled, standing.

"No, no, I was just trying to change channels—" Ian said, leaping up the few stairs in a single bound and fumbling for the remote. "I had no idea I had a roommate—"

"You didn't think we'd overlook a high security risk, did you?" the guard smirked.

Ian turned the set back on. He reached into a drawer and removed the bundle of neatly folded clothes with the clandestine MEphone inside.

"You don't mind me showering, do you, bud?"

"I prefer Kevin, if you don't mind," the guard said, sitting back down and staring at the game. "Live it up, Ian," he said, his eyes beginning to glaze over.

Ian unzipped his garment bag, pulled out his toiletry bag and lay the fresh clothes on the down comforter on the bed. He glanced at Kevin. He was leaning forward, intently staring at a ball game.

Ian felt for the MEphone. He snapped Kevin's picture and ran the face recognition app. After scrolling through the options, he copied and pasted a row of numbers into his notepad. Next, he tapped the Rawtooth on, copied the numbers from the notepad and pasted them into the box from the "advanced settings" pop-down menu. He punched through a few more options and aimed the mobile at the screen the guard was watching.

Two thin bars of static flickered across the screen; the hue changed momentarily, then reverted back to its normal state. Was it working? Ian satisfied himself that Kevin was too involved with the ball game to notice. He had risen and had begun interacting with the set. Perhaps this is what Robin meant. Ian tapped Rawtooth off. Again, the static flashed across the screen, followed by a barely perceptible, momentary change in hue. The man blinked and sat down. He yawned and began looking about the room.

Ian tapped Rawtooth back on. Static again, hue. Kevin stood once more and slowly began interacting with the screen.

Confidently, Ian headed for the shower. As instructed, after shaving, he wrapped the towel about himself and sat on the bed. It was 8:55. The guard was sitting down with his arm extended on the couch, his head turned as though there were someone next to him. "I told you you'd love this, Michelle," he said, stroking one of the pillows of the couch. One of the players hit a home run and Kevin stood, "Ooooh! Michelle! Look at that!" he put his hand over his eyes to shield an imaginary sun and strained to see the ball on the screen.

"Michelle?" Ian said. The guard didn't respond. Ian walked over to him. "Could you introduce me to your wife?"

"Oooh, look at her smile. But she's only my girlfriend!" Kevin beamed. "Oooooh! Just a sec—he sat back down and stared at the screen."

Ian disappeared back into the bathroom to look for some cologne in the drawers where he had noticed all kinds of goodies including a toothbrush, mouthwash and razor. He found a blow-dryer and absent-mindedly began styling his hair. It reminded him of the salon by Union Square where he once thought Barb took him when she was getting her hair straightened. What had he been doing there in fact, he wondered. Did the salon even exist? Did Barbi?

He turned off the dryer and returned to the bedroom. He put his feet up on the bed and sank into the fluffy quilt. It felt like clouds under his bare back. He sat up and stared out at the water over the partition. From this vantage point, the living room, screen and guard were not visible. Ian allowed his imagination to wander.

All his experiences in hotels had probably been fictitious. Or at least derived not from real occurrences, but from a combination of television images and real memories. Yet had he been any the less happy? On the contrary.

He wondered: As a prisoner, he had the illusion of frequenting hotels in exotic places. He thought he had been leading an idyllic life. Would freedom really be worth the price of giving up all these illusions? Had his life been truly empty, since he had spent most of it in a jail cell? Sure, his job had been fulfilling and he had been content, happy. Even joyful at times. Only that was before he knew of some of the distasteful consequences for humanity of his actions.

He remembered seeing footage of President Franklin Roosevelt calling for four essential freedoms: hadn't he enjoyed these? Freedom of worship, freedom from want, certainly. Freedom from fear—at least until now. And until he had woken up from the implant, he thought he enjoyed freedom of speech and expression. O.K, there could be a problem with that perhaps....

He focused on a fisherman casting a line on one of the jetties. The loud cheering on the television, along with the incessant babble of the announcer and guard, were making it impossible to think clearly.

His life. Images of hopping in his neighbor's yacht at the dock below his house and speeding through the Golden Gate; his 18th birthday party when he was in college and the humorous spread they served of Twinkies, Ho-hoes, Hostess Cupcakes, Spam, Velveta and all sorts of other retro American junk food—only he must have been in jail college the remaining years before he graduated, he realized.

Sitting on the grassy knolls at Dolores Park and taking in the view of San Francisco.... True, these memories had all been false. But did it really matter? Wasn't it more important to have an impression of a nice life, than to have lead a mediocre one?

If the powers-that-be had found a way to reduce suffering, enhance enjoyment, was it really so terrible to repay them with effortless labor?

He glanced at the clock. He still had fifteen minutes. He leapt off the bed, down the stairs, past the chattering guard, and slid open one of the glass doors. *Freedom from fear.* Not for him. Not for Robin, certainly. Freedom of expression to inform others about the way society was structured with the prisoners living an illusion? Not. They'd think him a nut. Was this freedom of expression then?

Obviously the freedoms did not apply to high security prisoners like Robin and him. Yet for the rest of the population, they were purely illusory, were they not?

A gust of cold June fog burst into the room. Ian wrapped his arms around his bare torso and peered over his back one more time at the oblivious guard. The afterglow from the hot shower, and perhaps his adrenalin, kept him warm. He flared his nostrils and breathed in the tangy salt air, something he had never before experienced, it seemed. He stood there with his head slightly back, trying to take in as much of the seductive aroma as he could. He glanced over his shoulder, but the guard was still involved in his program. Ian shut the glass door and, with it, the maddening noise of the screen.

From the far right side of his balcony, Ian could see a restaurant perched on the cliff he recognized from the screen as Sam's Chowder house. With its various leveled patios overlooking the sea and hillside adorned with fluorescent magenta ice-plants, the restaurant looked more like a luxury resort. Wouldn't it be lovely, Ian thought, to lounge in one of those outdoor deck chairs by the fire pits, while working on his photographs, momentarily resting his eyes on the curve of the peninsula and jetty, the calming hum of a fog horn on the horizon and the sound of waves lapping? Better still, he thought, what he'd give to go bounding through the incredibly beautiful waves of golden grasses and ice plant, alongside the sea, then do nothing more than lie for hours on the sand, staring up at the clouds. He flashed back to the female guard confiscating his room key and exhaled rather loudly.

Ian glanced down off the balcony to the sea walk. The fall onto the ice-plant below was not more than a story. A broken wrist or ankle at most. But he had no idea how the world out there really functioned. He'd have a greater chance with Robin, certainly. Unlike Ian, she obviously had no intention of returning to Plato's cave of ignorance. He wondered how long she had managed to function with her knowledge of the paradigm, how she had managed to cope with the horror of it. A thought occurred to him.

All right, he told himself. *Suppose things are great for us in the world of illusions, despite all the lies. Wouldn't you much rather be the ones who are making out like bandits from all our hard work?*

Obviously the wealthy were best off, the ones who really did own all the nice homes and resorts on the screen. The overhead was certainly low on whatever companies they ran with prison labor. Further, as Robin had pointed out, the prisoners put most of their earnings right back into the upkeep of their cells, including their own electronic mind control mechanisms. And they put money into the service industry during lunch and after work....

No—Ian shook his head. It wasn't right. Regardless of the perks.

The fabricators of this status quo were obviously wealthier than any class that had come before them. And if they shared this wealth with all the inmates—how would Ian's standard of living compare then?

It isn't right, he repeated to himself. Regardless of the quality of his former life. *What gives them the right?!*

People at least had a right to know the truth so they could make their own informed decision about leading a life of illusion, whether or not they made a decision which was against their collective interest. Whether or not they felt that ignorance was indeed bliss, as George Orwell had once written in 1984—a book he must have downloaded in prison! Or how?—

Surely if we all knew how we were being duped—we'd need a revolution certainly... Then we'd all have the opportunity to eat real food, live in real houses.

Then a somber thought struck him.

Had the majority somehow already agreed to implement the current order, knowing that only a small percentage of them would win the lottery, knowing that the compensation prize for the losers, the vast majority, would be blissful ignorance? What kinds of fools would have agreed to such a pact?

The stinging cold and anticipation of Robin's arrival drove Ian back inside, into the bathroom. There, with the door shut, he could continue his internal conversation, yet still hear her knock.

The knock came at 9:31, according to the digital numbers on the small screen in the bathroom. He bounded out. He knocked on the back of the front door to let Robin know he was there. He called over to the guard. "Do I get it?" To Robin he said, "Just a minute!" He approached the man and repeated his question. When Kevin continued nattering on about strategy, probably to his invisible girlfriend, Ian passed his hands up and down, before the guard's eyes. The man only waved him away and walked toward the screen.

Ian bounced back to the door and flung it open, smiling with unmistakable confidence.

Robin had changed into a short black miniskirt, black top and worn, black knee-high boots with thick rubber heels.

"Nice," Ian said, looking her over from top to bottom, his eyes lingering on her boots.

"My running shoes," she explained, looking over Ian's bare shoulders toward the guard.

He shut the door. He decidedly liked the mix of feminine and masculine attributes; her boots and short hair, low voice, direct, strong nature. A surprising image jumped into his mind. Hadn't he once been with another boy? Shawn! Had they been of legal age? One of the first real memories he recalled. He had just turned eighteen. Is this what landed him in jail? Had he been brainwashed to think he was het'?

Robin noticed his expression and strained with perceptible panic to view the guard.

"Oh, I'm sorry. Don't worry. He's at a ball game with his gal." Ian's ease with women—whether imagined or real—returned as he put his arms gently around her waist. She yielded like warm butter to his touch as he gazed into her sea-green eyes. His large hands slid up her body, cupping her face, one searching out her breast. *No doubt I'm bisexual then,* he thought to himself, almost laughing as he devoured her mouth with his. They stood intertwined like this inside the room's entryway for quite some time.

Finally Robin turned their bodies, leading Ian toward the bed. She looked intently into his eyes and pulled off her black spaghetti top, her generous breasts leaping out of a rotund, faded leopard skin bra—something she must have purchased before she was determined to be a high-security risk, Ian couldn't help contemplating.

The sound from the ballgame's final quarter was deafening, Kevin now yelling and shaking his fist at the screen without pause.

Robin pulled Ian toward her on the bed. His towel began to slide away from his waist.

"I don't know if I can handle a three way," Ian laughed nervously, tucking his towel back into place.

"Would you feel better if we were in the bathroom, with the door locked?" Robin sat up. I'm actually afraid where he'll go once the game's over."

Ian gathered the pillows and comforter from the bed, and Robin grabbed some extra bedding from the closet. They stepped inside the tiled room and locked the door. Next, they got to work on their nest, covering pillows with the comforter.

"Who gets to lie down first?" Robin joked, removing her tights and underwear.

"Me," Ian said, falling backward and removing his towel and mounting Robin on top of him in nearly a single gesture.

"Wait!" Robin said, pulling a pack of condoms out of her bra, before removing it entirely.

He brought her moaning mouth closer to his and sealed it in a kiss.

Through the door, Ian could hear that the television outside had switched into a program about Italy, Renata Tebaldi's operatic voice in the background. He thought he heard the guard snoring, and he allowed himself to become lost in Robin's body. Although he had made love to dozens of women, his body seemed to insist that Robin was the first. Never had his senses been so titillated, as though every pore, every cell in his body had suddenly come alive. His senses were overpowered, bursting with emotion he was unable to restrain. *This is one of the first times,* he realized. *One of the very first times I've really been awake making love to a woman, not a teenager or young adult.*

"I feel like I'm your virgin, Robin."

"Seriously? *You?* ...Although—-" She began laughing quietly.

Almost instantly, he reached climax, confirming his apprehensions. She wanted to keep going.

"Be careful, Love," he whispered, holding the bottom of the condom so the semen would not leak out.

Robin's motions became more rapid, heated. Finally, she threw her head back let out a soft cry and stopped. She collapsed in a heap on his chest.

Ian removed the condom with a snap. "Listen, Love," he said to her.

Robin lifted her head from his chest and allowed him to get up. "He's snoring!" she whispered.

They ran the tub and got in together. Ian gazed at Robin lying placidly against the porcelain in the steaming water, her body with freckles and moles unfolding delicate pink lips. A human flower he thought, kissing it under the water, intermittently coming up for air. He fumbled outside the tub for one of the condom packets Robin had brought and ripped it open with his teeth.

"One of the details they forgot to include in the hotel package!" he joked.

He made love to her once again.

"So this is ecstasy!" he said finally. "I mean this isn't a dream. This is real,"

"You bet it's real. See?" Robin said, biting him on the lip.

"This is the first time. I mean that I can remember," Ian said, suddenly wishing he hadn't. "You?—"

"More often than you want to know," she laughed.

"How?"

"With inmates. Like you. The guards don't prevent it. It took them a while to realize I was not in REM sleep. But..." Robin began kissing Ian's chest, "this is the first time probably that I've made love to someone who was awake. Let me tell you. It's much better!" She threw her head back in a laugh.

Ian felt himself flushing. "That's right. All those times in Tiburon...."

"You were in REM!" Robin laughed. "I'd get bored and come to your cell and listen to you rattle on and on about the sea and Sam's and things that were utter nonsense."

"How could you put up with that?" Ian was struck by a mixture of shame, curiosity and judgment. "Why?"

"Why? Like I said, I was bored. And horny," Robin grinned. "Plus, I don't know," she said almost shyly. She was playing with his chest hairs absentminded. "I thought you were hot."

"But then, you got fed up with me the night at Sam's supposedly. What was that about?"

"You're looks and moves stopped being enough for me. I got fed up with your world view, I guess. I wanted more."

"And now?" Ian gazed deeply, unreservedly into her eyes.

"Now," Robin kissed Ian deeply. Coming up intermittently for breaths she managed, "I think I'm starting to get my wish."

The kiss dissolved into more giggles, then laughter.

"I never imagined I'd like conferences this much," Ian grinned.

"We were lucky," Robin looked up. "They're about to get rid of them."

"Yeah, why would they go to the expense, since they can do it in REM time, can't they?"

Robin shrugged. "To keep fueling our memories with real sensory input? Perks for the managers? Did you know you look great when you laugh from this angle?" Robin began flirting again, then resumed kissing his torso. "I like that you haven't shaved."

Eventually they dragged themselves out of the tepid water and fell asleep in a wet heap on the comforter.

Ian thought he had been asleep for days when he felt Robin's lips on his back, her thin arms around him. "Wake up, babe," she repeated.

Ian sat up. "What time is it?"

"Three twenty-two. But you'll need some time to stomach what I'm about to tell you."

Through the door, he could hear the guard snoring over the television din. The noise from the set would help mask their conversation.

Cautiously, Ian opened the door. The guard was still sprawled on top of the large couch. Ian pulled a blanket out of the closet and threw it over the fellow, then returned to the makeshift bed in the bathroom where Robin lay. He shut the door and locked it. Robin put her head on Ian's chest and stared up intently into his dark eyes. "Do you know how long I've been waiting for someone like you." It was not a question. "Someone I was attracted to who could also understand what I'm about to say—"

XXII

IAN POKED HIS head outside the bathroom door to peer at Kevin. The blue glowing numbers on the dark screen by the bed said "6:22." The "Star-Spangled Banner" was playing on the screen in the living room by the guard and some cheerleaders with red, white and blue matching lipstick, hair and tattoos were singing along. The guard had turned over and the blanket had fallen off his shoulders. Ian glanced at Robin. "The blanket," he whispered.

"Let's leave him. We can turn the heat up," she whispered as she headed over to the control.

Ian entered the shower, shaking his head. "How many of us are there, then? I mean who are awake?" he yelled excitedly over the spray of water.

Robin opened the glass shower door. "Let's talk when you're out."

There was some frenetic motion behind the door. Then it snapped open.

"You miss talking to our guard?" Robin asked with irritation.

"I'm sorry," Ian said, grabbing a towel and scouring himself dry, leaving red marks. "I'm just—"

"Overwhelmed, overloaded with all the information I gave you? About water being our best weapon to wake folks? Crazy, isn't it?" Robin offered, fastening her bra behind her freckled back.

"Robin, come on now. I want to believe you. I want to believe that people are fighting back against our jailers.... but another part of me— I mean—Come on, Robin, you really expect me to believe there's a rebellion that's waking people up by pouring water on them?" Ian dabbed a Q-tip in his ear.

"O.K., Ian. You explain how it is that you first woke up." Robin crossed her arms and was pacing back and forth the length of the tub behind him. He watched her in the mirror.

"I'm not sure really. I had a bad headache. Probably because my chip was malfunctioning, my brain was rejecting it..."

"Come on, Ian," Robin turned him to face her. "Don't you remember all those sirens? Then the sprinklers and the lockdown? That was us!" she smiled triumphantly.

Ian had a terrible falling sensation again, like he was on an elevator that had arrived at its destination with a thud. Was Robin just having delusions again? And if so, was he not losing his mind as well, lying to himself because he had wanted to fall in love?

She noticed his expression. "What's wrong, babe?'

"Tell me this, Robin. "Why aren't folks waking up each time they shower or go out in the rain?"

"It takes a lot to jolt someone out of REM. The fire and alarm systems were designed to wake us in emergencies. As you know, when we wake up from deep sleep at night, we surface into walking REM and stay there until we're triggered through special visual or auditory stimuli in our earphones or from a screen into our waking states when we begin our commute or get to work. Sure alarms and sprinklers wake us completely as well, but it doesn't take much to persuade the mind that it was just a dream.... So we have to set the sprinklers off again and again, to trigger the alarms over and over. You had been woken half a dozen times before you snapped out of it. It's complicated, Ian. Routine showers only help wake you into a more alert walking REM, not completely."

Ian thought back to the morning he first found himself in the cell. Robin's story did seem to match up to his experience. As such, he allowed a spark of excitement about the news of a mounting rebellion to grow inside of him.

"If what you say is true, Robin, I'm surprised the resistance is able to keep pulling off these actions," he said finally.

"Things have gotten a bit hairy, since you woke up, actually. Not to mention the mildew buildup from the sprinklers going off so many times, so we've had to lay low." Robin stopped pacing back and forth to look directly at Ian. "Ian, ironically, the biggest problem we have right now is not so much with the authorities. It's with our fellow prisoners, our supposed allies. Seems like there's a growing movement among those who resent us for having awoken them—those who believe they were happier in their former ignorant somnambulistic state."

"I'm not surprised," Ian said, sarcastically. He waited for her response in silence, recalling his own moments of rage at having been awoken. Now that he had indeed awoken, and now that he had decided everyone else had a right to know the truth as well, his only hope lay in Robin's rebellion to wake the society. If everyone knew, he reasoned, they'd demand their fair share of the owners' wealth and privilege. Yet, he was afraid to ask about the odds. How large was this rebellion? Was it growing? After all, why would anyone want to risk his or her life in paradise for a distant hope that things would be better than a jail cell?

Wouldn't it just multiply the suffering instead of reducing it? The rebel's task paralleled that of Sisyphus, whose fate was to forever push a boulder up a hill. Just when the boulder was about to reach the apex, it would come crashing down.

Something occurred to Ian. "How did you learn all that you know, Robin? Who told you?" he inquired soberly.

The animation vanished from Robin's face. She looked down. "A friend from work. Before they terminated her."

Robin took a deep breath. "The person who told me withstood water-boarding for doing so. Because they can't do anything that leaves a trace. She nearly drowned and went into a coma. They took her off all life support, but then, I don't know, maybe because she used to work out in her cell, she snapped out of it. The owners still maintain they don't use torture."

Ian gasped self-consciously. They sat there in silence for some time. Finally Ian cleared his throat. "I'm so sorry, Love," he said sadly, putting his arm around her.

"But initially, when she told you—you believed her immediately? Or had you already been awake?"

"I sort of believed her. I think it helped me wake up."

Robin looked away, grinning with embarrassment. "I had a crush on her at the time."

"Do you regret it?" Ian asked.

"Sometimes," Robin said.

"Do you think it is selfish of us, even cruel to wake them?" Ian asked finally. "I mean my mother brought me up to leave the world a little better for people, which is what I thought we were doing at Bear-TT."

His own mention of his mother filled him with remorse and anxiety. Certainly she was still living out an illusory REM existence. She therefore was unaware of his communication privileges being revoked and was probably sick with worry about his whereabouts. Would he want to wake her? Or allow her to keep living inside the safety of Plato's cave? Her life had probably become nightmarish anyway, he rationalized.

"We owe the world a lot to restore our karma after working for that devil," Robin smirked.

"Huh?" Ian asked, still thinking of his mother. Suddenly cognizant of Robin's words, he rejoined the conversation. "Oh right."

They both remained silent for some time. Ian shook his head. Finally he spoke up. "Are we thinking of the world, of the inmates, or just ourselves by waking them?" he asked.

"Sometimes a part of me thinks it's crazy—wanting to wake them," Robin's tone was full of naked disdain and bitterness. She paused, bit her lip. "But my higher self knows better. For all it may accomplish, I guess they should have the right to make up their own mind. Isn't that what democracy is?"

At last Ian spoke. "Aren't they making up their minds when they decide not to wake up?"

Robin thought a second. "I don't think so. Not really,"

After a long pause, Ian forced himself to ask the question whose answer he did not want to hear. "So is the resistance diminishing?"

"Actually no," Robin's face softened with the recollection. "There are increasing resistors to our struggle, but there are far many more of those who are thankful to know the truth and are more focused on wanting to change it," she smiled triumphantly.

Ian put his hands on Robin's bare freckled shoulders and looked intently into her eyes. "Are they after you, Robin?"

"I'm a high security prisoner. I enjoy a lot less freedoms than the ones that are still tethered to the system. But you, you seem to be starting to go back off their radar, I think, since they think that your REM has begun to work again after your last operation. Your guard is just a precaution, I think. So we have a real chance with you on our side. Think you're interested in hearing how you can help?"

XXIII

THE GUARD WAS still snoring on the couch as Robin and Ian entwined themselves in a lengthy good-bye kiss. After closing the door softly behind Robin, Ian headed down to the living area. He flipped off the screen which the guard had been viewing, dressed, and stepped onto the balcony to digest the world Robin had dished him up for breakfast that dawn.

With what felt like sandpapered eyes, Ian watched as three fishermen with olive skin untangled a net they had cast. Behind them stood several buckets with rockfish and ling cod, a crab or two. The bay was silver and glassy, almost like wet paint under the thick cover of early morning fog. Though he hadn't slept much, the deliciously tangy and brisk morning salt air was invigorating, conducive to reflection.

Ian thought back on his life. There had been a gap when he hadn't lived in the jail after he had turned 18. Investing most of his energy into skateboarding, at the time, he had actually despised most cellular devices, poking fun at their brain-dead converts. Somehow he'd become one of these pod-people. His jobs became increasingly demanding, compelling him to acquire his first device. First lured by utility of an inferior product, then increasingly frustrated with its limitations and seduced by the slick, self-assured glow of MEphone and pad users, he sought out his first Bear-TT job with a subsidiary petrol company. He remembered his mother joking that it was like a new lover, keeping him up at night while he delved into unexplored territory. He'd spend hours learning all the facets of each option and program, shortcuts; then countless more hours organizing his data, calendar events, contacts, accounts, photographs and files. Sometimes he'd forget to sleep. His mother had been right, Ian chuckled—how he grew to adore his MEphone and the company that gave it to him. He remembered the same fascination when his company had issued his first MEpad at a discount. It was like double-timing, he joked—he didn't know which of the two he loved more nor could do without.

So that must have been when he first became so deeply tethered. Maybe that had been how his deep REM first got triggered, for he began having oodles of money to travel, then buy his Tiburon home... a sure sign of the jails.

This implied that inmates first entered the jails of their own volition. If this was so, would it be just as easy to leave? He would have to discuss this further with Robin.

Robin had told him that the society finally began allowing implants as a matter of convenience, the way GPS and airport retinal scans had first caught on in spite of a cacophony of objections by human rights groups fighting desperately to hold on to the antiquated constitutional notion of a right to privacy. Efficiency had won out, as implants afforded their hosts the option of breezing through long lines in banks, airports, stores, museums, theaters, bridges and public transport—all coincidentally rights-free zones. This was especially useful during commute hours. Thus the rights-free zones expanded with little objections.

This formula was of course repeated in various parts of the world. While in the poorer countries, where gross iniquities were coupled with increasing incarceration and objections to implants, the citizenry failed to mount a unified resistance. In the places where objections had led to uprisings and revolts, without the citizenry of the superpowers following the same course, progress was isolated and news about victories, blacked out. The result was popular adaptation to residing mostly within rights-free zones.

Thinking back to the tethered commuters, Ian wondered how much of his own commute had been real. Though he believed he was taking BART to the Ferry Building or a cable car to Pier 21, then catching the ferry to Tiburon, something had triggered his REM sleep state. Perhaps he had actually begun the commute, the cable car to the pier, then something in the terminal had triggered his REM and he had sleepwalked back to the jail like all the other commuters. Then he remembered his treadmill and the incline that had reminded him of the hills on the way to work. More likely, his REM sleep state had been triggered before he ever left the building—perhaps by the large screen by the fountain, or his MEphone—and he was merely taking the elevator back up to his jail cell, then getting on this treadmill. Some of the walks at lunch, or immediately after work could have been real. But upon more introspection, Ian got a sinking feeling. On Thursdays, his day off, —that ferry ride, that cable car, the walk occasionally to Coit Tower, that walk he so loved up Columbus from BART, past the Francis Ford Coppola building, past Vesuvio and City Lights on the way to Puccini, was nothing more than an elevated heart rate and incline on his treadmill.

Ian's thoughts were interrupted by some brusque noises below his balcony. Beneath the left side of the patio, by the jacuzzi, two women with dark complexions, one slender, one lovely and a bit stouter, were dragging aside heavy wooden lounge chairs, probably to make more seating room for the afternoon's conference luncheon. A third, who had been sweeping, had stooped to pick up some dog droppings with a napkin.

The women looked Mexican, Ian noted, refocusing his thoughts upon them through his new lens. Immigrants—whom Robin had christened *slaves*—were funneled directly into the inmate class, though they were not housed in the jails. Instead, they were kept in penal colony ghettos without any REM relief, similar to the underclass. The most unsavory, most arduous, worst paid jobs were reserved for these "slaves." These were the ones who worked in the excrement processing plants of the owners and cleaned out their sewers, who excavated their foundations and hauled their garbage; who mopped up their vomit; bled their beef and deplumed their chickens. They were the backbone of the society. Not only were they willing to carry out the work rejected by the more uppity inmates; they kept the latter in check as a reminder of how fortunate they were, reinforcing once again, the illusion of their privilege.

Just like inmates who possessed REM sleep-triggering implants that tethered them to the jails, immigrants were allowed to wander freely about, outside the jails. Their return to their penal colonies was guaranteed by its ability and willingness to crush even the most irresistible of toddlers and the most feeble of grandparents alive in the jaws of its economic or military machinery. This eternal state of war overseas drove these modern slaves out of their homelands and into a foreign caste system which effectively stripped them of all entitlement to anything vaguely resembling human rights. Thus they ferreted out an animal existence trotting from work to the jail slum, and from the jail slum to work and very little else because of the economic impossibility of their escape.

This new realization prompted by Robin's crass analysis, made Ian cringe as he watched the brown women below. His eyes alighted on a retired couple out for an early morning stroll down the beach path with their poodle. *Now, let's see,* Ian thought. *Obviously, part of the genuine owning class.* The neighboring homes were real and one belonged to this couple. The rest of the elderly—he had seen a few on the floor of his jail—resided mostly inside, almost always in REM sleep, probably until they got mad cow disease—what used to be commonly misdiagnosed as Alzheimer's in the old days, he reflected with cynicism. The few times they'd step outside to go to the store, the bank or other errands, the REM would be temporarily turned off, as it was for the working inmates whenever they left the prison. Probably their state-subsidized hearing aids, Ian thought.

So there were inmate pets and free pets too, Ian mused, as he stared at the poodle now lifting its leg on the bright pink ice-plant. What did its captive counterpart care if its home had bars on the windows?

In fact, the dogs of inmates fared better than those of the fringe population. Ian recalled the scraggly looking grey-haired hippie woman cradling a dog he had seen on his way to Puccini one evening. Now *there* was a problem for the owners. The hippie was obviously not an owner, but clearly not an inmate either. Ian thought of the beggars and homeless people camped on the sidewalk. Most had been jailed, without any respite of REM programming, but those who had been released or were on the brink of being caught were certainly a problem, considered to be free thinkers from the owner point of view. Or was it a problem, since they were marginalized as crazy and usually blamed themselves for the society's inhumanity?

There were some fringe people who could also be the offspring of owners—slackers. They were not be confused, since they ran little risk of ending up as inmates. Ian recalled having seen in Tiburon a dumpy thirty-five year old man with longish hair sitting on a park bench. Onto his t-shirt he had taped a lined essay paper with words in thick marker: "Study buddy." Since Ian had never lived in Tiburon, either the man was a composite of something he had dreamed or invented in REM or seen on the screen. Ingenious, he thought, how the utopian REM dreams were tainted with flaws like this, muggings, unfortunate events, which rendered them so realistic. But of course, dreams were that way.

Thinking back to the imaginary slacker or nut's sign, Ian pondered the status of students in this strange paradigm. Most ivy league and UC students would fall into the owner class, though there was sure to be some downward mobility, as well as upward, some *outsiders*.

How twisted is that? Ian thought. *How could we all have allowed things to decay to such a degree? The frogs failing to jump out of water coming to a slow boil phenomenon, like Robin alluded to.*

He pounded his fist on the railing and clenched his teeth. It was simply not right, and the criminals in charge had to be held to account.

He was awake all right. There was no going back. And something had to be done.

Yet as Ian recalled Robin's plan to integrate him into the rebellion, he began to get cold feet. It had seemed so much more rational, possible, with Robin standing next to him, combing her hair in the bathroom mirror, in the hour preceding her preparations for the conference's culminating workshops that dawn.

"Count me in, Love," he had told her. "What would you like me to do?"

She had looked at him coquettishly. He thought of the ensuing kiss and impassioned love-making.

"Is that all you wanted?" he laughed after they were sated.

"Well, there is one more little thing," she had laughed, then launched into his part in the next action.

Robin claimed that they had no way of knowing the size of their growing movement. It really made no difference, he reasoned with himself. Now that he had woken up, there was no returning to the comfort of sleep.

If they were in the majority, action made the most sense. But supposing they were a minority, then didn't he have even more of a responsibility to the rest of his fellow inmates for having been granted the gift of sight?

Ian thought back on his last minutes with Robin. At 7:00 am she had stuffed the MEphone in her bra.

Just don't wear any tight shirts," Ian had laughed.

She hesitated.

"What's wrong?"

"I guess we would have found out if my guard woke up already."

"And if we were wrong?"

"You won't see me at work," Robin said.

A long silence passed between them.

"Thinking of your friend? I know, Love," Ian gathered her up, stroked her hair.

"It was worth the risk, though. I mean to be with you." She looked up at him, then gave him a long drawn out kiss.

When they composed themselves Ian spoke. "We've got to get a lot more done before we can get caught," he winked. "When, how do we meet again to figure out the next steps once we've begun?" Ian asked before their final parting kiss. He realized he didn't even know where her cell was and inquired. "I'm on the 84th floor," he reminded her.

"Well I'm cell 84, if that makes it easier to remember," Robin said. "Only on the 19th floor. Kind of like the book by the same name."

"Too weird," Ian snickered.

"Like you'll be calling," she laughed. "We have to be cooler than ever now at work. In a month or two—depending on how well things go—I'll ask you to go to lunch in the Atrium. Make up something about why you have to leave suddenly—stomach cramps, whatever. Meet me by the main entrance, by the screen. I'll have the MEphone. We can try and see if we can really go to lunch again on the outside to plan the next action."

"And if that doesn't pan out? We'll talk after we're out of solitary?" Ian asked.

"If we ever get out. Stay clear of me until I signal you to go outside. I'm already on their hit list. There's some hope that you'll still be able to act if something happens to me. The commute is your best bet. We'll figure out a way to communicate." With that, Robin pressed her lips to his and melted into his embrace. She was so delicate, so soft, he thought, so, so, so real.

As Ian thought back to the past evening and morning, the anxiety and sadness of the past year began to be replaced with a sensation of lightness, like helium swelling his chest.

Savor it, he thought to himself, reflecting on the plan Robin and he discussed. *You'll probably need to remember what joy feels like for what could lie ahead.*

XXIV

IAN WAS SEATED on the rim of the tremendous cascading fountain, waiting for Richard to emerge from work and begin his march upstairs, back to his cell. His heart was pumping as though he had ingested a gallon of coffee trying to catch Robin at the coffee machine. From his vantage point at the corner of the fountain, just by slightly turning his head, he could keep his eyes on the entrance to his office, as well as the elevator bank.

A heavy set couple stumbled into the lobby and stood staring, wonder-eyed, up at all the cells as though mesmerized by one of King Ludwig's Bavarian castles. The look of child-like stupefaction on their faces evidenced that they were tourists. Tourists were forever tilting their heads up, looking skyward, which is why they were so susceptible to being assaulted, Ian reflected with malicious envy.

What about tourists, he wondered. He was in real non-REM time so they were not illusory; and they were not in jail, so they had to be owners. Realtime tourists were all owners, he realized. Then he remembered Robin's disclaimer. They could also be inmates on a two-week vacation? Either way, this explained the blissful look on their faces. Of course, he thought, recalling the tourists he had actually seen throughout North Beach. They looked ecstatic compared to the commuters, staring at the birds and trim on the tall buildings, not just because they were on vacation, but because they were not in jail the way he had been when he thought he had been sight-seeing.

Ian looked at the big digital numbers on the screen by the entrance, then nervously around for Richard. He wondered if he had missed him though he knew that, inevitably, Richard would have had to walk by him to get to the elevator. Patience, he told himself. He scanned the scene for signs that the guards had noticed his odd behavior.

Look up, like the tourists, tilt your head back, he told himself. The architecture seduced him as though for the first time. Again, he was struck by its duality. It was more like being trapped inside of one of Escher's paradoxes than he ever imagined: San Francisco luxury hotel and condo complex converted into a lofty office complex on the one hand, an insidious prison on the other. From a detached perspective, one could argue that the mirage was indeed ingenious.

Robin had pointed out that not even the lower security guards were aware that they were working inside a jail, for the balconies masked the bars from the ground floor. These were told that the hotel had been designed by an artist with an industrial flare, should they for some reason find themselves on an upper floor, wondering about the bars. Thus they believed they were simply guarding a trendy, industrial-style hotel in which some high-net worth individuals also resided.

The only security guards who could actually see the existence of the bars were the top-level guards who wore heat rays and special dark glasses with the same color and wave pattern as the glass. This enabled them to see beyond the balconies, through the bars, directly at all the prisoners in a given area spanning several floors. Thus it took only a handful of guards—just two per floor posted to the area not covered by the floors directly above and below—to see all the thousands of prisoners housed in the jail at once. More than anything, this is what helped perpetuate the illusion of a moderately guarded set of offices, rather than a jail.

These higher level security guards believed their job was to keep privileged but highly skilled terrorists, like Ian and Robin, under house arrest in their high tech condominium complex upon request of their employers. They thought nothing of invading their privacy by peering through the glass directly into their lives.

While Ian now had trouble imagining the scene as his coworkers saw it—without the well-concealed cell bars below the balconies—he foresaw the futility of communicating this to them during working hours or real, non-REM time. After all, from their view point, he must be a little off because he'd been admitted to a sanatorium for a brain operation. Without changing their REM sleep patterns to be awake once they left work, none of his coworkers would ever see any of the cells from their vantage point in their cubicles, the restaurant nor from any other point inside the lobby.

He missed Robin. It seemed as though months had transpired since their return from the conference, yet less than two weeks had passed. During that time, he had tried to distract himself by focusing on their action. Instead, his mind would eventually wander to their tryst in the bathroom of the Beach House Hotel. Over and over, he replayed their meeting, beginning with their first flirtations at work; the goose-bumps he got when she whispered in his ear, "Don't give up before your miracles;" her coy little sideways smile at him by the coffee machine, to their first interaction at the jacuzzi. He ran the reel of their affair over in his mind recounting as many details as possible, as though engraving tracks in the golden record of his mind for eternity. Inevitably, he'd be overtaken by desire. At this point, there was no way out but to force himself to refocus on their plan.

Richard was to be his test case.

It turned out, however, that Richard had chosen this evening to work late, keeping Ian on tender hooks for well over an hour. Ian debated whether or not to carry out his plan, since the commute crowd would be much thinner.

"What are you doing here?" Richard slapped Ian on the back, startling him.

"Richard! Oh, I just returned from too big a dinner and was contemplating getting a cab back to Tiburon, though I need the exercise," Ian lied. "You?"

"Working too much before I go on vacation."

"Where you going?" Ian said with boredom as they walked toward the entrance.

"Fiji or Tahiti or one of those "i" places. I forget exactly, but it's one of those islands where your hotel sits on stilts over that unreal, fluorescent aqua-colored lukewarm water," Richard said dreamily, automatically putting in his white earbuds.

"See ya," said Ian taking the cue. Richard deliberately changed course and began walking toward the elevators. He had slipped into REM.

Ian turned around and followed him, keeping a distance. As soon as Ian saw Richard entering the middle elevator, he turned and walked hastily toward the bank of elevators. "Shit, shit, shit,!" he feigned as though he had forgotten something upstairs. This absurd gesture, he felt, gave him license to gallop toward the elevators, though within seconds he realized that the behavior of inmates must always look erratic to guards, since they were responding to cues in REM sleep, not the real world.

Ian noticed Richard's elevator was now at the 32nd floor and began tapping his polished foot on the carpet. Finally, an elevator came. Rudely, Ian squeezed in, ahead of his turn. Richard's elevator was on the 41st floor. *These folks are asleep anyway*, he reassured himself. If Ian timed it right, he might catch him before the final corridor turn to his cell.

Ian's felt as though he had stuck his finger in a light socket. An old woman with a wire cart full of groceries blocked his way out of the elevator. Ian huffed and puffed, towering behind her. At last, she was out and he darted around her, and with his long legs, bound down the corridors with his briefcase, looking at an imaginary watch on his wrist for the benefit of the guards, he supposed. The crowds were thin and he easily saw that he had not yet caught up to Richard. Finally, he spied Richard's mile-long legs and perfectly pressed green-grey suit. As usual, no guards were within view.

Ian caught up to Richard from behind and pulled out his earbuds. Richard spun around to look at him, a look of bewilderment on his face. Ian pulled out a bottle of water and poured it on Richard. "Wake up, man," he shouted at him, slapping his cheeks.

Richard called out, then rubbed the water off his face. He began blinking rapidly, the beads of water falling from his dark lashes.

Ian's heart was doing cartwheels, sit-ups, sprinting into his throat. This was the decisive moment. "You're going to be O.K. Here, sit down on my briefcase." Ian propped the case on its side and helped his colleague perch on top of it. He used every ounce of his powers of persuasion, rubbing Richard's back with feigned confidence. He resisted the temptation to turn his head this way and that, looking out for guards. Out of the corner of his eye he could see to the end of the corridor, now and then a bored-looking commuter marching toward his or her cell.

"What happened? What happened?" Richard inquired, still blinking rapidly.

"You passed out, dude. But you're going to be, okay."

"Where are we?" Richard suddenly began turning his head, in what seemed to be the panicked gestures of a spooked horse. "What is this? What is this?"

It was working. "It's okay, Richard. You're going to be fine."

"What did I do? Why are we here?" Richard looked as pale as the dead, save for a little tell-tale splotch of pink on each cheek.

"Richard, you've been here for years. You just don't remember." Stooping, Ian put his arm around Richard's shoulder. Richard remained perched precariously on Ian's briefcase. He kept rubbing his head, rifling his short hair. He stood up.

"Let me show you the cell you've been living in."

"Are you crazy?" Richard threw Ian's hand off his shoulder. "Where the hell are we? Why am I soaking wet? I'm getting out of here!" Richard looked baffled. He craned his neck this way and that, looking for an exit.

"Go ahead, try to leave," Ian said, shaking his head.

"Why wouldn't I be able to? Look at all these other folks coming and going." Richard protested.

"Richard, they're all in REM sleep. They're not really awake."

"What?

"Look, if it's true that we can come and go, what difference would five minutes more of your time make."

"What are you saying, buddy?" The color had returned to Richard's face. He looked irritated now.

"Look," Ian began walking toward Richard's cell. "Does this look familiar?"

"What?" Richard followed. "Right around this corner... look."

Richard followed Ian, somewhat grudgingly.

"Does it look familiar?" Ian asked.

"What do you mean?"

"You have the key. Check your pocket."

Richard fumbled around in his slacks pocket. "What are you talking about? I don't have any keys on me. Listen!" Richard jingled change in his slacks.

"It's a card. You have it somewhere on you. Check the inner compartment of your suit jacket. May I?" Gently, Ian helped Richard retrieve the key that opened the cell from his left pocket. A green light flickered and Ian pushed the cell door open for Richard.

"How do you explain your having the key if you haven't been living here? Just look inside! Who are those photos of?"

"Roxanne, Trent... What?—" Richard turned to face Ian, a look of anguish on his face.

"What's going on? How long have I been here?"

"Maybe a decade, like me. Since you're older, you actually may have been here longer. Just not on my floor."

Richard sat down on his cot. "But I have an eight-year old. Where is he then?"

"Take it easy, Richard. He's all right. he's here too— The school is in the jail."

Richard collapsed against the wall. "Help me out here, buddy. What are you talking about? Wait, I'm just having a nightmare. Wake up!!!!"

"Take it easy, Bud. Let's just step outside again," cautioned Ian, who was still holding the cell door. This door will trigger some visitors if we open it again later. It's safer if we talk with all the noise of the commuters around us."

XXV

RICHARD WAS PLAYING it cool at work, Ian thought. He refused to discuss anything about his ordeal that had extended, with the aid of some bourbon, late into the previous evening. Ian hadn't left his cell until Richard finally collapsed into a fitful, drunken sleep. Finally Ian caught sight of him by the coffee machine when no one else was around. Ian congratulated himself; an entire evening and afternoon had passed and his curiosity and enthusiasm about his interaction with Richard had temporarily reseated his memories of Robin.

"Have you been able to notice the difference in how people behave here?" Ian inquired of a bleary-eyed Richard scanning a bloodshot eye to subtract the cost of coffee from his assets. "Remember, no one is in REM during work."

"Excuse me?" Richard stirred milk substitute into the black liquid.

"The paradigm we talked about last night," Ian said, looking about. "No one's around."

"Why are you acting so paranoid, , Bud?" Richard laughed.

"Cut it out, Richard. I'm serious," Ian said with irritation. "What do you remember about what we talked about."

"When?"

"Last night. After work. After you passed out."

Richard looked baffled.

"I passed out after work? I don't remember anything... except this weird dream. Yeah, yeah you were in the dream."

"That was no dream. It was real," Ian insisted.

"How could you know what my dream was?"

"That we're all in jail, right? That we've been in jail most of our lives and are going to remain here. That your life in Marin is an utter illusion. Sound familiar?"

Richard was silent. "Right, Ian," he said finally.

"That wasn't the dream? You don't remember what we talked about?" Ian almost pleaded.

Richard continued to look perplexed. Then his face took on a look of genuine concern. The same look, Ian reflected, when Ian was sent for his brain operation and Richard thought he had gone nuts.

"Why don't we talk more about this later? I have a pile of work. Excuse me," Richard said politely and headed back to his desk.

He had slipped into denial. The news had been too much for him, Ian thought sadly, lumbering back to his desk on legs of lead. At one point in the conversation the previous evening, Richard had become hopeless, desperate in his despair, it seemed. "Can we go back?" he had asked.

"You mean back into REM? I suppose you still could. For some reason, it's too late for me. But wouldn't you rather know the truth?"

"I'd rather be back in Marin,"

"Even if you knew it was an illusion."

"Of course! I was happy then," Richard said sadly. "I just want to be happy. Don't we all?"

They had traversed the circumference of the floor a dozen times that evening. A few more commuters passed by them, one fidgeting in his pocket for his cell key.

"But we're enslaved. Enslaved to this pursuit of illusory happiness!" Ian stopped suddenly and leaned over the railing, looking down into the lobby. "Enslaved to the corporations that own this prison! It's not right. Don't you think it's not right?"

"No, it's not right," Richard agreed sadly. He clasped his hands and bowed his head. Then he cocked it, looking over at Ian. "But what can we do? Just look around you! What could we possibly do?"

"Wake everyone up." Ian was pacing back and forth. "If we woke everyone, we could stop this. Then would you still want to live your deluded life in Marin?"

"If things were fair, I might give it up. If there was a way to reclaim that lifestyle, I suppose—"

Ian sat back down next to Richard. "And if your lifestyle was not that idyllic, but more people could live decent lives? Would you be willing to give up some of your luxuries? Or would you rather go back to REM sleep, back to your Marin?"

"I'm tired," was all Richard had to say at that point. "I guess I'll check into my cell and get some rest."

XXVI

8:25 AM. WEDNESDAY morning. The office was still pretty empty. Ian closed the bathroom stall and fumbled in his coat pocket for a felt tip.

"Woke up, but he forgot paradigm. Again?" he wrote.

Back at his desk, he sealed it in an envelope and dropped it on Robin's desk.

Hours turned painstakingly into days.

During this time, Ian began to oscillate back and forth about their plan, about their motive. After all, what awaited people like him and Robin but a perilous life filled with many hardships and few immediate rewards?

Ian recalled a foggy summer Sunday he'd spent with his neighbor, Angela, viewing the Claude Monet Exhibit at the Palace of the Legion of Honor. It seemed as though the two of them had spent a couple of weeks along the French coast watching a storm come and go; the wind rising up along the cliffs upsetting the clouds and grasses; strolling along the hot beach in too much clothing; swimming in that warm, aqua green-blue water together and wriggling their toes in that clean, white, grainy French sand.

After the exhibit, they saw all this again from the large transparent windows of the Cliff House, seated directly above the Camera Obscura, after the exhibit. His camera had captured the gulls soaring over the enraged San Francisco sea crashing on the dramatic rock formations, echoing Monet's psychedelic stone arcs and stormier pallet; Angela's black hair streaked with fog, her full lips, lovely Japanese almond eyes.

Back in Tiburon, the fog had succumbed to summer. Ian took a stroll along the bay via the Tiburon green, Monet's paintings merging with the dramatic seaside scenery, San Francisco in the backdrop. He was asking Richard to give up the belief of a life full of days like this one. Once awake, some false memories might persist, but most would begin to disappear, depending on the strength of the individual's denial system.

Ian would never set foot again in Tiburon. Nor would he be able to afford places like the Cliff House, nor even special museum exhibits.

He stared at the waves and thought of what he had that was real. He could walk with Robin on the sea wall by the Camera Obscura, gaze at the waves, climb down to the ruins of the Sutro Baths, explore the sea cave and kiss in front of the opening where the waves came in, knowing that what they had was theirs, was genuine, was right.

Suddenly, now as he contemplated the mirage that had been his life. Supposing his mirage life had been real—even with the sporadic moments in a nice Tiburon home or enjoying exotic tourist destinations—the bulk of his life had been whittled away in that rat box of a work cubicle creating what amounted to mostly utter nonsense, or worse yet, toxic nonsense. Yes, the idea of simply walking freely by the sea at his leisure with Robin, leaving, at worst, mere footprints in the sand, was more than enough.

Finally Friday, he received a note in an unaddressed envelope. Inside was a wad of T.P., with the following:

"NO. Wait."

That's all there was. Ian shoved the note in his pocket and headed toward the latrine.

Weeks grudgingly turned to a month, then another. Work had never seemed so laborious, now that Ian knew the truth about the society. He was an inmate, a slave, and his employer—not his supervisors but the company's actual owner—or owners, he corrected himself—the stockholders—were gaining from his lack of freedom. He was acutely aware of this, and as such, now resented every task demanded of him. Moreover, he was painfully aware that anything he did well would only add another link on the chain that bound him and his colleagues in prison. He found himself increasingly tempted by a desire to perform his job poorly, to sabotage it, in fact. But he knew this would arouse too much attention, and to carry out what he and Robin had discussed, they had to slip under the radar.

So he suffered through the most inane staff meetings, the most humiliating and dull trainings and retreats, fighting the urge to make snide little comments during patronizing ice-breakers and team-building games designed for social klutzes with a developmental age of four. Instead, he obediently mooed like a cow through his blindfold, listening for other cows in a farm full of roosters, dogs, cats, horses and sheep. At the retreat, he went along with the team-building shootout, in spite of the tennis ball size bruises on his thigh and having had the wind knocked out of him by Black-RAW's black paint pellets.

Late one night in his cell, Ian remembered once exiting the North

Beach garage in Chinatown in Barbi's car. Barb had insisted on parking in the overpriced garage because she said it was an experience in itself, with elegant bamboo growing up three floors high. On each space, a fortune was painted in the bright paint color assigned to distinguish each floor. One Ian particularly loved read: "One day you won't be here."

"Why do you like that one so much?" the mirage called Barbi had asked. Had she been another inmate or completely made up, like a dream?

"Life, no matter how challenging, looks like paradise from the eyes of the grave," Ian had responded.

Whatever she was, she hadn't appreciated the sentiment. Perhaps because she wasn't really alive.

Another fortune read: "Perception is not reality."

"Park here," he remembered saying to Barb: "Look, 'You are very close to the place you've always dreamed of.'" She continued up to the roof. "Here!" But she passed up, "A wish will be granted after a long delay."

"I like the view here," his dream Barbi had said. The space they finally landed in read,

"Everything will now come your way."

Funny, Ian thought; the following week had been the one in which his censor began malfunctioning and he woke up to the reality of jail. Perhaps it was a good thing after all. Robin had certainly been a stroke of luck, he smiled.

He recalled that it had been dusk when he and Barb got out of the space. He had looked out at the bracelets of lights on the Bay Bridge, over the water, Coit Tower on the left. Farther West, pale blue lights illumined the spires of Saints Peter & Paul's Parish; Alcatraz in the distance. Behind them was the Transamerica pyramid. It had inspired him to finally take Barbi in his arms and kiss her, right there on the roof of the North Beach garage, even if they did get charged for an extra hour for taking too long to exit.

The rest of the evening had been strained. Both had been embarrassed about the kiss and wanted to revert back to the safety of their friendship—she perhaps more than he because of her back and forth with Kennedy.

Now in retrospect, Ian was glad he had kissed her. What would it have mattered had he stripped her of her clothes right on the spot, since her boyfriend, Kennedy, and the situation was probably as fictitious as was she?

Ian had noticed the lot before because whenever he had passed it on the way to dinner in Chinatown from work—a real memory—he had noticed the glass elevators with the passengers riding with their backs to the beautiful view, staring blindly at the doors, waiting for them to open. Their myopia symbolized to him something he despised in humanity. But now with new eyes he realized they might have been in REM—or afraid of heights.

On the way out of the lot with Barb, something strange had occurred. Blue and red emergency lights were going off on all the floors, yet there was no sound, even with the window down. He also realized Barbi had complained about the fan running in the car, yet there had been no sound. He had had a terrible sensation at the time, as though he had been dreaming and couldn't wake up, and something was going wrong. This must have been the case, because the memory was based on screen images.

Maybe the mute had been on, Ian thought with some bemusement.

Now, looking out past the gulls, over the Bay, Ian searched his memories for clues that Barb was a real person. He had met her at Puccini, he realized, his heart leaping with happiness. It had been for lunch. Yes, lunchtime, so he would not have been in REM yet. Or at least it was daylight out, and warm. Even if he had met her at Puccini's in the hour or so following work in the summer, since this was one of his programmed routes, there would have been a good chance that he would not have been dreaming.

Then he realized it had been on a day off—the time he would have been in REM sleep in the cell. Did she live in the hotel-prison with him? The Embarcadero Multiplex was large enough that he might not have run into her over the last few years. *Of course! Barbie and Ken dolls!* he thought sadly, feeling foolish.

He got up and paced on the treadmill. He began to think back on his friends and relatives with equal apprehension: Sandy, Adriana, Silja, Kitty... his cousins Sarah, Andy... Hope and Mary Ann, Mechthild and Javier, Noah and Diana, Ben and Lee, Trini and Luis J. Rodriguez.... Flesh and blood friends with middle and last names. Lynn K., Tracy Tyler, Abena Songbird, Jennifer Boysen, Elaine Katzenberger, Jesse Clarke—although maybe not after their falling out—Chris Carlsson, Roger Burbach.... Real? If they had been inmates why hadn't he run into them? A sense of loss overwhelmed him. As though they had all been wiped out in the last San Francisco earthquake. Or they had been, not his friends, but those of a cruel author who was having a good laugh toying with a protagonist that was really Ian.

Did Robin ever feel like that, he wondered. He had to discuss these things with Robin. Robin, he thought, and his heart began to swell up again. Now he had Robin.

He sat back down on his cot and stared at the bars. Suddenly, he was struck by a question. Why the bars at all? For a high-security prisoner such as Robin and himself they made sense. But if the others, the overwhelming majority of the prison workforce, were allowed to mostly come and go at their leisure, with keys to their own cell doors, why the bars? It wouldn't make sense—*unless!* The hypothesis made him giddy. *Unless there was a large number of prisoners who had become or eventually would become high security risks!* Perhaps a much larger number of prisoners were already in resistance than was evident. Apparently, the owners lived in fear of a rebellion! He remembered the scratch marks in the wall of his own cell. He had little sleep that night thinking about this, about what Robin would have to say about it.

XXVII

"PAY DAY," ALICE winked at Ian as he stepped into the office. Don't forget to check your account online. You keep forgetting."

Ian smirked and slogged over to his desk. It was all so meaningless to him now. He logged into his account and stared at the screen. He had accrued 89 days of vacation leave. He laughed aloud at the absurdity. Before his implant malfunctioned, this meant months in his cell, thinking that he was in Paros or Paris. Now it would mean staring at his three walls for days on end without any respite. Not that work was any better. He'd be able to read, lie in bed. Plot a rebellion with Robin?

There was no telling exactly how large their movement was, nor who the members were. Probably they would not achieve any kind of victory in their lifetimes. Still, he knew he had to try just the same, like Robin, for that one in a trillion chance that victory was possible. For the truth of it was, he had concluded after endless internal debates, that he could no longer lie to himself; no longer could he continue to hide inside what Robin was always calling Plato's cave. Moreover, he felt compelled to help others emerge from the cave as well. There was no denying Robin had inspired his new awareness. Whether his decision to aid the rebellion was primarily motivated by a desire to win her approval, or an earnest sense of moral duty, he simply had no alternative but to act.

He strode up to Alice's desk. "Any chance I can trade my vacation days for pay?" Something real and concrete that Robin and he might actually use, he reasoned.

"All work and no play makes Ian a dull boy!" Alice said sarcastically. "I'll see what I can do," she smiled, standing up to head toward the boss's door. She turned around. Sympathetically she added softly, "Are you—?" Then, awkwardly, after seeing his dejected expression: "Never mind."

Ian headed back to his desk. Someone had placed a blank #10 envelope on top of his stack of papers. Eagerly, he turned it over and saw that it was sealed with something puffy, like cotton inside. He opened it and found Robin's note, scrawled as usual on toilet paper so that he could dispose of it easily:

The dahlias refuse to wither, as flowers will, in unlucky love affairs, or so they say.

Each time i gaze at them, i'm caught by surprise, seduced into yet a deeper layer of labyrinth, more beautiful, more intricate, more mysterious than the last. "It is enough if one tries merely to comprehend a little of this mystery each day," Einstein once said. Loving you is like that.

Ian's spirits soared. Yet he could feel his heart pounding in his throat. The time had arrived to attempt their rendezvous on the outside.

"When I ask you to go to lunch in the Atrium, meet me by the main entrance screen. Make up some excuse about why you have to leave early," was his recollection of what she had told him. Now all he had to do was exercise patience.

The minutes limped by on crutches, painfully dragging themselves into hours. His stomach was grumbling. He began to wonder whether he had misunderstood Robin about attempting the breakout the same day as his receiving her letter. Twice he resisted the temptation to walk toward Robin's cubicle after getting up to retrieve a cup of coffee.

He wondered what their risks were. Were the guards themselves even aware of the power of a reprogrammed jail-broken MEphone to trigger their REM sleep? Suppose Robin boldly pulled hers out and aimed at some screen? Unless they mistook it for a weapon and fired, which they were more likely to do than not; they might simply find it amusing.

No, the danger lay in a failure to notice guards cognizant of their escape. Someone they had not seen who was aware of their identity from a different floor—Perhaps a higher level guard posing as a lower level guard. They could be shot at. Or locked up in solitary, as he had been for trying to have lunch on the outside with Richard. That was optimistic. Treason inevitably meant termination—if they were fortunate.

Ian's stomach remained in knots well past the lunch hour. In fact, it was four o'clock, he realized. He decided he couldn't eat anyway. Had something happened to Robin?

The next day, his stomach was just as upset. All morning, Ian felt all pins and needles, as though he had overdosed on niacin. Finally, at a quarter to one, he caught sight of Robin and let out a sigh.

"Want to get some lunch at the Atrium," she grinned. She was glowing. She had obviously just trimmed and re-dyed her hair, the new red streaks really highlighting the green in her eyes.

"Great, I'm starving," Ian smiled. He tried not to look too long at Robin, for fear that their emotions would be acknowledged by unfriendly witnesses.

"Got you a present," she said coquettishly. "Try them on!"

They were a pair of Polaroid sunglasses. "How much did these set you back?"

"Two for one sale. Besides, What else can I spend my generous salary on? A bigger house? A vacation?" she laughed, putting her own on. "Let's see."

It would be a good idea to conceal their eyes from the guards, he realized.

As they approached the entrance to the building, under the large screens, where three guards stood—only one wearing the glasses—Robin fumbled in her purse. She kept her jacket draped over the purse, so the MEphone could remain hidden from plain view. Ian peered more carefully over her shoulder. Discreetly, she scrolled through a document of long numbers, copied a line of them, turned off the Rawtooth and pasted the numbers into the "advanced settings" box. She aimed her mobile at one of the screens by the entrance. There was no flickering. The guards didn't seem to change from their present course of action.

Robin discreetly snapped a picture of one of the guards. She opened the face recognition app and flipped through the screens until the ME chimed. She scrolled through the options and stopped on an image and referenced the tall, bald and elegant African American guard who was distracted giving an entering tourist directions to the front desk. Ian nodded. "That's him! Are the others part of his group?"

"We'll find out," Robin said as she copied the numbers, then pulled down a menu and pasted the line of numbers next to the picture into the appropriate Rawtooth box, hit a few more options, then aimed the mobile at the screen again.

Suddenly the bald guard stopped talking to the tourist, and lifted his head toward the screen, nodding vacantly. Ian noticed he had been holding his breath and exhaled. He glanced at the other two guards. One, a slender Filipino man with pockmarked skin, headed out the door to talk to one of the valets. Ian had overlooked all the valet parking personnel outside. No telling how many lurked out there.

"What about the valets?" Ian whispered anxiously.

"Not their job. Too busy fetching and parking to keep track of inmates." Robin assessed the tall blonde guard with short parted gold hair done in the style of an old 50s movie star and two white wires sprouting from his ears. Ian studied him for a change in appearance. The guard rubbed one of his eyes. His features were handsome, except one hazel eye seemed asymmetrical. He looked like an arrogant fellow, probably unaware of the bald spot in the center of his head when he looked in the mirror, Ian thought to himself. His back was to the door, as he looked the guests over, bidding them a good afternoon as they departed. Now and then he seemed to scan the lobby, then the visible floors for irregular patterns.

Robin aimed her mobile at the guard's belt, where a MEphone hung. The guard took several steps back and stared up at one of the screens by the entrance. He remained there, transfixed.

Ian noticed the African-American guard was still staring up at the screen as well.

"Ready?" Robin smiled, her words seeming to escape from the corner of her sexy mouth without her having moved her lips.

"What happened that first time? Some other guards somewhere else are in REM now too?" Ian asked.

Robin shrugged.

"And our third buddy with the valets?"

"It's getting late," Robin said cryptically.

Ian walked confidently next to Robin out of the entrance where they came face to face with the Filipino guard. The man stared at the couple. Ian's heart stopped. There was a small screen by the cashier, but...

"Can I get your auto?" the man inquired politely.

"Oh no thanks," Robin smiled and walked on. Ian followed her lead. She was talking about getting something into the mail on time to make a deadline. Ian played along as they walked up Drumm Street towards Jackson Street. He dared not look back. He expected the guards to come after them, tackle them from behind with heat rays and bullets at any moment. Robin stopped at the corner to wait for the light. Ian stared down at the ivory mosaic swirls that were the signature sidewalk of the Embarcadero shopping center. Casually, he moved his head enough to search for the guards discreetly. To his relief, he spied only pedestrians.

"That guard wasn't part of the group?" he asked.

"Low level. Just supervises the valets," Robin snickered.

"How did you know he wouldn't come after us?"

"I didn't," Robin smirked and headed toward the bay.

Now, out in the sharp autumn sunlight for the first time in a couple of months, Ian was grateful for the sunglasses. The sky was piercing blue, satin, he reflected, suddenly aware of the chill in the air. Ian caught sight of the gargantuan apartment complex on their left along Jackson, with its basement boutiques, gym and supermarket spanning three-square- blocks. "I never realized these luxury condo deals were actually prisons," Ian laughed.

"Yup. At least four around here," Robin pointed out. "One at Battery, at Front, at Davis and Drumm."

Robin stopped as they approached the Embarcadero plaza and fountain. She headed for one of the metal tables on the eating court directly across from the fountain, peeled off her leather jacket and rolled it into a pillow. She stopped, and pulled out her MEphone from the pocket and set it carefully on the table in its red and black case. "Oops. I'd better be more careful with that. Although, who knows. Sometimes it seems like we don't even need it." She promptly sat down and stretched out like a feline, head back on the make-shift pillow to catch the rays of sun.

Ian sat down rather stiffly and looked around.

"Relax, Ian. We're free again," Robin said through her teeth, lips barely moving. Her eyes were shut, and her mouth parted ever so slightly in a sideways grin. "This is so amazing!" she began laughing. I can't remember feeling anything so good… Try it," she said, stretching out her long legs even further so as to lie as prostrate as possible, though face up, in the chair.

"You don't, do you?!" Ian teased, suddenly straddling Robin. He bent over her, lifted her face toward his and locked her into a long, sensual kiss.

"I meant besides—!" Robin laughed, coming up for air, but he didn't allow her to finish her sentence.

Ian stood and adjusted his trousers. "Shouldn't we get going, Robin?" he riffled his hair.

"We just got here!" She laughed.

"Robin, don't you think that's enough, now?" Ian pulled at her wrist.

"Out here there are just inmates and owners. Guards aren't really needed. It's all under control. Remember?" she said, pulling her arm away and putting it behind her head. Ian noticed the unusual size of her biceps as she stretched her bare arms out. "We're free, babe," she repeated, turning toward him, stretching her arm toward him. "Have a seat."

Ian allowed himself to sit down. Habitually, he checked his shirt pocket to retrieve his MEphone, found it empty, took a breath and looked around, somewhat anxiously. After a while, he stretched out, lifting his face to the sun as well. The heat felt wonderful on his skin. It was actually a relief that all his gadgets, his tethers, were broken. He grinned. "I've really missed this," he laughed. "Really? We're free?" He had been so naïve when she had first jail broken them to go to Puccini, then Vesuvio.

"As free as its going to get. What kills me is that we probably could have done this weeks ago, maybe even without the MEphone. Just walked out together. I think I've just gotten used to being overly—"

"Paranoid?"

"I was thinking more, 'cautious.'"

"You don't think writing on toilet paper is—"

"All right. Maybe that was a little over the top. But I'm on their radar, remember, you're apparently not!"

Ian sat up and looked at the Dr. Seuss-like fountain: half a dozen waterfalls issuing from gigantic angled rectangular tunnels of cement over a small emerald lake, over which children skipped on floating cement steps through the torrents of water. A little boy fell in and the father scooped him back out. The child wailed on the edge as his parents figured out how to dry him off for the journey home.

Ian instinctively removed his own coat and began to stand as though to offer it to the child. Almost at the same time, the father removed his sweatshirt, buttoned his jean jacket around his bare torso and exchanged it for his son's wet top and sweater. The sweatshirt covered most of the boy's wet legs.

Ian sat back down. "Why go back at all?" Ian laughed. He could hear his stomach rumbling again.

"Because we have some work to do there, remember?" Robin said. "And I don't mean for Bear-TT."

"Right," Ian sobered.

"And it's so easy to leave!" Robin laughed.

"Glorious!" Ian exclaimed, standing. "Where to now?"

Suddenly the afternoon and the future's uncalculated possibilities stretched out before them like the sapphire blue of the Bay past the ferry building clock tower. "How about The Waterfront!" He was speaking rapidly, with a slightly higher pitch, like an excited child. "I used to go there on special occasions. In REM. I want to see what it's really like."

"How about Delancy Street," Robin said soberly. "At least once we're on the outside we'll still be able to afford it occasionally... but the Waterfront—"

Ian thought about the clearly superior food at Delancy Street, the exaggerated number of waiters and bus boys and the fact that the bill always came to a fourth of comparable restaurants. "What's the deal there,?" Ian riffled his hair with his hands.

"Non-profit. Run by some of us on the outside."

"Oh that makes sense now!" Ian reflected. "So we'll still be able to go there, come the revolution?" he laughed.

"Absolutely."

"How about we take advantage of the Waterfront while we still can. View's a little better over the water."

Robin shrugged.

The stroll through the Embarcadero docks was lovely in July, lavish baskets of hanging flowers adorning the wooden walkways over the water. They emerged just shy of Broadway and made their way into the restaurant. A most hospitable, elegant Indian maître d' led Ian and Robin past an enclosed patio hanging over the water, upstairs to a mezzanine. Before them, the Bay Bridge unfolded over the green water, toward the shores of Oakland. Gulls flew lazily back and forth over a long fishing pier in the foreground. High up on one of the Oakland hills, Ian could make out the white shape of what he knew to be the Mormon Temple near where a famous couple of writers lived, though how he knew this was beyond him.

"Well?" Ian smiled, taking Robin's hand in his. "Pretty spectacular, isn't it?"

"Is it better than hyper-REM?" Robin smiled. Her eyes seemed to him the same color as the water.

"I feel like I'm sitting on that ship over there," Ian pointed out a white Southern-style barge that looked like it belonged on the Mississippi. "Just cruising around the Bay like a tourist," he beamed.

Robin laughed. "I remember being pretty happy in REM as well. But this is—"

"Real?" Ian laughed. He watched a large cargo ship the size of a few blocks pass under the Bay. With global warming, the clearance was getting tighter each year. There was something about the scenery, the real non-REM moment that made him feel more alive than he'd ever felt. The new scents and sensations were quasi-orgasmic. A wonderful sensation of calm, as well as joy seemed to percolate inside him. Perhaps it was Robin. "Do you feel as though you're using all your senses for the first time?"

"Something like that," Robin agreed.

A nice looking waitress with her blonde hair tied back in a pony tail interrupted their reverie. They decided on an appetizer of pancetta wrapped prawns, Caesar and grilled swordfish to share.

"How much time do we have?" Ian asked Robin, once the waitress had left to put in their order. Should we start talking about a plan?"

"They think I'm off at a convention. They seem more lax when I disappear by myself after one of those, because they sometimes run until midnight. What did you say?"

"I told Alice that I had a bunch of pain—a kidney stone—and needed to make an emergency visit to urgent care. She told me to leave immediately."

"Wouldn't it be nice to spend the night somewhere?" Robin asked dreamily. Robin leaned forward and whispered. "For all they know, you're at the hospital and I'm at the convention."

"Where to?" Ian smiled, wrapping his leg over Robin's thigh.

"I know this kind of funky place in North Beach. It was a poet's old studio in an SRO—"

"How about the Saint Francis overlooking Union Square?"

"Why so decadent, babe?" Robin smiled her lopsided smile, concealing a laugh.

Ian looked nonplussed. "It's a historical landmark! It's the only one on Union Square."

"Ian, when are you going to break your addiction. You don't like how this society imprisons its workers, yet you're not willing to give up some of the chains."

"Come on, preacher-lady. What are you afraid of? That you won't be able to make your own mortgage payments? Haven't you saved quite a bit of money since you stopped taking imaginary trips?"

"We'll need money for our plan, Ian." Robin looked concerned.

Ian shook his head. "What a scam. Who gets all that real money of ours for virtual things? Can you spell it out?"

"First of all, money, by nature is virtual and its value arbitrarily decided by those in power. That's why we have our own barter system in the movement. Our own currency. But getting back to your question, all money streams lead to the owners eventually. Don't forget there are also owners of your virtual mortgage, owners of your virtual vacations—dozens of parasites. The owners of our prison are just some of the parasites." Robin smirked.

Once the feast was before them, Ian and Robin's conversation stopped. They savored each morsel sensually, staring silently into each other's eyes, as though contemplating in a church. Now and then one of them would break into giggles.

It was Ian who spoke first. "Doesn't this seem like the best meal you ever had?'

"It probably is," Robin said. They both laughed. And laughed harder, as though it were one of the funniest jokes they'd ever heard.

Then Robin got down to business again, discussing strategy.

When they were finished, Ian automatically picked up the electronic slate and allowed it to scan his retina. Several accounts flashed on the screen and he tapped the appropriate one, then entered a tip.

"What are you doing?" Robin grabbed the slate. "They'll see where we are!"

"They know where we are," Ian said flatly, tapping his brow where he believed the implant lay. "Remember?"

"You don't understand. Out of the ordinary activity will trigger a flag. Patterns of flags will put you on their radar. You don't think they're always monitoring you, do you?"

"You seem to think so."

"That's me, because I'm considered a threat to their order. Remember, this is only a police state for those the state deems a threat. I'm now on the outside, so I'm considered a terrorist. They still think you are on the inside. For you, it's easy to break out of the grid as long as you don't set off any flags by changing your routine. No problem if this were Puccini or some place you normally went to on your lunch break." In a flash, Robin scanned her own retina and pressed send before really reviewing the amount.

"But you're a high security risk!" Ian protested, rising with a hoarse whisper.

"Relax, babe," Robin said with some amusement. "Supposedly I'm at a convention, so I can get away with it this time. We'll need our cash to support that bourgeois habit of yours."

Robin and Ian walked down Embarcadero, through the tangle of people at Fisherman's Wharf and after a half hour of waiting in line, caught a cable car up Powell to Union Square. They were fortunate to end up in an outside seat facing the moving scenery, despite being in such a desirable owner-magnet city. Robin reclined into Ian's arms. The other tourists—whether owners or inmates on two-week sabbatical— were too busy looking at Ghirardelli Square, the crab shacks, seals and Aquatic Park, to notice Robin and Ian kissing the entire way. Finally, past all the commotion, the couple came up for air.

"You know what your biggest threat is?"

"You," Ian laughed, wrinkling his nose at Robin.

"Close," Robin grinned. "Getting back to the conversation we were having after our food came—"

"You do have a one-track mind," Ian said with a trace of irritation. "That's what you were thinking about all this time?"

"Not while—" Robin blushed. "But seriously, Ian. Actually, your biggest threat is other inmates, not the state. It can only function with the complicity of the inmates. I know it sounds silly, but just remember that, when you're waking people up. The opposition can get pretty intense."

"Think we have a chance of—"

"Not that we'll ever see, probably," Robin looked down at the tracks.

"But!" Ian remembered the bars. "Were there huge uprisings before? Did they almost succeed?" He was speaking rapidly, his voice higher-pitched with urgency

"Absolutely. Don't forget this movement is global. Just give thanks that you're in an owner-magnet city where security is pretty relaxed, not some prison city like Fresno, Houston or Tucson."

The cable car stopped in front of a series of Victorians with peeling paint, one with a broken window.

"Look Ian. Those are the movement's squats," Robin whispered. That's an occupied café where different committees meet. That's our library, taken over during one of the closures, and behind that's Club Gaomotion, kind of a cultural center with films and bands and art shows. It was named after an anarchist collective in the Mission District back in the last two decades of the twentieth century. Speaking of the Mission, you know that beautiful old building that used to be New College on Valencia, then a string of clubs and bars? It's now the Free School, where teach-ins and classes take place. One of the buildings was turned into our hospital where there is also a women's clinic and free health care."

"So it's like an alternative society?' Ian asked.

"Exactly. Underground but above ground. You know where we have to go?" Robin began speaking quickly, like an excited child. "Radio Habana! It used to be owned by this Cuban, Victor Navarete. This artist. He put this crazy Salvador Dali-esque 3-D art all over the walls, framed pictures of the poets that used to frequent the café like, uh, Jack Hirschman and, uh, whatshisname Jorge Argueta, Alejandro Murguía, Alfonso Texidor, Margot Pepper—a realistic fleshy hand coming out of the frame; a real typewriter on the wall, grotesque politico heads with Barbie doll bodies; a dummy hanging from the ceiling dressed like a punk rocker—it's all been preserved like a historical landmark. The collective that took it over after Victor and Leila passed away gets its money from workers that come in at lunch time and the owners that took over the Mission. Then they feed us free!"

"So this has been going on a while?" Ian asked.

"Since the early part of this century. Let's see this is '84. Around eighty or more years ago!"

"But you were telling me about the huge uprisings… Was there one here?" Ian persisted.

"Well there was at least one major one I know of." Robin said.

"When?" Ian's tone was eager.

"I'm not sure exactly. I know it was before REM. And after almost everything had become rights-free zones, not just airports and workplaces. The occupy-inspired resistance was at its height then. There was lots of repression, like in the third world, then the REM, though I might be mixing up events."

"That's the only explanation for bars on our cells then," Ian posited.

"Maybe," Robin forced a smile.

Ian stared at the pastel Victorians, some with intricate gold trim. Some had drawn curtains. In one or two, an inhabitant could be seen walking or sitting at a table or desk. "So besides the occasional occupied buildings, who lives in all these if most of our society is in jail?"

"The small percentage of owners, mostly. A single owner often owns dozens, even hundreds of houses, so most of these—I'd say about 80%—are vacant, waiting for their owners to go on holiday or on business trips. Some are rented to young people who don't have their third strike yet. College kids, maybe. People who've fallen through the cracks. And like you noticed, there are some jail-broken prisoners who are living in some of the houses, underground or off the grid."

"Would we be able to rent one eventually, you think?"

"It would be easier to squat, both logistically and morally, no?"

"Occupy! I love it," Ian said. "Onto the Saint Francis?"

"You're bad," Robin laughed, leaning into Ian.

XXVIII

ON THE OTHER side of consciousness, someone was knocking at the door. Ian stirred. His back felt magnificent. The soft wonder-top mattress beneath him reminded him of his Divine® bed back home in Tiburon. He stretched and curled Robin into his arms, kissed her. She continued snoring lightly, like a little animal. Quietly, Ian pushed aside the down comforter and swung his legs over the king-size bed.

Another knock on the door. The screen clock said 10:23. Housekeeping, he assumed. He decided to ignore it.

The knocking stopped.

Ian stretched and walked barefoot to the window, marveling at how clean the carpet beneath his feet was. The large windows at the foot of the room boasted a view of Union Square opposite Il Caffé, Macy's to the right.

For a minute Ian felt a wave of nausea. What had he been thinking? Tiburon was not real. How could this be? What if his REM sleep implant had started working again?

Another knock. This time, louder, more insistent, male. Clearly not housekeeping.

Wait, hadn't he and Robin escaped the jail? So this was real.

A more threatening pounding nearly sent him into a panic. The knock could be—

"Let me grab a robe," Ian called out reflexively, heading into the walk-in closet to buy time to think. His mind was assaulted by images of armed guards demanding to confirm his identity. He inhaled deeply, trying to orient himself. Could the authorities have discovered the couple's whereabouts so quickly? The prospect of their capture sent blood pounding through his arteries. What if they had heard their plot the previous night through Robin's MEphone? He closed the closet door and stood there in the dark.

Robin had been right. At least they had enjoyed one last, dreamlike tryst.

Ian tried to relive the events of the previous afternoon in the flash of a second, as though preserving an anodyne for the poisonous prospects of what lay ahead, on the other side of the door.

...Robin had sweet-talked their way into a room in the historical wing of the Saint Francis built in 1902 that survived the SF earthquake and fire. They had sat at the large desk, overlooking the city streets barricaded for what Ian assumed was the Chinese New Year celebration. Ian recounted his experience with Richard in full detail. Then Robin filled him in on the next action.

"So we have to walk by Chinatown on the way home. Pick up some of those black market smoking fireworks left over from the Fourth."

"The Fourth? You mean the New Year's celebration."

"Right," Robin laughed mysteriously.

"It wouldn't be too unusual for an inmate to have brought one home?" Ian inquired.

"Not after the Fourth of July. That shit goes on all summer! I mean, Chinese New Year, whatever," Robin tucked her head under Ian's chin.

"What luck!" Ian exclaimed. "Did you know about the parade going right under our room?"

"That's why I picked it!" Robin giggled.

"So now I get to participate in the movement from the outside," Ian said kissing the top of Robin's head. "I thought I'd been in an accident. Then, that there had been some kind of disaster. Fire."

"Those have been pulled off too. Too risky."

"Haven't the guards figured out your tricks by now?"

Robin laughed. "If they can remember. Plus, the turn over. If there's one thing we have on our side, it's amnesia. It's inherent in this system. The system couldn't function without it."

For a while they stared dreamily at the airbrushed wisps of fog brushing the azure backdrop of sky behind the Transamerica pyramid downtown. Billboards loomed on the nearby high-rises. Finally, Robin said, "I have some friends in our complex. By now they've probably found others."

"How do you know they are not agents?" Ian asked sarcastically.

"Stop it! How do I know you're not an agent?" Robin half grinned out of the corner of her mouth, but her brows and eyes seemed to betray concern.

"Like this," Ian said, taking her face in his hands and bringing her lips to his.

After a while, Robin wiped her lipstick and laughed. "Seriously, one of the ways you can tell is whether they agree to go to lunch on the outside or not, whether they can or if guards start to follow them.

Another is by tethering them to the MEphone. If it works on them."

"How convenient," Ian smiled. "Tell me more about your friends."

"Angelina I've known since fourth grade. She'll be easy for you to spot. Plus, you know where you saw her? You saw her in passing at the Beach House conference. Part Italian, part Puerto-Rican. Green almond eyes, double-size lips."

Ian looked at Robin blankly.

"Just look for the prettiest woman on the floor—like a Brat doll."

"That would be you. Especially the brat part," Ian winked.

"Thanks, but pay attention. Mary Liz is cute too with light brown eyes and brown wavy hair, full lips. I went to a screening of a documentary she had made that won her high security status. We're kindred souls. As for Rickey, he's a brilliant writer. Professor of Ethnic Studies now. I've known him since the pseudo-college days from the jail we thought was a dorm. We were both working in the kitchen. Look for a handsome light-skinned African American man." Robin said.

Finally they agreed on a strategy and since Ian seemed to be finally off the radar, that it would be best for him to be the one to execute it.

With the details in place, Robin slowly sidled up to Ian for another kiss and began removing her clothes.

She fell back on the wonder-top Saint Francis bed with a wide grin, arms folded behind her head.

"You look like you're enjoying yourself quite a bit," Ian smiled.

"It's going to take generations for this paradigm to change and I'm not going to waste the moments that are truly mine in the meantime, " Robin commented.

"Or the opportunity to create them, I see. You remind me of the Greek and Roman Stoics," Ian said.

"Hardly Stoic. Try a closet hedonist," Robin grinned devilishly.

Ian could barely resist her and overtook her with his body. Between kisses he explained that the Stoics had been a combination of hedonists as well as cynics: those who tried to minimize what they needed from life, according to the ancient Greeks. "Stoics were not only lovers of tranquility and joy, but they had a strong sense of social commitment; and a philosophy of life—like you—to leave life better for humanity."

"While enjoying life as well!" Robin had laughed. "I just don't need all this crap to do it!" she had said, punching a pillow.

They made love late into the evening, trying out various facets of the room besides the bed: the chaise lounge and bathtub with double shower head.

Eventually they developed quite an appetite again.

Just then, the crab-encrusted Halibut and green mashed potatoes from the Oak room downstairs arrived on a white table cloth under two steaming silver lids.

"I don't feel like getting dressed until tomorrow," Robin said, throwing on a hotel robe.

It seemed to Ian as though the day had stretched on and on with endless indulgence, conversation and relaxation.

Only when they seated themselves at the table, did Ian notice the Chinese New Year parade marching around Union Square, past Macy's on Geary, flamboyant Chinese lions on stilts and endless golden illuminated dragons zigzagging under their windows stories below on Powell Street before winding their way back down on Post. A team of white, glitter-adorned horses pulled a Bear-TT chariot full of children and beautiful bikinied women. Ian turned on the screen to view better. He could hear drumming and fireworks.

"We are so fortunate to be right over this!" Ian exclaimed. He ran over to the window and tried to open it to better hear all the music coming from the television. "Wow, pretty good insulation!" he noted. The window wouldn't budge. Finally, with the aid of one of the dining knives, Ian unscrewed the window guard and managed to get his head through the pane.

"Hey! Where did everyone go?" He looked up and down the street. "That's crazy!" He turned to talk to Robin, and the parade reappeared.

Robin was laughing.

"What's going on?!" He shouted. Inside the room the parade was in full swing. He stuck his head outside again and it vanished.

Robin was now laughing so hard she had rolled over onto the bed and was holding her side.

"What's happening? Tell me, Robin!" Ian pounced on her and kissed her neck. "Tell me, come on, babe!"

Robin wiped the tears from her eyes and quieted herself. "Chinese New Year in July, Ian? Come on!"

Ian felt foolish. "So it's a mirage."

"Projected on the window with the same technology as the GPS bifocals. Manufactured for tourists on command. You were not supposed to open the window, Ian. Disappointed?" Robin burst into laughter again.

After dinner Ian couldn't remember when each of his senses felt so fully sated. It was the last thought he coherently pieced together before he and Robin fell asleep in each other's arms, legs intertwined.

The knocking persisted. "Mr. W—" a deep male voice called from the other side of the doors. He couldn't just leave Robin to be discovered while he cowered in his hiding place. He opened the closet door and made his way cautiously to the front door.

Whatever the consequences of their adventure, at least Ian had been granted the opportunity to be truly alive in his body and mind, truly inhabiting all of his senses. He had truly loved and been loved. Moreover, he had come into possession of the truth.

Would he rather have been Richard, still clinging to his virtual delusion? For the first time Ian felt confident about his choice. Boldly, he opened the door. "Yes?"

"Room service, Sir," smiled a tall African-American man. Ian laughed as he beheld the rolling table complete with tablecloth and carnations, iced water glasses, a basket of croissants and a tremendous crab omelet with hash-browns and two plates—probably the rest of their cash, Ian reflected with a sudden new apprehension.

"Everything okay?" the waiter inquired, perplexed.

"I'm sorry. It's not you. Everything's perfect!" Ian smiled.

The waiter wheeled the table in front of another window overlooking Union Square, then took his leave.

When Robin emerged from the bathroom in a robe, she turned up her nose at the decadence.

"Ian, your addiction to this kind of luxury—this, the Waterfront— is what's enslaving our society!"

"I know, I know. Don't worry. We'll have to give it all up soon enough. Meanwhile, why not enjoy!" Ian said through bulging cheeks full of crab and melted cheese. He was so overcome with excitement, Robin cracked a smile.

"Look at you! You're like a little kid!"

He managed to distract her by making love to her a final time. They enjoyed each other as though it were their last time together. Afterward, they dressed in silence, Robin finally hungrily devouring her portion of omelet, and Ian polishing off the last of his larger half. Then they headed back to the prison.

XXIX

FIVE-ELEVEN, FRIDAY evening. Commuters were so thick, Ian had trouble stopping to fumble with his briefcase. He had trouble locating the hidden firecrackers and lighter through his badly scratched and now too-dark sunglasses he hoped would better conceal his motivations.

He turned to a commuter that was in REM and slapped him on the back. "Hey, dude!"

The man stopped and smiled, almost automatically, as though Ian were someone he knew. Realizing he wasn't, his smile began to turn upside down.

"TGIF!" Ian called out, lighting the firecrackers and placing them inside a planter attached to the balcony. The man laughed and stepped back.

The firecrackers began smoking and cracking. Some commuters turned to look.

Ian walked on to his cell as though nothing had happened. Very quickly the smoke filled the passageway and the smell permeated his cell. Outside his cell he could hear shouting.

"What's going on?"

"Fire!"

"No, it's just some idiot celebrating."

The sprinklers came on in his cell, soaking the furniture. He could hear startled shouts of some inmates whose cells had also become shower stalls. Ian had stored the few books he had in his desk; his clothes were in the closet. He grabbed a wooden ruler from his desk and exited his cell. The scene looked surreal, somewhat like a conservative version of the wet-T-shirt crowd scene in a Bollywood film. The sprinklers throughout the building were drenching everyone.

Many of the people had stopped, looked bewildered. Ian began running down the hall, ratting the bars with his ruler.

"Wake up! Look at where you are!" Ian rattled the bars. "You're in a jail! Wake up!"

More and more prisoners stopped as they noticed others doing the same. Ian paused to observe their reactions. One or two seemed to be waking up to their surroundings of their own accord, without any interference on his part at all.

He stopped the next person he saw, a man in his fifties in a soaked pin-striped suit.

The man blinked stupidly, water falling from his lashes. His lips sputtered with water.

"Where am I?" he choked.

Ian put his hands around some cell bars. "You're in jail! You've always been in jail. It's a work camp. Don't let those stylish prison clothes fool you! But it's easier to break out than it looks!"

"How? But what—Agnes!" the man moaned. "She was just here. Where are you, Agnes?" he began weaving down the hall, lost.

Ian ran to a pair of young women jiggling and giggling in the shower of water. He could see one woman's nipples through her thin wet sweater; another's red bra.

"Girls! Wake up! We've been jailed unjustly and it's time to get out!"

"What do you mean? How?" the red-head with side pony tail laughed.

Just the thought of the work ahead was dizzying to Ian.

One of the two young women screamed and fell to her knees. "Help! How did I get here! Help me! I want to go home!"

Her friends tried in vain to console her. Suddenly, three young men who looked like wealthy college jocks rushed over to the girls. "Close your eyes. He's only trying to confuse you. Shut it out," they insisted. Two tried to comfort the distraught girl, while the third told Ian to get lost.

"It's under control, dude," the jock repeated. "They don't need your help."

"But you don't understand. We've been jailed unjustly and..."

"I understand full well, dude. We are happy where we are. LEAVE US ALONE! Tina, Tina! Close your eyes!"

"If you could just let me explain," Ian persisted.

"Look Bud. I know exactly what you're up to and I'm calling the guards!"

"Ian?"

Ian turned around abruptly at the mention of his name. He was staring at a dark-haired girl with green eyes. He recognized her cartoon goldfish lips with gold lipstick from the conference. Obviously, Robin had not wanted their association known at the time or she would have introduced them formally. Angelina was with a good-looking, dark-skinned man with a strong chin and tight kinky black curls.

Alarms began sounding throughout the building. More screaming indicated guards had shown up.

"Angelina and Rickey!"

Angelina nodded. "Let's go back to your place," she said, hastily leading Ian by the elbow. "Did you burn dinner again? Is that what all the smoke was?"

"Exactly," Ian responded. He picked up his pace and turned his head. "The guards may be after us," he said under his breath. "That fellow and his friends—"

"It'll take a sec to catch up to us, then more time for the stool pigeons to fink you out." Angelina said, between breaths as they sped up.

"Lost cause," Rickey muttered about the jocks, leading Ian back toward his cell. "They're too lame to find a guard and remember your description. Crowds are too thick right now; the guards, too busy."

"They have a right to be upset, you have to agree," Angelina said to Rickey, then turning to Ian, "We'll catch you up in a minute."

"Nice to meet you," Ian whispered when they were safely inside his cell.

"There's a pretty strong opposition movement," Rickey explained. "We found it more productive to focus on waking folks. Or, on the fence sitters: those who've woken up but haven't decided what to do about it. The friends of that snitch are pretty much a lost cause."

"He means they're entitled to their point of view," Angelina said, with some irritation that was more directed at Rickey than at the jocks.

"Now if you two folks could be so kind as to enlighten me. How do you go about waking folks?" Ian inserted.

"Just what you were doing. It's been a real slow process," Rickey rolled his eyes.

"It does depend a lot on the target," Angelina offered. "Obviously, the tricky part is figuring out where a complete stranger will stand. While it's true that trying to convert the opposition is generally not as effective as targeting fence sitters." She turned to Rickey now, "I think the movement should start targeting more guards. Like there's this one tall, handsome, bald African-American guard I've been talking to. I'm pretty certain we can win him over."

"Come on, Angelina," Rickey said with irritation. "Of course a guy would say anything to you to—"

"Shut!" Angelina interrupted, before Rickey could finish, folding into a tight pout, arms crossed.

"Handsome. Come on, Angelina," Rickey grabbed Angelina and spun her around to look at him. "This is serious, Angelina! You're playing with fire. Not fire, more like nuclear waste! Talking to a guard could tip him off to the rebellion's strategy," Rickey whispered tersely, as not to yell.

"Relax, honey. I haven't told him anything. I'm not a moron. But you have to hear me. This guy has made all kinds of comments that seem to indicate he's more on our side than his bosses. That's why I even considered talking to him at all."

"How do you know he's not some kind of plant."

"I don't. But look, Rickey. Either way, we're screwed. The state is all too powerful. They have all the weaponry. They have all the money. And they have the ultimate brainwashing, numbing tool at their disposal that turns their opposition into a bunch of obedient zombies. For the movement to succeed, we have to win over those in charge of putting our rebellion down or at least get them to stand aside. Hugo Chávez won in Venezuela at the turn of this century because the military took his side and defended him against a right wing coup. Before that, in the Depression era, the unemployed miners in Pennsylvania illegally mined coal on company property and sold it themselves below the company's commercial rate. Local juries refused to convict them and jailers refused to imprison them.

As Emma Goldman says,

'How long would authority and private property exist, if not for the willingness of the mass to become soldiers, policemen, jailers and hangmen?'

At work the next day, in spite of the heightened security in the building, it was business as usual. At about three, when the two colleagues both usually needed a jolt to snap them out of the painful, weighty afternoon lethargy that always set in an hour or so after lunch, Ian bumped into Richard at the coffee machine.

"Any idea why afternoons seem to drag so?" Richard scanned a blood-shot eye and glanced over at Ian.

"Probably because you're looking forward to getting out of here. Consider yourself, fortunate," Ian said.

"Not exactly," Richard grumbled. "I'm not looking forward to a full body scan and all that other nonsense just to leave the building now, thanks to those fricken terrorists."

"Don't you think they're trying to help us?"

Richard paused and looked hard at Ian. "I don't understand. How is turning this place into a police state helping us?"

"Never mind," Ian mumbled and headed back to his desk.

That evening, back at the prison, there was a surge in the number of higher level security guards. Unaware security guards and Embarcadero Multiplex "residents" were informed that there were terrorists in their midst.

Over the next week, according to plan, Robin and Ian studiously avoided each other. The number of higher level security guards in the building increased. The incident had to be repeated on the same floor, same approximate time, to work on as many of the same inmates as before in order to avert the "Richard" effect of selective amnesia. Once the workers went to sleep, then surfaced into hyper-REM upon waking, their memories would, in effect, reset. They'd only truly awake from REM once they entered the workplace. Robin and Ian had to ensure that the memory of the jail would be powerful enough to be recalled at a later date, indentified as reality not just as a nightmare.

Ian waited for a guard-free gap in the commute crowd to repeat the incident on the same floor. Finally, ten days later at 6:24, in the far corner by the stairs across the hall from his cell, he found such a gap and lit the firecrackers, reciting the numbers he remembered in Cantonese as well as a massacred "Happy New Year," his closest approximation of happy Independence Day.

"Gout, Bot, Sep, Gung Hay Fat Choy!"

Instantly the hall was flooded with the acrid stench of smoke; the air began to get thick. Within seconds, a terrible alarm began sounding, causing people to cover their ears, then walk frantically toward the elevator or into their cells. The sprinklers went off, almost instantly soaking all the "commuters."

"Wake up!" Ian screamed at them through the deafening sound of alarms. "You've been enslaved your whole work life! Wake up! Look at your bars! They are real!"

He ran through the crowd, screaming and shaking the inmates.

A tall, elderly man with a crescent of white ostrich hair on his head began to cry out; his wife, a tiny, older woman with a page boy hair cut, turned about like a ballerina in a daze, covering her head; a group of two suited men, and a woman in a business outfit, peered inside the cell bars as though for the first time, while others ran frantically toward the elevator in a panic to escape. Cries of "Let me out!" began to flood the halls, igniting more panic.

Ian emulated the same behavior, spinning and darting erratically down the hallways until he found his cell. Confident that no one was watching, he waved his key and stepped inside. He reached for the umbrella he kept by the door, opened it, put his briefcase on his soggy cot, sat carefully upon it and listened.

The alarms sounded less imposing, but still intolerable. He could make out moaning, anguished cries, sobbing. Then, he could hear shouting, struggling. The guards. He felt a helium-like sensation in his chest, originating in his navel and traveling up, buoying his heart. Resistance to them was increasing!

XXX

WHAT IAN HAD not realized was that while, indeed, the sounds he had heard were of resistance, some of the scuffles had been skirmishes between the rebels and counter resistance. These were prisoners who were cognizant about having been repeatedly startled awake to such a dismal reality and were determined to punish those who had deprived them of their previous comforts. They didn't hesitate to call on the guards for help.

For the next couple of months, the rebels carried out a dozen more actions on various floors. Angelina helped their group gain confidence using her and Robin's MEphones to activate the guard's REM sleep states during the actions, to increase the likelihood of their forgetting the incidents. Judging from the number of actions they were able to get away with, apparently their plan was working. The frequency of their encounters with the counter-resistance, however, indicated that opposition to their movement among inmates was also growing.

A few days before Ian was scheduled to help set off the alarms in the entire building, two blonde men recognized Ian in the elevator on his way back to his cell after work.

"Isn't that him?" said the handsome one with hazel eyes.

"That is, dude! Hey, my friend!" shouted the one with hair like porcupine bristles. He put his hand on Ian's shoulder as they stepped off the elevator. "We've been looking for you to thank you. You're the one who woke us up, aren't you!" They continued walking down the hall.

Bristle-head stopped. He grabbed Ian to stop him; looked at him hard. "Yes you are. Dark. Good looking. I'll never forget your face."

"You've been staring at it in your ME enough," his friend snickered.

Bristle-head scanned Ian with his ME and scrolled through the face recognition software options. Ian's identity came up along with a match in Bristle-head's ME photo album. "Good thing I capt you for security the evening you did this. I think we have a match, don't you think?" He showed Ian the photo of himself. "This your twin?"

Ian's face flushed.

"I don't know what you did, buddy," Bristle's tone became lower, menacing. "I don't know what the fuck happened, but I can't get home now. It's all gone. My Marina townhouse, my walks there, my second home in Tahiti right on the water. They operated on me, told me I'm crazy. But I know it's you. What did you do to it all?"

"I don't know but I want to kill him," the other said.

"Good idea," said Bristle-head. "You watch out, dude. Watch out for your life. You got 24 hours to put it all back."

Ian refused to walk back to his cell until the men left. "I'll call for the guards," he threatened.

"You know how quick they'll be to respond," Bristle head smirked.

"Yeah, especially when you let them know why we're after you," his friend added.

"I had a respectable life. Why did you do it, dude? Why?"

"You got the wrong guy," Ian said.

"We capt you, dude. It's a match and you know it!" Bristle shouted, flashing his phone at Ian with Ian's image and the identifier.

"Remember, now. We'll catch up with you, if you don't put it all back," the other man said.

Ian was shaking when he waved his key at his door.

The following day, Ian managed to get Robin's attention at the coffee machine.

"Lots of work lately?" He muttered.

"Yeah," she said without looking up.

"Some nuts threatened me," Ian mumbled.

Robin felt Ian's forehead, then feigned touching a sizzling surface with her index finger. "Ouch! Hot! You poor thing. You should stay home tomorrow," Robin said cryptically. "I can take over your ad assignment tomorrow."

"That's unnecessary," Ian responded. "I'll be fine, but, hey, thanks." He did not want Robin to put herself at such risk because of her terrorist status. The chances of her being recognized and apprehended were even greater.

They argued back and forth.

"Tomorrow, don't bother coming. I'm taking over the work on the ad whether you're here or not," she hissed her warning and strode back to her desk.

That evening Ian could not sleep worrying about Robin and the fall-back plan they had discussed for emergencies back at the Saint Francis. He began to have second thoughts. He recalled his conversation about whether it was cruel or humane to wake the inmates. In a democracy, they would have the right to make up their own minds, Robin said. But clearly, the men who had threatened Ian were telling him that given a choice, they would choose to remain deluded. Was he wrong to ignore their wishes? In a genuine democracy, wouldn't that point of view be respected as well?

His mother would undoubtedly choose the truth. But if by some miracle they were able to find her, let alone wake her, they'd put her at risk. Sadly, he realized the situation was a lose-lose and best forgotten altogether for now.

XXXI

IT WAS FIVE forty-seven in the early evening. Ian was around the corner from his cell on his floor. He had intentionally spilled the contents of his briefcase and had nearly finished sorting through it and putting it neatly back. Still, the alarm and sprinkler system had failed to activate. He could feel his pulse throbbing in the side of his neck, his heart skipping irregularly. What if Robin and the others had been caught? The closest bank of elevators to where she was positioned was quite some distance away. Could they have been apprehended after attempting to escape in the elevator? Ian milled about as long as he could without arousing suspicion. Finally he returned to his cell.

He spent a long night wondering whether he'd ever see Robin again, anticipating an unwelcome knock at the door. Sometime, near dawn, he fell asleep.

The next day, he was late for the second time.

"Sick?" Alice smiled.

He just nodded and rubbed his hair. "Coffee," he grunted and headed for the machine. When he saw Robin trot up behind him, waiting her turn, he felt like a scuba diver whose oxygen had been turned on again after too dangerous a hiatus.

"What are you doing here?" she said. "You're supposed to be in bed." Then, barely audible, she whispered as they parted. "Duds. Next week, same time. Lay low for a while."

Ian was on the elevator when the alarms went off in the lobby. A guard was in the elevator as well. Ian made eye contact with him, feigning confusion. To throw the guard off, he exited on the 25th floor. No sooner did Ian step off the elevator, than he could hear shouts and cries issuing from the lobby and floors below. He was immediately soaked by water. Some of the resistance must have set off the sprinklers throughout the building. He knew Robin was among them. Ian ran through the halls shouting as usual, trying to wake the fellow inmates. He took the stairs down to the next floor to continue his routine there.

"Oh thank goodness! Ian! What is happening? Why are we here?" Carmence, the Chinese woman who owned the North Beach dry cleaning store suddenly embraced and clung to Ian as though to a raft in a flood. Tears shone in her eyes and Ian could see she was trying to suppress them. After explaining to her, as best he could, what was taking place, Ian asked for her key. He waved it until one of the cell doors opened.

"See, this must be your cell," he showed her.

"Oh, no. Let's not go in there," she said. She stopped cold when she noticed her son, husband and two daughters inside. They were soaked, sitting on their drenched cots, staring, arms folded, at a black screen, looking miserable.

"Quickly! Come!" she motioned them.

"But ma, that's not the problem," said her oldest daughter, standing. She was taller than her mother. "The door is open. But just look. I'm not going out there. What are we doing here?"

Her husband began speaking to her sharply in a low voice in Cantonese. It was the first time Ian had ever seen the anonymous genius that mended and altered all the clothes he had brought in to Ko & Co. over the years. Real money for real work, he realized, not virtual.

"I knew it," Carmence shook her head. "I just knew it," she sank down on the cot. "I made mistake on the taxes."

"No, no, no!" Ian tried to console her. "We've all been here for years. We're all guilty of something minor, but that's just a pretext. You have implants that make you all think you live in that nice house in South San Francisco that you're always painting on your weekends."

"Why have they rounded us up again?" her husband demanded of Ian, standing, as if he hadn't heard anything he just said. "Is there another war?" Then turning to his wife he asked in Cantonese, "Who is this?" He glared at Ian suspiciously.

"This is Ian. Customer," Carmence stammered awkwardly. "You know the one who gave us the orchid?"

"Oh, yes. Pleased to meet you," Mr. Gao's expression softened as he forced a smile. "But why they rounding you up too? Why you the enemy?"

"Relax, Mr. Gao. This is not a concentration camp," Ian offered. He continued with his usual, practiced refrain about their situation. The two girls and Carmence knit their brows, nodding intermittently. Mr. Gao's temple throbbed. He nodded too. In spite of the signs of a black out, his son was determined to get the screen to turn on. After Ian finished, Mr. Gao stood as though to show Ian to the cell door.

"I had no idea. No idea," Carmence was shaking her head. "You're right, something has to be done."

Mr. Gao shouted some questions at Carmence. She argued back

and they disputed some point in Cantonese.

"He says, why should we believe you?"

"Why would I make this up?" Ian asked. "Don't you think others have a right to know what's going on?"

"He not crazy. He very good person," Carmence said to her family. She began speaking to them in Cantonese. "Something has to be done," she repeated in English. Mr. Gao shook his head, arguing in Cantonese. Carmence sounded passionate. This continued for some time. "I give up." Carmence said, finally, then to Ian, "He stubborn." She stood.

"Ready?" She motioned for her children to join her and Ian beyond the cell doors. The daughter who had shown apprehension about the chaos outside volunteered to stay in the cell with her brother, but Mr. Gao wanted everyone to stay together. The couple argued some more and Carmence began to disappear into the commotion. That's all it took to get Mr. Gao out, after his wife. Determined to keep his family intact, he shouted after his children, who followed him immediately. Mostly they kept Ian company as he tried to wake the others. Every now and then, Carmence would join in, shouting and explaining to confused inmates about their situation. The bolder daughter listened attentively, then began doing the same.

For about an hour, there was mayhem. More and more people were waking up. Now and then Ian noticed a recently-awakened inmate trying to wake the others. At times, there would be resistance between inmates, and scuffling, which Ian began to realize was the counter-resistance.

While watching one of these clashes, Ian thought he recognized Richard, passionately arguing against the waking of other prisoners. He told Carmence he'd be right back and snaked his way over to his colleague.

Richard looked at Ian, but didn't acknowledge him. Instead, he went on shouting at some kids with black leather jackets and colored hair to leave his neighbors in peace.

"These kids are just trying to help, aren't they?" Ian offered in their defense.

"What do you know about it, Ian!" Richard snapped. "They're luddites. They're really screwing things up. Is this the reality you want to live in? How could you prefer this to the tranquility of your Tiburon mansion? You are insane!"

Somehow Richard was awake now, Ian realized. Only he had

crossed over to the wrong side. "What are you doing on this floor?" Ian inquired finally.

Suddenly, loud alarms resounded throughout the building, as though from every floor. Then there was some blaring on loud speakers.

"One of the terrorists is by the west side of the fountain. Repeat, she is by the fountain."

Ian bolted out of the cell and peered over the railing. Far down below he could see armed guards with helmets scuffling by the fountain. A shot rang out and the smoke trail lifted towards him.

"One of the terrorists has been apprehended! Repeat, one of the terrorists has been apprehended!"

Ian felt as though he had fallen through ice to drown in shocking Arctic water beneath.

Carmence and her family had joined him in looking to see what the commotion was.

"What's going on?" Carmence inquired. "You don't look good, Ian. Come, sit down." She tried to get him to go back to her cell.

"That's okay," he said.

"Return to your homes," came the edict from the loud speakers.

"It's not OK. Your face is all white. Like snow. All white." She stood with him, patting his back for a while. Her family stood, waiting, peering at the commotion below. Mr. Gao stared at his polished shoes, shuffling them nervously, then readjusted his gold-framed glasses on his thin nose. Carmence and he exchanged a meaningful look.

"Return to your homes," blared the loud speakers.

"What we do now?" Carmence asked finally.

"I don't know," Ian choked. "Return to our cells."

After helping Carmence's family find their way, he stumbled toward the stairwell. Lights were flashing. Once in the stairwell, he could hear the stairwell door being slammed shut somewhere above him, probably bolted by the guards. He ran toward the nineteenth floor, with his heart in his throat.

"Please not her," he found himself saying through gritted teeth.

"Evacuate the stairwell. It is not safe. For your good, evacuate the stairwell," a guard blared on a speaker system. Ian looked up. He could see the guard peering over the stairs, staring at him. Ian headed toward the door on the next level down. He opened it and shut it and hid along a wall inside the stairwell, where the guard could not see him. He heard other doors opening and closing. Footsteps, running.

"Evacuate the stairwell!" the loudspeaker continued.

Ian began running down the stairs. He made it several more flights before he heard heavy boots coming his way. He looked up and saw three armed guards. He saluted them respectfully and made a beeline for the door. Floor 20 it said.

He cursed under his breath and opened it. A few stragglers wandered around, looking lost. A young bicyclist with long, blonde curls was trying to incite others to break out, followed by a group of three or four other young people. An inmate pointed the cyclist out to the group of armed guards. They turned and headed toward the bicyclist and his cadre.

"This is a lock down," one bellowed on a load-speaker. "Return to your homes."

Ian headed in the opposite direction at a fast clip.

"Hey, young man with the briefcase," one of the guards called after him. Ian turned a corner and began sprinting toward the stairwell on the other end.

"Young man! Stop or we'll shoot!" one of the guards announced through a speaker. Ian had his hand on the stairwell door when he heard a shot. Rather than turn, he ducked into the stairwell and bolted down the stairs. He was all right. He heard the stairwell door open and the guards clomping down the stairs. He clung to the wall as far out of sight as he could.

"Robin, Robin, Robin," was all he could think. He opened the door silently on the 19th floor and galloped toward her cell. He listened for the door to open again and the guards to burst forth, but they didn't. Perhaps he had lost them. He turned the corner and his heart settled down from his throat back into his chest. He passed a few people marching back to their cells.

"Don't go back!" an older man in jeans was shouting at them. "This is our chance! They've had us captive here for years making oodles of money off our sweat!"

When Ian approached Robin's cell, he could hear sobbing. Was it her neighbors? Someone else who knew her, he thought. The sobbing grew louder. It was coming from inside her cell. He ran up to the door.

"Robin! Please—" he cried out, peering into the cell. Someone was hiding in the closet behind a pile of clothes obstructing a direct view. The crying stopped.

"Robin? It's Ian!" he cried. He noticed he was literally holding his breath and exhaled. Suddenly, he realized his mistake. What if it was a trap and the guards, having apprehended Robin, were inside her cell waiting for him now?!

A flash of blonde and red hair poked out. Ian braced himself for the sight of a gunshot wound. Next, he anticipated his own skin and blood aflame, then perhaps, the fatal bullet.

"Robin?"

To his relief, she did emerge. He was beside himself when he saw her run to the door.

"You shouldn't be here," she whispered. Then she opened the door and threw herself into his arms.

He looked cautiously beyond her shoulder. To his relief, they were alone.

"Angelina," Robin said and began wailing again. "They got Angelina, bastards!"

XXXII

PREDICTABLY, LOCKDOWNS FOLLOWED each alarm incident. After a good night's sleep, many inmates and guards had little memory of what had taken place. Management tried to counter this with guard trainings and adding more top level guards. Many inmates who were still living virtual lives complained about the added layer of security.

On the opposite side of the fence, the counter-resistance demanded more protection against the growing terrorist threat. Their fears were not unfounded. More and more people were managing to remain awake and adding to the resistance. Carmence Gao was among these. She lived a few floors from Rickey. Now with Angelina gone, Rickey took some relief from his grief by dedicating his spare time to training Carmence in the movement's latest strategies. Rickey had shown Carmence in principal how to put a group of guards into REM, but he could not convince her to try it out on a real situation. With all the added security, it was easy to find a target. He spotted three high level guards with dark sunglasses at the end of the corridor. It was past dinner time and the commuter crowd had thinned.

"There's your target, Carmence. It's all set. Just scan them and run the face recognition app right here."

"Oh, but they'll see me, don't you think?" Carmence hesitated.

"We're in a good position, right in front of a screen. They have to look at it to see us." Rickey stared at the guards. Then he recognized the tall, bald elegant African American guard Angelina had claimed was friendly trailing a bit behind the other two. "Carmence, excuse me. Can I see the ME a sec?" He punched at the screen frantically until it chimed. "It's a match. Look of all these, I think it's this one. Reginald N. Perry! There, you capt him, Carmence, group number 103,678-N! Check one of the other ones to confirm they belong to the same group. It's done by shifts, so unless there's something unusual going on—"

"Oh, is this a match?" Carmence asked with some excitement. "I get it now. Yes! Same group. 103,678-N, right?"

"Good. Select them, copy them, then the pop down Rawtooth menu. No, no. Pop-down menu. The Rawtooth box."

"I know, but I don't see where."

The guards were now within several feet of them. Carmence was too busy to notice. "Activate REM, send, done!"

"The screen!" shouted Ian, "Not the guard, the screen!"

Carmence aimed the ME at the screen.

"Can I help you find a good a channel, Miss?"

Carmence looked up and recognized the wide nose and greasy receding hairline she had scanned now aiming a conventional gun at her heart.

"That ME belongs to Angelina Bella, correct?" the officer said.

Carmence remained speechless. Slowly she put her hands up, still holding onto the ME.

"Thank you. Mind if I take this? It's not going to work on us, what she taught you to do, isn't that right, Reg?" The officer glanced at Panther as he reached up for the phone. He placed it in his pocket, then he waved his gun at Rickey, who complied by raising his hands in the air as well.

"Shit! That's what talking to a cop gets you," Rickey muttered under his breath, scowling at Panther.

The greasy-headed guard motioned the pair toward the opposite end of the hall, toward the elevator. As they walked, he turned his chin up toward the screen as though what CNN had to say was suddenly more important. The third guard followed suit.

Carmence looked at Rickey. He nodded imperceptibly, turned the corners of his mouth ever so slightly into a smile.

Carmence cleared her throat. "Sir, would you mind lending me your MEphone to call my husband to pick me up? Someone just walked away with my purse!" Carmence said sublimating all her anxiety into the fictitious scenario.

"Certainly." Panther slid the phone from his colleagues hand and handed Carmence back the phone with a wink.

"Good job. I think that's enough training for one night," Rickey said patting Carmence on the back. They both burst into nervous laughter as they headed back to their cells.

Suddenly he stopped and turned back looking at the guards still intently watching the screen. "One more thing, Carmence," Rickey added. "So see that black, bald dude there? Watch out for him. I think he's been the high security leak for our side."

The next action was scaled back and scheduled for Carmence's floor. The proximity of the counter-resistance prompted Robin to urge Ian to stay in his cell for the next month, but he refused.

"But they must know that we're counting on your low security status for all those actions," Robin begged Ian.

"The chances of that mob finding me in a building with this many people is pretty, slim," he insisted. "They can get me on my way back from work... anytime, really. If they were that intent on it, they would have done it by now, don't you think?"

"Not necessarily."

"I'll make sure I'm not alone."

It was 5:34 Wednesday evening, when Ian emerged from the elevator after work on the 25th floor. Within minutes, he heard several loud cracks, followed by shouts and cheers of "Happy Birthday!"

He walked toward the designated stairwell, shouting to wake the commuters, rattling bars. He spotted Carmence and Rickey a few feet ahead doing the same. They had been joined by others he'd never seen before. Rickey was issuing instructions to Carmence. His eyes were still bereft of their former spark, Ian reflected, his face deadened, as though his soul had been extracted, leaving behind just a shell of a human being.

"Oh no, it's real! I knew it! It's real!" came an agonized cry through the alarm. Several people were hunched down, sobbing. "What are we supposed to do?!" one man wailed.

Carmence rushed over and began explaining to him what was taking place.

"You're right. This did happen to you before. You been in jail for years...." Carmence began to deconstruct reality for the men. Rickey and the others in the group continued on to wake more prisoners, turning the corner. Ian smiled as he watched the men begin to follow Carmence.

He decided to work on the opposite end of the corridor. A man was crouched and sobbing.

"I want to kill myself," he said. Ian leaned down to console him.

"Kill him! This is the one! Kill the motherf—!!!" someone shouted. Ian looked up in time to recognize the two blonde men who had assaulted him earlier. They were joined by over a dozen others.

"It's all his fault!" they screamed to everyone on the floor.

"He's one of the biggest reasons we're here and not back in our homes. He took it all away. Get him!"

Ian could not believe his eyes. The man he'd been consoling stood up and looked at him with a mixture of confusion and anger. He took several steps back and joined the crowd. More people were approaching, standing over Ian with their arms crossed, some rolling up their sleeves.

The blonde, beefy guy with the bristle hair cut repeated his case to the crowd. He became impassioned. "Aren't you ashamed of yourself, creating so much misery? Do these people look happy to you? Don't they deserve to live their quiet, decent, contented lives? How can you live with yourself!" he screamed.

"Hey take it easy," Ian heard a man in a plaid flannel shirt address Bristle-Head. Suddenly he recognized the man in the flannel shirt as Richard.

"Richard! Help me, buddy! Tell your friend—"

Richard shook his head. "He has a point, Ian. You can't blame us for being angry."

"That's right!" someone protested.

"He shouldn't live with himself!" someone else shouted.

"That's right!" the crowed began to yell.

"Hey wait!" he heard Richard say, as he tried to hold Bristle-Head's arm back.

That was one of the last things he remembered before a crowd fell upon him with briefcases, and blows. The last face he saw before he sank into the hollow, ringing white noise of unconsciousness was Panther's. Was he trying to break up the mob, like Richard, or was he egging them on?

XXXIII

THE BLADE GLIDED skillfully over Ian's face, carefully averting the area by the left ear where the skin was still healing from the removed stitches. Ian grasped the razor as firmly as he could in his right hand with thumb and three fingers, so as to avoid further injury. It was these sorts of tasks that were so difficult to grow accustomed to without the use of a little finger. Never had he imagined how vital the flange really was.

The pain had been so acute when it had been crushed and severed from his palm, it was as though the circuit that connected all his nerves had shorted, and he passed out instantly. After the accidental amputation was re-cut and sewn closer to the palm, the wound was not treated with antibiotics and Ian nearly died from the fever. Had it not been for Robin secretly rallying the other workers, they would have let him die in the hospital from "complications." While Richard was among those coming to Ian's defense, Robin had remained somewhat skeptical about his sincerity.

Richard had also been one of the first to visit Ian in the hospital wing of the jail once he was out of intensive care. He had stood along the edges of the room, not looking at Ian, but examining everything along the periphery, the stainless steel sink and faucets, plastic drinking pitcher, the gold curtain separating the next patient. He didn't notice Ian sinking deeper inside his sheets as though Richard was going to suddenly lash out and grab the bandaged hand that was tractioned like a piñata from the center of the bed.

"I'm so sorry, Ian," Richard said finally. He sat on the bed and took Ian's good hand in his, assessing the appendage that hung from the cord between them. "I tried—" Richard offered awkwardly.

"I know you did," Ian said. "You actually tried to stop them, didn't you?"

"Absolutely!"

Silence.

Ian spoke up. "Do you know who did it? Were they friends of yours?"

"Allies maybe, not friends," Richard corrected. His brows were knit and the vein in his temple pulsed with discomfort. He stared at Ian's hand inquisitively.

"They couldn't save my little finger."

"Let's see, that's your right hand."

Ian nodded sadly.

"Obviously there's no excuse for that kind of violence," Richard said finally. He changed the subject and they talked about the weather and office politics in Ian's absence. Tracie had suffered some burns in a terrible car accident.

Ian felt a twinge of guilt for his feelings of both sadness and satisfaction at the news. To change the subject, he almost asked after Robin, but stopped himself. He shifted to get some water and felt an electric surge of pain in his right hand and cringed. He cleared his throat. "Do you know—did anything ever happen to the guys who did this to me? Or are they still at large?"

Richard shook his head. He remained silent, staring at the floor. It occurred to Ian he was not saying "no," but was shaking his head instead in disapproval. "What about what you and your group did to us?" he retorted. He shook his head more resolutely and looked hard at Ian. "Have you thought of that? Have you thought of the kind of life you've imprisoned us in? What's the consequence for that?"

"Richard, I didn't do that to you. The owners did," Ian almost whispered.

With that Richard backed out of the curtain that represented Ian's room. "Gotta go, Ian. Hope you get better. Keep taking your Vicodin. See you at work."

The day before Ian was discharged from the hospital, his bedside phone rang, waking him from his sleep with such startling volume, there was no confusing dream and reality. He had been especially sensitive to the ring tone, not having heard it in such close proximity in over a year.

"Ian? Ian, Darling! Is that really you?" The voice was slightly quaky, but elegant. It felt like a hand, a lifeline reaching out to rescue him from the other side of a chasm.

"Mom! Mom!" Ian choked. "It's me, Ian."

"Are you all right? How are you, Darling?"

"I'm getting better, Mom. I lost a finger, but it's not life-threatening or anything."

"Oh no... Ian." He could tell his mother had begun crying and tried to console her. After much silence she managed a single word, "How?"

"It's a long story and I can't go into it now, Mom. Mom you have to listen to me. I've been in prison. That's why I haven't been able to reach you."

"Oh, golly! I don't understand. Let me sit down."

"Mom, are you okay?"

"I'm fine. What's—I don't understand...."

"I'm in prison, Mom. It's not as bad as you think at all. Relax. I got placed there for standing up for my principles. It's okay, Mom. They're treating me as well as they treat you."

"I don't understand. But if you say so. But why?"

"Mom, for standing up for my principles, Mom."

"Good for you, I guess. I know you did the right thing. You always do in the end," His mother laughed through her tears.

"I can't talk about it right this minute. But trust me."

"Of course I trust you, Ian. No, no, don't say these things on the phone. Not if you're in jail.

"Do you know when you're getting out? Of jail, I mean."

"No I don't, Mom. I don't."

"Wait! Where can I reach you? What jail?" She became frantic. She began sobbing again.

"I'm not sure, Mom. Mom if you ever find yourself in a similar situation, just know there's a movement afoot to change all that... to get you out. That you won't be there long. Just have faith."

"I don't know what you're talking about Ian, but it's ok," his mother laughed unexpectedly. "I love you, son," she said in earnest. " Just know I love you." Then to Ian's surprise she added, "I'm proud of you, Ian. Wherever you are. Please remember, I'm proud of you. Promise?"

Now, many months later, back in his cell, Ian was guarded very carefully. The answer to Richard's question regarding the consequence for having woken him, Ian thought, was that the state had declared Ian a terrorist, perhaps guilty of treason, a high security prisoner. He was escorted to and from work and to and from the Atrium restaurant at 12 noon for lunch. The escorts came wearing the masks of "new coworkers" or "friends" from Facelift®, but they spared no time in letting Ian know exactly what the consequences would be, should he not follow their suggestions: twenty-four hour brightly lit solitary without work privileges; excruciating interrogations.

Yet Ian's spirits were the best they had ever been—at least since the old days when he had been content in his delusion. Who could blame those poor sods like Richard, he thought, for hating those who burst their bubble.

"You can't blame us for being angry. Have you thought of the kind of life you've imprisoned us in?" Ian tried to shake the memory of Richard from his mind.

Besides those who reviled him, a surprising number were equally as indebted to him for having dragged them out of Plato's cave of ignorance into the light of truth, though this truth in itself was hideous to behold. It was they who were now carrying the movement forward, along with Robin, Rickey, Carmence and the countless others he had met in his new community, since he could not. And the rest—those that lay in between—they were indifferent, like sheep to be led by whosoever claimed the reins of power.

But it was Ian's growing interdependence on his new community that filled him with unparalleled joy. His new friends kept him abreast of the latest developments in the resistance community; two schools had been liberated. One reclaimed school had been renamed Lakeside Elementary, resurrecting one of the first occupied schools in the nation that had been recaptured by the owners, then destroyed. Artists were already busy painting the second school with the Chiapas mural that had been burned down and reproduced on the City Lights Bookstore wall, Robin proudly announced.

Ian couldn't deny that his joy at all this news was somewhat mixed up with his growing infatuation and love for Robin. But he had never felt so needed, so loved. As though his existence on earth actually mattered and made a difference. And this knowledge, this new sense of purpose made all the discomforts worthwhile.

For how long, though, he wondered. Long enough to get over his addiction to his devices, what Robin chided were his vices, like the Waterfront and Saint Francis?

Sadly, Ian's thoughts returned to his friend. Or former friend, he wondered. Now that Ian was better, Richard had been avoiding him and had been quite aloof during their few interactions. It was clear that, while he did not believe Ian deserved the death penalty for waking him, he would never forgive him for depriving him of his happiness. After all, absent Ian's sense of purpose and community, and now stripped of his luxuries, what was really left for Richard?

You wish well on your friends. You want nothing more than their happiness. While I'm ultimately not responsible for Richard's suffering, without my help he would still be happy. Can I ever forgive myself for that? Regardless of the lives we're enriching.

"There is nothing more precious than a single life, a single heart-beat," he kept hearing his mother and her mother before her repeat.

How he missed her. *"Please remember, I'm proud of you. Promise?"*

He had to let go or he'd go nuts. Whatever prison she actually resided in, there were others who would attempt to wake her. He had to have faith in their movement. For now, perhaps until her dying day, he was just going to have to let go, he would have to learn to live with the uncertainty.

Then, almost as though she could read his mind, he received a letter with a newspaper clipping with his mother's handwriting: "Thought you might need to know this. Never forget how much I love you and how proud I am of you." The clip was a study about happiness. A year after winning the lottery, winners were just as happy as they had been before their good fortune, or equally as miserable, depending on their disposition prior to winning. The same was true of paraplegics: a year after their accidents, they were just as happy as they were before their misfortune or just as unhappy. Circumstances had less effect than did the propensity for joy.

XXXIV

AT 8:12, THE time the morning commute was in full swing, the alarms sounded with such intensity, Ian had trouble gathering his thoughts. He had finally fallen into deep sleep near dawn and now had trouble rising. Within seconds, a cold rain fell down on his head, before he could run for cover under the counter. Water dripped from his lashes and soaked his running pants. The sprinkler system in the entire building must have been activated.

Then an odd thing happened. All the lights shut off. The opaque milky balconies turned clear, exposing the cell bars to the cells opposite the chasm. All this would be certain to wake more of them, incite far more to join the rebellion.

The interactive screens blared orders in unison: "Terrorists have set fire to this building. Evacuate all quarters! Convene downstairs in lobby!"

"Fuck that!" Ian heard some people yelling. It took a superhuman effort not to grin and risk guilt by association. Ian wondered whether or not the resistance had resorted to a real fire this time.

Others were screaming, "Where are we?"

"What is this? Let me out!"

"What am I doing here?!!"

Ian threw on a suit. Now for the first time, the bars on his cell made sense in order to stop an imminent rebellion, Ian realized, as he stepped in line with those inmates who had chosen to obediently follow the directions to evacuate to the lobby. Ian expected to see someone outside his cell waiting to escort him, and happily found none. Apparently the escort was badly-needed elsewhere. It seemed as though more than half the prisoners were headed in the opposite direction as the orders, some banding together to huddle inside a stairwell, even a cell.

"What are we doing here? Who's in charge?!!!" a man in a soaked suit and tie screamed.

"I demand to see a lawyer! You're going to have quite a lawsuit!" a heavy woman in a blue and white flowered dress and pearl necklace yelled.

"Let's just bust down the place," others were suggesting.

"You're going to regret it, believe me. I've known this was like this for some time," a female voice fell on deaf ears.

A crowd of angry people charged past Ian. "This way!"

A terrible lock down of all prisoners would clearly follow what seemed like an inevitable rebellion. Doors would be permanently sealed with the pretext of keeping the terrorists from escaping.

The elevators were filled beyond capacity. Fortunately, thanks to the first large-scale U.S. terrorist attack earlier that century that hit two New York skyscrapers, the evacuation protocol favored the inmates on the upper floors. Ian reminded himself that because the society was not a traditional police state, the number of top-level guards would be insufficient, although they did have an army of weapons at their disposal.

Ian managed to squeeze through the crowd in the elevator toward the panel of buttons. A guard was trying to block his access, but with so many bodies, Ian was able to press 19 fairly easily without the guard's acknowledgment. Ian stared up at the illuminated numbers. 22, 21, 20, 19, 18. The doors did not open. In this chaos it would be difficult to find Robin. Out of desperation, Ian managed to push the alarm button. The elevator jolted to a stop on the fourteenth floor. Ian jammed the "open" button and pushed his way out. The guard went after him, but was immediately pushed aside by the crowd in a mad panic to access the elevators. Ian made his way to the stairwell.

Up he climbed, his heart racing either from sheer fear or from physical activity, he didn't know which. Regardless, never had racing up five flights of stairs seemed so effortless.

Ian emerged on the 19th floor stairwell where he and Robin had agreed to meet in such an emergency, and glanced around for signs of her. Finding none, he crouched down on the hall carpet and waited.

"What's going on?"

Ian spun around at the sound of Rickey's voice. He was standing next to Mary Liz and apparently had come with a large group.

Mary Liz twisted the water out of her long, wavy hair. A tear welled up in one of her large brown eyes and cascaded down her wet cheeks. She wiped it and busied herself with introductions, as though nothing had happened.

Ian looked at Rickey apprehensively.

"She just misses Angelina," Rickey sighed. His light brown eyes flickered with pain.

At least his eyes don't look deadened anymore, Ian thought to himself.

Another crowd of people descended the stairwell. The tail end of the crowd stopped and made its way onto the floor. Ian counted about twenty more people, of various ethnicities.

Suddenly, he noticed a bald African American guard with dark glasses staring in his direction. The guard was walking toward him, straining over the heads of the intervening crowd to keep Ian in his line of vision, it seemed to him. It was also now clear to Ian that this was Panther. No sooner did he recognize him, than he disappeared from view.

Then, Ian felt an arm on his shoulder. He spun around, his gut in his throat.

"Hey," Robin said, forcing a smile. She was wearing a backpack-purse, which seemed to be the only dry article on her. More people descended the stairs and poured onto the floor.

One woman pushed her way toward Ian, calling for him. He walked toward the sound.

"Carmence!"

They embraced for a while. "My daughter too!" she beamed.

The group, now numbering close to 40 stood, waiting. Motion on the stairwell stopped. One of the young men walked back toward the stairs, looking up.

"I think that's all of us," he said. People edged toward the stairs again, extending their hands. Ian took Robin and a young Asian man's hand. They began making a slow descent down the stairs, allowing other, more panic-stricken inmates to pass them.

At last, the group emerged in the lobby. They continued linking hands. Resisting the motion herding them toward the center, they managed to snake their way along the walls toward a source of natural light: a side exit. Several times they had to stop and wait as one of the group was broken off.

"Ma! My mom!" Ian heard Carmence's daughter screaming.

"We've lost Carmence!" someone a male voice shouted. "Stay with us! Stay with us," others were calling to her daughter.

Ian felt lead sink from his belly toward his ankles. "I've got to go!" Ian said.

Robin held firmly to his hand. The Asian man next to Ian explained that Rickey and two other people were already designated to find people in Carmence's situation. The linked hands began pulling forward, toward the light.

Robin explained. "Rickey has Angelina's MEphone with the most frequent access codes."

Ian was relieved to hear the guards hadn't gotten a hold of it. Then a sad thought occurred to him. "Is that why they got her? The GPS?"

"Actually, the opposite. It's because she gave it to someone else," Robin panted as they walked on. "Working on a weaker spot. She thought they'd need it more."

"I need to find Carmence," Ian shook his head. "I'm the one who got her involved in all this—"

"There's a plan in place to help her. Don't abandon the plan now, babe," Robin said. She brought his linked hand toward her other hand which was holding the MEphone in an attempt to aim it at the screen. "It's a good one."

"Hold it. Freeze right there!" Ian recognized the large guard with the lumpy, stubbly head, broom mustache and icy, blue eyes. He was joined by several other guards who had also removed their sunglasses. To his dismay, Ian recognized Panther. He must have spotted them on Robin's floor, then alerted the other guards to the group. They were onto their plan.

"Hi!" Ian said weekly, looking at Panther.

Lumpy Potato-Head pointed a tazer at Ian. Before he could blink, Robin's linked hands were going up above her head. Instinctively, both she and Ian aimed the hidden mobile at the nearest screen.

Unfortunately the camera and flash function had accidentally been triggered in the shuffle.

A shot was fired in response. "Drop the object in your hands!" Potato-Head demanded.

Ian dropped his hands and fell to the floor, hoping to buy more time.

"Freeze!" Potato-Head screamed. Suddenly, his eyes began blinking stupidly.

Robin looked inquisitively at Ian. "We didn't do that," she noted.

Ian shrugged. "Someone else in the group!" He stood back up with the others. The human chain of rebels slinked past the guards toward the side exit. There they encountered two more guards, one female; most were involved in trying to contain the prisoners in the lobby. The guards instructed them to sit.

"What?" shouted Robin, suddenly cognizant that these guards belonged to a different user group and would require capting. She spun away from the group, turned off the flash and snapped some pics of the chunky female guard with short, dull brown hair. Next, crouching with her back to the guards, she huddled over her ME, scrolling through the various images and group numbers.

"What's she doing?" The female guard raced toward Robin with her gun aimed at her back. "Hey! Put your arms in the air and turn around!"

"What's wrong with your security guards over there? The inmates are all escaping!" A bearded man in the counter-resistance shouted angrily as he helplessly watched other prisoners, who had discovered the drugged-like state of their captors, heading toward the exits.

"Back up!" The remaining guard at the side exit screamed at his female colleague before sprinting toward the commotion.

Once her colleague was out of view, the female guard turned back to Robin.

"Hand over that ME right now, little lady."

Robin held up her palms with the ME. The female cop examined the phone. "You're under arrest, she said, handcuffing Robin to the exit door handle. "This should serve as a deterrent to your friends. We'll just wait right here."

Ian stood motionless, staring. Suddenly he felt a heat ray braise his back and cried out in pain. "We meet again, my friend," said a husky, familiar voice. "Keep moving."

"Toward—"

"That's right, Ian. Right toward your sweetheart, Robin Banks."

Ian's back was throbbing from the brief exposure to the heat ray. For some reason, the fear sparked the horrifying image of Ethel Rosenberg in the electric chair falsely accused of nearly treason the previous century, plumes of smoke rising from her head.

Panther said something to the female guard and she handed him Robin's ME. He grinned and flipped through the screens. Robin glanced at Ian with a heart-wrenching look that made him want to gather her up in his arms.

The female guard stumbled away from them and began staring at a screen near one of the exits, suddenly mesmerized by a screen game show.

Two more guards joined Panther and began talking. One of them scanned an electronic device along Robin's cuffs, unlocking them. "Here," Panther said, and handed Robin back her ME. "I assume this is yours."

"Thank you." Robin cleared her throat, looking at the guards with bemusement. "Why are you doing this?'

The one who had unlocked her, smiled. "Well I know I'm not an owner, so whose side do you think I'm on?"

Ian almost choked on an unexpected burst of laughter, so overwhelming was the sense of relief.

"Well?" Panther said, opening the doors wide for Robin, Ian and the crowd that had formed behind them. "What are you waiting for? Isn't this what Angelina wanted?"

Robin and Ian exchanged another look of incredulity. Robin beamed as she watched more members of her group pour past the remaining stupefied female guard, through the doors, into the sunlight. She began laughing so hard she could barely move. "Thank you, Reginald!" She laughed even harder at the fact that she knew his name.

"No prob, Robin," he winked. "You all would have gotten out there eventually. Most folks are just walking out. The actual physical barriers to your freedom have never been as great as those imposed by the mind."

As the mass of nearby prisoners felt the draft from the open doors and beheld the others fleeing, they burst forth like a dam, pushing their way toward the exit to their freedom.

XXXV

THE MECHANICAL WHIR of police helicopter blades could be heard in the distance. Not an hour after the Embarcadero Multiplex jailbreak, Ian, and Robin and their co-conspirators were dashing madly toward Market St. The plan was for the group to disperse and meet up May 1st, a week after the jailbreak, at the crest of Dolores Park, overlooking the City. The May 1st plan was being mirrored by other jail-broken inmates in cities all over the world. Similar May 1st actions had gathered momentum over the last few decades. Word spread like fire to the freed conscripts.

Shots and screaming broke out as the guards tried to round up the tail end of those who had managed to escape. Inevitably there would be a death toll. Robin and Ian had argued about such potential casualties when she had first informed him at the Saint Francis Hotel of the strategy for escape.

"But what kind of life do we have anyway—those of us who've woken up?" Ian had argued. "I've been living like the walking dead since I found out. I'm ready, I think, to risk dying to begin living."

"That's you," Robin said flatly. "An entire state of prisons in the Midwest rebelled two years ago and ultimately lost. They disappeared down the memory hole, and the governor made the lives of those who had woken up living hell. There were some gains in strategy, which we're using now. Change is a long process. Like I said, we probably won't see victory in our lifetimes. Can you live with that? You willing to die for *that*? For me it's a game of resistance *and* endurance."

By endurance, Ian knew she meant trying to squeeze the most joy out of whatever pleasure there was to be had on the outside. *A true Stoic in the Greek sense*, he thought with a tinge of envy.

"Endurance but with a healthy amount of hedonism, right?" he smirked.

"Of course! But I don't want to party alone. Isn't it all about helping as many others as you can to join you in—"

"...in this ephemeral... journey?" Ian interjected.

"Dance!" Robin exclaimed, waving her arms above her head. Celebration! Wonder! ...Life! Why focus on 'ephemeral'?"

"Because we have six billion years left at most. By then our beloved sun will—" Ian flared his fingers like a firework "—begin its trillion year process to extinguish itself. It'll swell to a red giant, consume

Mercury and Venus and fry us, though humanity will have gone extinct long before, thank goodness."

Robin laughed, shaking her head. "Ian! What are you saying?"

"You haven't heard? Sorry to break it to you, babe, but in about a half a billion years, give or take, when the sun is ten percent hotter, as our CO_2 diminishes, along with plant life, animals begin going extinct, the largest first. Optimistic predictions give us three billion years, 2.8 I think I heard, when the sun is forty percent brighter and the oceans are all boiling, or gone along with even cockroaches and bacteria."

"But what are you saying, Ian?" Robin repeated, laughing. "We shouldn't try to stop global warming then? The greenhouse effect will happen anyway when the sun is in its death throes? Screw the resistance? Are you giving up?"

Ian chuckled. "I'm just saying none of the other insanity beyond this moment will really matter. It'll all be gone. Socrates. Shakespeare… Some predictions have all the stars going extinct eventually, leaving nothingness, like before the big bang."

"Sappho, Emma Goldman… Galeano, Chomsky… oh no!" Robin inserted wistfully. "Probably there would be another big bang, don't you think? Maybe this is the trillionth one."

"Possibly… But that doesn't help Marx and Adam Smith… Devoured by the collision of the Andromeda and Milky Way in four billion years. Humbling, isn't it? Their life's work reduced to stardust, our origins."

"But don't you think our heroes and loved ones would continue living in the cosmic consciousness?" Robin proposed.

"The end of the universe could also put an end to that."

"Momentarily, until the next one is formed. Maybe there have already been a trillion Earths, a trillion Martin Luther King Jrs., a trillion Ians, just like maybe some cells on this planet have existed before?"

Ian smiled. He leaned over the table and took her face in his hands for a long, sensual kiss.

"There's something to be said about the moment," Robin said smiling, when they finally paused. "Regardless of the fate of the universe. When I think of the inevitable death of our sun, or all suns, I'm left with… moments, as you say…." She gazed out of the window, up at the sky. "It makes me realize what a miracle life is. How impossible it is to be here, looking out this window, thinking these thoughts. How we can't waste this gift." She looked at Ian and their gaze locked. Quickly, she turned again toward Union Square, her eyes catching a figure painfully pushing a shopping cart full of belongings uphill. "But also, I want the satisfaction of having helped others enjoy this 'ephemeral' dance of life. I want to feel good about how I lived my life, with integrity and convictions. That to me is real freedom. At least then you can meet the end feeling better about it. Don't you think?"

As Ian heard the shots, he longed for the luxurious days of philosophizing and conspiring with Robin. The reality now was chilling and far more tragic than he could have imagined. Their victory at the jail, the uprisings in other jails, might not amount to anything tangible in his day. While he ran, he remembered Robin's words reminiscent of those of his mother and grandmother: "A single life is the most sacred, wondrous thing in the universe." Now, one of those sacred lives, Robin's closest friend, Angelina, was gone and Rickey and Carmence were missing.

Thanks to some ingenious hacking, Robin managed to tangle her and Angelina's identities together in the Fatherland Security database so that a retinal scan of Robin would produce Angelina's information current to the year prior to her passing. As part of the plan, members of the resistance had exchanged personal information and passwords for this purpose. This had bought Robin some time. It seemed apparent that Ian was still off the radar, since he had not yet been apprehended. However, just how long the couple would be able to remain undetected underground remained uncertain.

Given the fate of the Midwest prison activists, the Embarcadero Multiplex resistance had decided that once an attempt had been made to awaken the entire prison, it would be too dangerous for any of the plan's conspirators to remain on the inside.

Police helicopters began circling overhead to put down the terrorist rebellion. *How many more of us will now be caught, tortured to find out our plans and allies?* Ian pondered. He wondered sadly about whether he'd ever see Carmence and Rickey again. Even if Intelligence learned about the plans to reprogram countless MEphones to hack into the system, what could be done? Recall all the MEphones and bring down Bear-TT and its stock-holders? *Wouldn't it be great,* Ian mused, *if they had to shut everything off?!*

More likely the guards and police would be sent to the hospitals for new implants. The rebels had planned to weed out infiltrators at their next meeting by rolling in a big screen and triggering police into REM sleep with their hacked and jail-broken mobiles. At least the resistance strategies were beginning to give screens and MEs a bad rep, Robin had jested. When she went on about liberating the masses from their insidious drug, Ian accused her of being a Luddite. She was quick to retort that they wouldn't have escaped without technology, without the ME. "Obviously it's a powerful tool," she stated flatly. "What I'm saying is it's not good to get addicted to anything."

"Except me," Ian laughed, kissing her neck.

"I said, thing, not person," Robin exhaled her laughter.

What most worried Ian was that the size and force of the counter-resistance had been underestimated. As Robin said, the work was cut out for them; it could take generations to turn the tide. It had been understood by Ian, Robin and the rest of the rebels in their community that, like their predecessors, they would seek lives on the outside if possible, from where they would continue to agitate and awaken prisoners, both inside and outside the jails. Those who had recently awoken during the last uprising would need guidance and support.

As they had for decades, the members of the movement would continue to disappear into the many empty flats that abounded in the city; squatting in the vacant vacation homes of the owners; using a barter system to get by, they'd announce themselves as house-sitters, carpenters, painters, plumbers, visiting professors, school-teachers, artists and pet sitters... They'd continue running their underground schools, cultural centers, bookstores, movie theatres and cafés. They'd merge into the morning and evening commute, like the other inmates and occasional owners, becoming as invisible as they had been for centuries upon centuries, waiting like bamboo roots to pop up again in fertile soil.

Robin's squat idea for her and Ian was a condo formerly owned by the daughter of a former San Francisco Poet-Laureate, Jack Hirschman. The political rebel had been a poetic genius in the old order. His books had lined City Lights' shelves and he had held court in a bar called Specs in Saroyan Alley. A patron had subsidized his meager existence in a second story SRO in the heart of North Beach, then after his death, his daughter had bought the condo and preserved it as a historical curio until she could no longer afford the Home Owner Association fees. It was then snatched up by a speculator in Japan who expected to travel to

San Francisco, yet never had.

Robin led Ian up Broadway to Columbus, past the strip joints and hookers peddling their wares in broad daylight. At the light, they overheard a tall blonde woman and a brunette with ironed hair that was beginning to frizz from the fog.

"But can he slip it in and out?" the brunette asked.

"Yeh."

"But how?"

"The rubber holds it in."

"Things never change," Ian scoffed.

"What do you think they're talking about?" Robin asked, grinning.

"What do you think?"

"Not. They're taking about their MEphones and belt clips. See—" Robin passed the two young women. They were both holding their MEphones, examining them. "Remind you of any other obsessive people?"

Ian patted Robin on the rear and they laughed as they proceeded right on Columbus, up the hill. After several blocks, Robin led Ian through a narrow doorway between two restaurants and up some stairs. Instead of a card slot, the door had an old fashioned brass door knob. While all the condominiums had been expanded to include state-of-the-art bathrooms and kitchens, this one had been left intact as a historical monument. Robin inserted a small stick she had picked up into the key hole and worked it until the door opened.

The walls of the flat were covered with psychedelic swirls and streaks of paint reminiscent of Jackson Pollock. A few bold abstract canvases, with hues of much black and white, hung on the walls as well. There was a small porcelain sink, still stained with paint and urine, since the bathroom was still a long jaunt down the hall.

There was a small shelf that served as a desk, a twin size mattress, an easel displaying an unfinished abstract painting, and cans of dried up paint, the brushes still in them.

"Now doesn't this blow the Saint Francis out of the water?!" Robin boasted.

"Well, at least it's real! Like the sand, the sea…." Ian offered.

"It's ours for now. So it has to be the best!" Robin winked.

They gathered each other up and kissed for what seemed like hours, somehow managing to remove their clothes without seeming to untangle themselves from each other. They could hear rain softly patting the sills. They made love into the dawn, then the next day, until finally hunger drove them out into the night in search of a community garden, or underground barter co-op café.

The rain had stopped, and it was so late, only one or two screens still blared. Mostly the streets were silent. The red and green lights of the traffic signals were reflected on the wet pavement. Now and then a car would pass, hissing water under its tires. It was wondrous to hear this sound, Ian reflected, as though for the first time; glorious to be walking the streets without listening to his MEphone jabber or play music, without hearing stores calling out his name announcing special enticing offers; magnificent to be with so much silence.

Even Caffé Puccini was closed. They walked past City Lights. They could hear Vesuvio taking a last call. When they got to Ko & Company Dry Cleaning, Ian noticed a light. Carmence was ironing clothes behind the counter!

Ian and Robin tapped excitedly on the glass. Carmence motioned for them to be quiet.

"Family asleep," she whispered, unlocking the glass door and motioning behind her to the other rooms. "I got a microwave and hot plate, and now we have everything here. More comfy than the jail," she laughed in whispers. "No one suspects. Cops and guards walk by all day long, come in, do business, smile and go again." She giggled quietly like a little child staying up past her bed time, trying to contain her laughter so it wouldn't wake her husband and kids.

"That's right. You never made the high security list. They would just think you're working as usual," Robin laughed.

"Oh you know, I've seen your friend, Rickey, too. Rickey and Mary Liz have both stopped by," Carmence grinned.

"Mary Liz? Rickey?" Robin bubbled. "How are they?!"

"Pretty good. Together now. Mary Liz and Rickey, I mean. Mary Liz, I think, is living at that place on the Embarcadero. That really nice one across from the water with the geraniums in the window boxes— With the cafe—"

"No! Delancy Street?" Robin asked.

"Yup, that is the one. She said she won the lottery to live there. She even has a view of the water! Can you believe it? A real view of the bay! Imagine!"

"How did she score that?" Robin's voice cracked as she smiled with feigned jealousy.

"I don't know. I think Mary Liz is working on a movie for Delancy Street. Educational. Something like that. Rickey is staying there. Of course, in the living room."

"Good for him!" Ian laughed.

"I hope it works out for him," Robin sighed.

They talked in whispers for a good hour, catching each other up on events and making plans. But since Robin and Ian didn't have the heart to impose on Carmence's hospitality, Ian's grumbling stomach urged them onward.

Along Montgomery at California Street, the sparkles in the sidewalk caught the street lights, looking like leaping particles of fairy dust. Everything to Ian seemed so vivid, so colorful and alive. He had never felt so immersed in life, his senses so full.

Just like hundreds of other rebels, he and Robin would disappear into the mass of commuting prisoners and owners of the neo-feudal society. And even though they would carry on with their lives like Achilles, with the threat of annihilation at best, decades of sterile torture at worst, should they be discovered, now with his senses dancing in the symphony of lights around him, Ian could think only of how fulfilled he felt in the moment.

Never could he remember feeling so alive and ecstatic, so free, unfettered. Unfettered, untethered, connected to humanity instead of death, Ian thought to himself. So secure in his truth; the truth, bare and shivering, withstanding 24-hour surveillance lights, stripped of illusion and clutter. Despite dire consequences, for the moment he had chosen to fully embrace life, with all its boundless beauty and crushing cruelty; with all its heartbreak, discomfort and transitory joy.

And so Robin and Ian walked on in their eternal moment, giggling, gathering each other up in their embrace, the way lovers do strolling through parks on Sunday, grateful for the love in their life, as if it were ever-lasting.

"There is nothing in all the world greater than freedom. It is worth paying for; it is worth going to jail for. I would rather die in abject poverty with my convictions than live in inordinate riches with the lack of self-respect."   –Dr. Martin Luther King Jr.

ABOUT THE AUTHOR

MARGOT EVE PEPPER was born in Mexico City, the daughter of Economist Jeanette Pepper and blacklisted Hollywood producer, George Pepper, who fled the United States to escape persecution for their political beliefs during Senator Joseph McCarthy's inquisition. (Under the pseudonym George Werker, George Pepper's film credits include *Robinson Crusoe* and *The Young One (La Jóven,)* both directed by Luis Buñuel.) Margot Pepper's fiction, poetry, articles and translations have appeared in the *Utne Reader, Common Dreams, Z-net, Counterpunch, Monthly Review, Dollars & Sense, NACLA, Rethinking Schools,* the *San Francisco Bay Guardian, City Lights anthologies, Race, Poverty & the Environment, Hampton Brown's A Chorus of Cultures, Prensa Latina, El Tecolote, El Andar, Canada's The Scoop* and elsewhere, and can be found at http://www.margotpepper.com and http://freedomvoices.org. She is the author of a memoir about her year working in Cuba, (*Through the Wall: A Year in Havana,*) a book of poetry, (*At This Very Moment*) and a forthcoming book of short magic realism, (*The Acrobat, and Other Stories for Dark Times.*)

THROUGH THE WALL: A YEAR IN HAVANA

IN 1992, MARGOT PEPPER was one of a handful of foreign journalists granted a year-long visa to remain on the blockaded island of Cuba. Rave reviews of her 2005 memoir of that period claim that *Through the Wall: A Year in Havana* succeeded in breaking through the blockade to deliver a lyrical, honest, eye-opening account of life in Cuba. Reviewers have judged *Through the Wall* to be "a truly significant book" and "a vital contribution to history"(LIP.) The San Francisco Bay Guardian heralded it "well-researched, witty and thought-provoking.... graceful and lyrical even as Pepper delves into complex economic theory and politically-sophisticated analysis." *Through the Wall: A Year in Havana* is carried by nearly 50 libraries including by Harvard, Brown, Rutgers, and Melbourne universities. It is available through Freedom Voices (http://www.freedomvoices.org,) Amazon, or your local book store thanks to AK Press Distribution (http://www.akpress.org.)

ACKNOWLEDGEMENTS

UN TREMENDO ABRAZOTE de gracias to my *editor-jefe,* Jess Clarke for his indefatigable genius; to Freedom Voices, my ever-present editors, Eric Robertson, Kitty Costello and copy editor Maketa Smith-Groves; to the multi-gifted Christine Joy Ferrer for the amazing cover design, website and beyond; to Mary Liz Thomson, Jim Smith and Art Hazelwood for their enthusiasm and advice; Luis J. Rodriguez, Roger Burbach and Dr. Robin Balliger for their uncompromising inspiration; Joel Pitney for the brilliant book campaign; my mother, Jeanette and nine-year old son, Rafael, who led me to Chabot's telescopes that, with the help of the starry hot tub at the Sea & Sand, inspired me to expand the final scene regarding the fate of the universe; to Chris Carlsson for extensive feedback on the first draft, also to Mickey Ellinger and Juliana Mojica and to some of my muses, sadly now in the great *ayá*: George Pepper, Cleo and Dalton Trumbo, Suzie Dodd Thomas *y* Piri Thomas, Gerry Gillerman, John Ross, Beth Stanford, Mary Tallmountain, Ben Pleasants, Csaba Polony, Robin Williams, Aaron Swartz; and all the Oscar Grants, Trayvon Martins, Darius Simmons, Jonathan Ferrells, Michael Browns, James Foleys, U.S. drone strike victims, U.S.-sponsored childhood tragedies and fatalities and other human sacrifices that perpetuate the American Day Dream; as well as other immortals: Jack Hirschman, Avotcja, Juana Alicia, Doug Minkler, Christine Hanlon, Lawrence Ferlinghetti, Noam Chomsky, Richard D. Wolff, Mitch Jeserich, Amy Goodman, Alice Walker, Mumia Abu Jamal, Julian Assange, Edward Snowden, *y a* Chelsea Elizabeth Manning, all for setting the truth free.

THE AUTHOR AT WORK

WISHES TO BESTOW a bow of gratitude as well to Peter Maravelis, Elaine Katzenberger *y gente* at City Lights Bookstore, AK press, KPFA, Terry Messman at *Street Spirit* and Donna Longmore at the *Scoop,* all for their example and loyal support; to Susan Chasson for her wisdom; to Kaiser Oakland, Lenore Arnoux, Drs. Neuman, Scott, King-Angel and Joseph Panicali, and especially the Psychiatry and Education departments, heroic Dr. Tim A. Brown and students, and to Graciano Luchesi for letting me hog the back window table at Caffé Puccini for countless hours in order to write this book; *a* Dolores, Areli, Telma, Facundo, Gelzer, Esdras, Silvia, Yadira *y* Patricia *también.*

Many thanks as well to other inspiring and generous San Francisco venues, some for allowing me to stay and work long enough to witness work shift changes or to capture scenery for this story, despite some of the most coveted views and cuisines in California; others for feeding my soul or caring for my mother and child that I might write. Un *fuerte abrazote en particular para todos los trabajadores, cocinadores,* chefs, servers, bussers, drivers, gardeners, caregivers and cleaners *en* Café Boheme, La Rondalla, Blue Fig, Red Poppy, the Mission Cultural Center, Modern Times Bookstore and Radio Habana Social Club; San Francisco's Delancy Street Restaurant and garden Café, the Samovar Tea Garden, Cliff House, Hyatt Regency and Waterfront Restaurant; Karen Ko at Ko & Company, Calzones, Savoy Tivoli, Specs and

Vesuvio's Bar in North Beach; Macy's workers, Il Caffé, and Cheesecake Factory on Union Square; San Francisco Cable Car, BART and the San Francisco Bay Ferry; Berkeley's Café Babette, Café Strada, Café Milano, Café Durant, House of Curries, Skates and Jupiter; Oakland's Spasso Café, the Montclair Egg Shop, Cole Coffee, Diggery Inn, Crepevine, Ultimate Grounds, Cesar's, Scott's Seafood, Rumbo al Sur, Lake Chalet, Boca Nova and SoleSpace; Paul Chervatin, Jeffrey A. Lee, Michelle Moir, Jim Jr. and Sr. Thompson and company at the Oakland Hills Tennis Club; Mario, counselors, Riva and Sarah herself at Sarah's Science Camp as well as the breathtaking East Bay Regional Park District; the San Pablo Reservoir; the Coalition on Homelessness; Andy Woodner, Jennifer Boysen, Dentist Dr. Javier Torres, Jaime Espinoza and Mechthild Weber, Zerina, Nasim and Postal Plus Oakland; Hope Gillerman Organics and the American Center for Alexander Technique; Wages and the Natural Cleaning Cooperative, Kevin Rath, Geneva Ziaoure, and Peggy Watson at MANOS homecare; Zenaida, Zinnia, Ruby, Ana, Shahid, Janet, Rheda, Stephanie and Piedmont Gardens workers; Fiduciary Molly Hill, Oracle Vivian, dear ones Noah Nelson, Diana Hines, Sandy Costa, Sarah Jackson, Mary Ann Capehart, David Hucklesby, Steven LaVoie, nap-smelling Xochi and little squishy, fuzzy, purring Minou Chompsky; Calistoga's Indian Springs, Euro Spa Inn, Solage Sol Bar, Café Sarafornia, the Hyrdro and Village Inn Restaurant; the Beach House Hotel, Half Moon Bay Lodge, Miramar Restaurant and Sam's Chowder House in Half Moon Bay; the Water's Edge Hotel, Sam's Anchor Café, Guaymas Restaurant and Captain Maggie and her Ferry Sunset Cruise in Tiburon; the Rose Café in Venice Beach; Loews Beach Hotel in Santa Monica, Tía Chucha Centro Cultural, Monterey Plaza Hotel, Sea & Sand Inn and the Ideal Bar & Grill in Santa Cruz; Hotel Montecarlo in Mexico City, Hotel Lagunitas en Yelapa, Hotel Catalina in Zihuatanejo, Las Brisas, Ron and Bruce and the Rio Villa Beach Resort and the Village Inn in the Russian River, and the Saint Francis Hotel (longest uninterrupted and complimentary 17-hour work period without having to budge from a table looking out over Union Square except to use the latrine, not to mention the complimentary crab omelet that lasted all day!) And a special thanks to Cathy Campbell and the Berkeley Federation of Teachers, Wai Lee, Matt, Thea, Juan and the gang at M.A.C., the Apple geniuses at "the bar" and Apple without whose Airbook and iPhone this story may never have been written.

American Day Dream (Columbus Tower and Transamerica Pyramid)
©2015 by Margot Pepper